THE MERCURY
FOUNTAIN

THE MERCURY
FOUNTAIN

by Eliza Factor

Published by Akashic Books
©2012 by Eliza Factor

ISBN-13: 978-1-61775-036-6
Library of Congress Control Number: 2011923110

Akashic Books
PO Box 1456
New York, NY 10009
info@akashicbooks.com
www.akashicbooks.com

to my parents

1900

♥

T he scream must have come from Casa Grande. There were no other houses, no trees or huts, no jackals, only the bone-white road, the dusty scrub. Now all was quiet. The buzz of insects filled Ysidro's ears, and far away, a mining blast. Maybe he had misheard, maybe nothing was wrong. He was twelve years old, unarmed, and not allowed anywhere near Casa Grande on a school day.

It happened again, definitely a scream, definitely coming from the Scraperton house. Ysidro scrambled up the hill, up the forbidden steps of the veranda, to the front door, but its grandeur overcame him. Silence again, except for his own raggedy breath. He headed toward the back door, the planks of the porch creaking under his feet. The windows were all shuttered, until around the corner of the house he came to an open one. There she was. He gaped.

She didn't look a bit like the Mrs. Scraperton the men pretended not to look at. Her hair was clammed around her skull. Her skin was the color of a sick moon. A trickle of something that looked like blood ran down her chin. She doubled over and screamed again, the veins standing out in her temples. She rose back up—only then did Ysidro notice her belly. It was huge, monstrously round. He understood, and as he understood the floor of the porch seemed to move an inch or two. He felt as was as if he were standing on the banks of the Rio Bravo, right on the border of the quicksand. He had to put his hand onto the house to steady himself.

"Ysidro!" Aunt Alma pounded up the back stairs of the veranda. Her cheeks were red, her hair was flying out of her braid.

"I think Mrs. Scraperton needs the doctor," he managed to say.

"He's coming. He's on his way." Alma stood over him, panting unevenly, hands on hips. "What are you doing here? What's wrong with you? You look green."

"I'm fine."

Alma frowned.

"I am." He wasn't lying. The floorboards were getting solid again.

Alma kneaded her forehead, looking from him to Mrs. Scraperton and back again. "Are you all right to get Mr. Scraperton?"

The boy didn't move for a moment, stunned by this turn of events. Get Mr. Scraperton? He, Ysidro Herrida, would get to deliver this message? It was unbelievable, the kind of wonderful thing that he imagined for himself, those hours dawdling down by the fishing hole, but that he never expected to really happen.

"Go. Hurry. He needs to be here. The baby is coming."

A mile he raced, over burning sand, toward the mining workings, the scaffolding and towers brave and big and sharply visible against the desert flat. The sickening feeling that had overtaken him on the porch was all but forgotten. *Get Mr. Scraperton!* The order resounded with each slap of his huaraches. *Get Mr. Scraperton!* How would he announce it? *Mrs. Scraperton is having a baby.* No, not respectful enough. *Sir, your wife is in labor.* That was better, more manful. Maybe he'd get to shake his hand again. He'd only shook hands with him once but he'd remember it forever: like the energy of the whole planet had pulsed through him and he felt strong and warm and capable of doing all the amazing things that Mr. Scraperton wanted him to do.

At Independence Avenue, his lungs felt like they were going to crack open his chest. He swerved through the carts and horses and women bringing home food for supper. "Ysidro!" yelled Gwen, from the steps of Offitz & Carruthers. He pretended not to hear and plowed straight into a group of Anglo ladies. They jumped around, yelling angrily and calling for a patrol. He sped around a corner. Footsteps sounded behind him. He could not let himself get caught. The patrol would hassle him for hours. He shot around another corner, the footsteps close at his heels. He didn't understand. The patrols were wrecks, a cinch to outrun. He pushed himself as fast as he could, still the footsteps gained. And gained. They were right beside him.

It wasn't a patrol. It was Gwen. He should have known. She was the fastest girl in school. "Hi," she said, matching him stride for stride. "Don't worry about that patrol back there. It was just Poc. He didn't see who you were."

No way he could speak, he could barely breathe, and now a stitch pinched his ribs. They kept running, only one more block to Pristina HQ. "I wanted to thank you," Gwen said between breaths. "You know, yesterday, for helping me out when I had to do that recitation." She could run and smile at the same time. Her lips were pale, the color of the pink sand they had out by the quarry. And her hair was red, almost like Mrs. Scraperton's, when Mrs. Scraperton looked like Mrs. Scraperton, her hair all shiny and coppery, piled on top of her head with little ringlets dripping down.

He flew forward and skidded across the hard packed dirt. "You okay?" Gwen asked, fluttering around, touching his back and arm. He pushed himself back to his feet, but he was breathing too hard to stand up straight. She put a hand on his shoulder. "You might not be the best runner," she said, "but you sure are the best speaker. I swear, if they let anyone win the oration contest two years in a row, you would."

"I've got to go," he said between big gulps of air. "I've got to deliver an important message."

"Wait." She dug in her pocket. "Here." She handed him a caramel. "I'm sorry, it's a little mushed up."

He squeezed it, mushing it more. "Thanks, Gwen." She smiled, pale lips and a little freckle on her nose. He stumbled backward.

At Pristina HQ, Grierson looked at him skeptically. "Mr. Scraperton's not here. He's in Shaft 8, won't be back till six or seven."

This was the time to give the message to Grierson, who would give it to a mine messenger, who would deliver it to Shaft 8. But what of that handshake? What of that beautiful phrase—*Sir, your wife is in labor*—which he had said in his head until the words seemed to glow with import and beauty? Hadn't Alma said: *Get Mr. Scraperton*? She hadn't said: *Get a messenger, tell Grierson.* Shaft 8 was on the other side of town, past the school, the warehouses, the jaw crusher. It was the deepest shaft of all, the Glory Hole, the richest mercury load in the whole new world. In only a year he could work there, if all went well, but not until he was thirteen.

He got to the fence that encircled the mine and slipped through the hole. A group of men neared, slowly lugging equipment and grumbling about the lift. He hid behind a pile of tailings. When they were gone, he ran up the slope to the shaft building and scrambled inside. It was so dark and musty he couldn't see a thing. When his eyes adjusted, he made out gears bigger than wagon wheels. Shadowy men hovered about them, shining their lanterns and talking in low, hard voices.

Someone grabbed Ysidro from behind. "Where do you think you're going?" The boy could barely breathe, his collar was being pulled so tightly. "Speak, kid." A giant Anglo poked his chest. "Where do you think you're going?"

"Hey!" José María appeared out of the murk, mustached and handsome in his engineer's suit.

"Found him sneaking around," the Anglo muttered resentfully. "He won't tell me what he was doing."

Ysidro drew himself up as tall as he could. "I have a message for Mr. Scraperton."

"Yeah?" said José María. "And what is it?"

"I'm not supposed to tell," Ysidro answered. "It's personal and confidential." He'd seen the phrase on an envelope at Offitz & Carruthers.

The Anglo laughed, bits of spit spraying out. "Ha! Personal and confidential. Some kid, hey!" The man pounded him on the back, as if they were all of a sudden friends, but his pats were so strong that Ysidro bent over coughing.

José María regarded him steadily. "You can't go down there, son. As you well know." He nodded at the Anglo. "You, get back to work." A surge of pride shot through Ysidro. José María had proved himself so smart, he could boss around even the Anglos. When the man had left, José María patted Ysidro's shoulder. "Give me the message." His gaze had the effect of making Ysidro want to please him, but he couldn't give up, not so easily. José María smiled. "A messenger is no job for a boy with such skinny legs."

"My legs aren't skinny."

José María laughed.

"I can run fast."

"The lift is out. Did you know that?"

Ysidro shrugged. What was a lift? Shafts 2 and 5 didn't even have them; his cousins scaled up and down miles of ladders every day.

José María gave him directions. Ysidro understood them well enough; he knew the layout of the mine from the maps at school. And he had no trouble adjusting the headlamp—he'd had plenty of practice with his father's.

"Take a sip before you go," José María said, handing him the canteen. "It's hot down there."

"Thank you." Ysidro gulped down the tinny water. Then he grabbed onto the emergency shaft ladder and began his descent. The mine air wrapped around him, a rotten-egg smell of sulfur, made worse by the heat. He had smelled it before, on his father's clothes, on the winds that swept through town, but never so strong. After a while he could detect whiffs of sweetness mixed into the rottenness, bits of earth amidst the sulfur and piss and sweat and smoke. He got to a ledge where the first ladder ended and another began. The shaft grew darker. Hotter. His hands were greasy with sweat. Usually heat felt sharp, like a slap. You protected yourself from it with hats and white cotton, but this was different, slimy. He wiped his hands on his pants, spat at them, wiped them again. Down he went, rung after rung. Below, he could see nothing but an endless well of boiling black. But it wasn't endless. It was 428 feet—not that deep for a mine—and at the bottom he figured he would find Mr. Scraperton.

His foot hit solid ground. What was this? He couldn't be at the bottom, not yet. Where were the miners? He was all alone, on some sort of platform. His headlamp lit up tunnels filled with waste rock and numbers painted on the walls. He saw the beginning of another ladder and hurried toward it, then heard something. In front of him an old cardboard box marked *Hercules Blasting Caps* moved. He jumped back. A rat came out, a weird, slow-moving rat that rolled over and jerked its head sideways. He edged around it uneasily.

On the third ladder, the light from the top of the shaft completely disappeared. He couldn't hear anything. No men. None of the swearing or singing or drilling or hauling he'd learned about, no vigorous clamor of noble labor, none of that, only his own breath and the slip of his shoes on the iron rungs. How could this be Shaft 8? The Glory Hole? The walls narrowed. Maybe José María had tricked him, sent him down a dead hole as punishment for trying to sneak in. He shook his arms out, one at a time. The air seemed to resist him and seep into him at once. The smell was even worse now, sourer than it had been up at the top, and hotter. Like terrible breath. His abuela said there were brujas that lived in the mountains, witches that put spells on men and tried to lure them into their caves. He imagined that they'd have breath like this, hot and thick and black. They'd breathe on you and blind you.

He puffed out his cheeks and blew away the bad thought. It was wrong to think this way. Superstitions eroded your faculties.

The air got hotter and pressed in closer. He could barely breathe. You had to keep your faculties clear. Otherwise, you wouldn't be able to merge into the anatomy of the planet. But what did that mean, the anatomy of the planet? Merging into it? It was black. He couldn't see. He could have been lured. He was scaling down a bruja's throat. He had to stop. She might swallow.

A whistle blew, sharp and clear and no-nonsense. Then a blast, and the ladder quivered against the rock. Ysidro hung on, whooping and laughing. Afterward, catching his breath, he experienced a different kind of heat, a hot well of shame that bubbled inside him. He'd been acting like a peon, taking brujas seriously. He'd almost betrayed Nature. He scrambled as quickly as he could, ignoring the rubbery feeling in his legs. Finally, a light glowed beneath him. He went even faster, fully understanding why moths dive into lanterns. The walls of the shaft gave way, and he entered a giant cavern. Fires blazed at the base, men shouted, mules brayed. He jumped to the ground, rubbed the cramp out of his hands, and made his way to the West Tunnel.

The West Tunnel was supported by beams of cottonwood and strung with lamps, quieter than the big cavern until he neared a working area and the banging of metal and stone filled his ears. He turned a corner and found himself in a small cavern with blood-red walls and a fire at its center. Four or five men hurled picks and crowbars at the overhang. Their bodies were covered by a coat of red dust made redder still by the reflection of the flames. Their muscles glided under their skin like fishes caught inside their bodies. Ysidro shouted, but no one heard. He stepped closer, blinking each time the miners struck. The biggest man there turned around. Red dust had taken over every part of his face except for his eyes which glowed white and watery.

"Ysidro," the man said; it would have been a scary voice, save for the bit of friendliness tucked into it. Ysidro recognized his uncle, Jorge Rivera, and asked him if he was going the right way.

"As far as I know," said Jorge. "He was down there after lunch. You've got a ways to go. Better hurry."

He thanked his uncle and ran down a succession of crosscuts, trying to go as fast as a real messenger would. After a while, the tram tracks ended and the lanterns were replaced by candles stabbed onto stakes. A headlamp shone in the darkness ahead; it got brighter, and the tunnel filled with the sharp smell of a tanatero bent under his load. A moment later, another came, stooped low and running very fast. Then another. The tanateros were haulers who carried the ore in rawhide sacks strapped to their foreheads. Most were peons, and Ysidro gave them a wide berth. You didn't want to mess with peons. They polluted the mines with their virgins and altars and sullen attitudes. Ysidro kept an eye out for Javier, his cousin, who wasn't a peon, but a brave, strong tanatero who always placed in the ladder races. He didn't see him, but he saw many others. They looked straight ahead with their strange white eyes, and their breath came out gasping. One of them stopped to tell him that if he didn't watch out, he'd bump into Mr. Scraperton.

"I'm looking for Mr. Scraperton," he said.

The tanatero laughed. He shouted something that Ysidro didn't understand to the man in front of him. The other man laughed and their laughter echoed down the sweaty tunnel. Then it faded and the candles thinned. Ysidro was all alone. He hurried onward until he had to stop, his legs too jiggly to go on. He'd never realized how big the mine was. It was bigger than Pristina, bigger even than the distance from Pristina to Casa Grande, maybe even bigger than the distance between Pristina and his fishing spot. He came to a precipice. The only way down was a gallina ladder, which wasn't really a ladder, but a tree trunk, with the bark skinned off and shallow toeholds hacked in. He hugged it tight. He'd never been on a gallina ladder before. The first few notches were pretty shaky, but he quickly got used to it. That's when he noticed the smell. Wood. He buried his nose in a toehold. Yes, definitely. You could still smell the tree. He imagined the ladder before it was skinned and hacked, a shade-giving alamo down by the creek. He used to watch the sun coming through their leafy branches. It was a shame they'd cut them all down, but they'd had to. That's what his abuela didn't understand:

they'd had to. You needed to cut down the alamos to let the mercury out.

He reached the bottom and continued along a narrow dark tunnel, wondering how much farther it could possibly be. Something appeared in front of him. A shaggy white face with a long nose and pointy ears. A burro. But a strange burro; it stood so quietly and its eyes were blue. It seemed like an apparition. Ysidro took a breath and forced himself to touch it. It snorted. A real burro snort.

A headlamp shone at the end of the tunnel. Ysidro squinted. The light came closer and a man pushed Ysidro aside and grabbed the reins. "Thought you could get away? Heh?" He glared at Ysidro, like the boy was responsible for the beast running off, then whacked the burro's rump and the two of them moved off. "You ain't never getting out of here, Sam, not until the meat slips off your bones."

They disappeared. All was silent and black. Ysidro felt like he had been in the mine forever. His legs hurt. His lungs hurt. He walked as fast as he could. After some time, his pace slowed even more. What if he had turned down the wrong tunnel? It didn't seem possible it would take this long. He tripped. He had to get up, but his body was too attached to the ground. He closed his eyes. His face seemed to be bleeding. He tasted his blood and thought about Mrs. Scraperton, not like she was today, but like she was supposed to be, riding on her horse, kicking up dust. She would be okay. She had to. He pushed himself up. She was Mrs. Scraperton, not his mother. He'd never met his mother, only heard from everyone how good she'd been. The sickness he'd felt when he saw Mrs. Scraperton's belly rose up in him. He was in the ground: inside the hard rocks of the ground. They were solid. But they weren't. They were flickering and curving and shaking, and hidden within them was a creaking moan. He wondered about his mother, he'd never really thought of her as real before, just a sweetness hanging over him. Move. Get up. He found Gwen's caramel and bit into it, too tired to even unwrap it. The rich buttery flavor filled his mouth. He spat out the wrapper and wobbled forward.

T he boy stood in the red swirling dust, his mouth moving like that of a fish out of water.

"Who's that?" Owen walked toward him. Under the mine grit, he could barely make out the fine features of Herrida's son. "Ysidro? Is that you? What are you doing down here?" The boy was too young. "Who let you down? Who let you down? Speak!"

"I came from Casa Grande, sir. Alma sent me."

The heat and clamor gave way to a cold still, the only sound now the steady *drip drip drip* of the mine. Owen leaned closer to Ysidro. The kid's eyes were glassy with exhaustion and something else too, something more troubling. He almost didn't hear the rest of the sentence.

"Mrs. Scraperton is in labor."

"What?" He shook the boy.

"Mrs. Scraperton, sir—"

But Owen had heard. Warmth poured back into him. "Why didn't you say so?" He laughed and jumped up, the good throb of Nature rushing through his veins. "Hear that, men?"

The miners, who had been diligently pretending not to listen, crowded around, each one grinning larger than the last.

"What about that! Can't make it on time for dinner, but when it comes to the important stuff, blast it all! She's early." His men broke into a rowdy cheer, and Owen tossed his stopwatch in the air. It somersaulted in a high narrow arc, glittering in the dark. "Mother Dolores!" he boomed, catching the watch. "Hear that, boys? Feel that? That earthly shift and quiver!"

He raced down the tunnel, hardly needing his torch, so firmly connected was he to its jags and dips. Past ore-laden tanateros, up gallina ladders. No one knew, not one of them even had a clue. Dolores had been terribly secretive about the entire thing. Now finally there would be no more quiet. He would shout it from the roof! He climbed up the emergency exit, his calloused hands slapping each rung with a grudging pleasure.

He reached the top barely winded, not bad for fifty, and barreled past his men to the sweet-smelling afternoon, noting with pleasure the blueness of the sky. Exactly as it should be. He hopped on his bay and spurred her through town, panicking the chickens and almost running over Cleofas's wreck of a grandmother, but she didn't bother him now, no one did. Dolores! His Doe! His impossible D! Past the town, into blazing ocotillo and yellow-blossomed creosote. Lovely her, bringing him a son! A spring-born son! No Kronos he, he'd been waiting for this day ever since he first saw her, a tangled wave of hair flying behind her, galloping, even before she knew him, straight toward him, as if she knew too. He squeezed the horse's flanks. Come on, you old bucket. She'd let him put his palm on her belly. He'd felt a single kick, then a valiant battery. It had to be a boy, with a volley that strenuous. They'd name him Theodore, after the young general of San Juan Hill. Theo Scraperton, pounding not up, but down into the drifts and stopes, with an army of miners as hybrid as the rough riders, and a campaign more true and glory-filled. Come on, you old bucket. Giddyap! He shot up the hill to his house. A son! A son! He shouted his arrival, but got drowned out by an earth-shaking scream.

The sound lingered on, even after he could no longer hear it, a silent emanation of it agitating his temples, rendering him immobile. The French doors swung open, and the doctor trotted down the steps.

"No cause for alarm," Badinoe said, smiling, squinting up at him. "Your wife's got her vocal chords in order, that's all."

"Of course," said Owen, regaining himself. He hopped to the ground and slapped the horse. "Well, I made it. Sounds like the babe's still clinging in there."

"Yes."

"Can I see her?"

"I don't think that would be wise."

"I see," said Owen. He'd been hoping that Dolores would change her mind. He frowned at the house. She screamed again. "It should be soon, right? The screams are coming close together."

Badinoe shook his head. "You can't always tell."

"She's not too early, is she? I thought you told us to expect a baby mid-April. It's only April first."

"That was just an estimate. She sure looks big enough." Badinoe smiled as if they were sharing an observation, but she'd kept herself so shrouded up that Owen had barely been able to see her. He rocked back on his heels, trying to mask his aggravation. Badinoe chuckled. "In all this time, I don't believe I've ever seen you straight from the mine."

It took Owen a moment to realize what the doctor meant. He hadn't de-ored. His suit was cracked and stiff with cinnabar dust and his hands were stained a flagrant red. He had raced right past the shower house. He rubbed a clump of mineral-laden dirt off his suit, astonished at himself. He took great pride in following the rules along with everyone else. "I must have forgotten," he said as much to himself as Badinoe. "I'll have to pay the fine." He stood stunned a moment longer until he realized that he could turn this into an oration. We must strive not to let immediate excitements blind us to long-term considerations. We must train ourselves to see near and far simultaneously.

She screamed. The words running through his head withered into nothingness. "Is there no method to speed it up?"

"I wish there were."

Owen growled in disgust. He paced backward and forward across the driveway, not wanting to look at the doctor, whose uselessness mirrored his own. She screamed. The mine dust drifted off him, getting lost in the dirt. "Do I have time to run back to the shower house?"

Badinoe regarded him thoughtfully. "That is probably a good idea. Alma and I have things under control here."

Owen hurried back to his bay. Anything was better than waiting, and he could at least salvage what dust remained. The shower house and the accompanying laundry were equipped with a drainage system that took the grit from the miners' skin and clothes and rerouted it to the furnace. This way, every last cinnabar mote was captured and refined. He trotted down the driveway, wondering how much ore was caught in his knuckles, fingerprints, palm lines. It would be interesting to measure it, to know how much dust you carried away with you, the exact quantity. Dust that, because of you, will remain dust instead of turning into something of value.

Another scream, fainter, but still plenty loud. He stopped to listen. After she had finished, he kept staring at his red-crusted hands. A bolt of understanding shook through him and he laughed. He had not made a mistake. He was meant to have forgotten. This dust, this dust on his hands and suit and hair, wanted to be here, to witness, to honor the arrival of his son. It had clung to him purposefully.

He returned to his house. Dolores screamed, but now he

heard the deep reservoir of strength within her. Why had he been so distraught? She was not one for doing things quietly and serenely. And why should she? Births were tumultuous. That was Nature's Way. Great things were born of great up-heavals. His very own mercury was born of volcanic erup-tions. He dismounted firmly and led the bay into the dark, straw-scented stables. In the next stall, Generalissimo, Dolo-res's stallion, tossed his head and pawed the ground. Owen strode over to him. "She's doing great," he said. "Bringing forth a big one." The stallion looked at him fiercely and flared his prodigious nostrils.

Owen had first seen Dolores on Generalissimo, skimming across the Coahuilan plain, nothing like the side-saddled women he'd grown up with. It was incredible to him, find-ing her. Religion had warped every woman he had met to one extreme or another. And there in Mexico, with the whole country under the pall of dictators and priests, Dolores rode on her horse, free as the day she was born.

The stallion eyed him distrustfully. "You miss her, huh?" Owen laughed. They were competitors, and Owen was in the lead. "But you're not that far behind," he said.

He could picture her so clearly, galloping out to the crum-bling gate of her parents' hacienda. That time when Genera-lissimo had looked like a poor circus beast, his mane strung with red and gold ribbons. "In honor of your visit," Dolores had said, explaining that the horse and she both had to look their best, for they came together. He'd started toward the hacienda, but she shook her head, trotting in the other direc-tion. Her entire family had gathered there. "Toda la familia." She widened her eyes, evoking a natural disaster on the scale of the great Lisbon earthquake. "But don't worry, I brought you a bite to eat." She took a bun from her pannier. It was still warm, glazed with honey, a lone raisin at the top. "The staff of life," she said, "a horse and bread. Without them," she drew her finger across her neck, gesturing decapitation, then laughed and spurred Generalissimo. He had chased her. But she didn't—she never let herself be caught.

He now returned to his house, almost too grand a house, with double chimneys and plate glass windows. When he was alone, he'd lived in town, happy in a couple of rooms across from his office. But Dolores needed her Casa Grande, and children needed space, and he did love the view from the roof. He entered by the back way, quietly so as not to alarm Dolores, though not so quietly as to feel that he was sneaking onto his own property. Upstairs, in the room that Dolores had prepared for the baby, everything was so clean and new, a hobbyhorse, a rocking chair, quilts piled up in an open trunk, a washstand painted with spotted horses. Framed, above the crib, was his sole contribution: the Principles of Pristina. The baby would be too young to read it, but perhaps the ideas would have some influence nonetheless. He looked it over, his brow creasing.

The Principles of Pristina
Drink of this Cup & Rejoice

That which Man has hitherto understood to be God is in fact a sublime apperception of the Beauty of Nature. In obscuring this most basic Fact, the religions of the world have caused great confusion and unhappiness. We at Pristina honor the Wisdom and Beauty of Nature and proudly follow her Laws and Principles.

Clarity
Without Clarity, Man cannot directly apprehend Nature and thus is wrenched from Natural Law, Purpose, Knowledge, and Satisfaction. To achieve Clarity, the following Obscurants must be abolished:

—Alcohol, opium, tobacco, and other such narcotics and excitements that confuse Man's sense of time and proportion.
—Gambling or any other such pursuit that encourages irresponsibility, idleness, and superstition.
—Superstition, that is Artificial Knowledge, knowledge not directly acquired. Artificial Knowledge erodes the faculties and senses, depriving Man of his capacity for original, unmediated, natural thought. For example: Christianity in its various cults and sects, Judaism, Hindooism, Mohammedism, Spiritualism, Theosophy, Masonism, Witch Doctory & Etc.

Unity

As white light seen through a prism reveals a spectrum, so too does the essence of Man. Man is comprised of many races, races that by their very survival have proven themselves fit and ingenious. Consider the Mestizo, who felicitously combines the Nobility of the Spaniard with the Bravery of the Indian. In the Future, he will be further refined through the addition, either through Association of Amalgamation or Anglo Ingenuity, though truly, at that point he will no longer be a Mestizo. He will be a Pristinian, a Unified Man, inherently suited to his Labor.

Purpose

Labor is no punishment for sin. Labor is our Means and our Pleasure. Labor is how we participate in the Symbiotic Relationship between Nature and Mankind that characterizes the History of Civilization. Labor is the key to a unified society and a catalyst for Social Evolution. Labor is the birthplace of Happiness, Pride, and Beauty. Labor is to be cherished and honored as our bridge to the Future.

Never before had the words seemed overbearing. He had

not intended a list of no's. He did not want rejection, but a colossal embrace of all the beauty and force that Nature so willingly gave when people threw off their shackles and dared to receive. That was it exactly, a world generated by a colossal pure-minded *Yes!*

Another bout of screaming began. Owen pressed his forehead to the window. Huge cumuli had formed, enormous stacks of cloud billowing, glowing so brightly they hardly seemed real. From behind, rays of sun illuminated patches of desert and gilded the thick coils of smoke that rose from the reduction works. A strange new scream broke forth, its pitch cutting into the marrow of his bones. He hesitated, the possibility that it would not be a boy, or a girl either, flitting into his mind. He had heard of nameless things, finned or hoofed, caught between male and female. But it would be impossible for he and Dolores to produce something like that. It would be a boy. Theodore. He'd felt the kicks—and listen to that scream, far more healthy and fulsome than the last. The girls would come afterward. He had a name waiting for the first. Victoria. The next century's Victoria, more virtuous than the last, on account of the Republican blood coursing through her veins. He appreciated the rough democracy of names. The colored were always naming their offspring after the prestigious and monumental. He'd known two George Washingtons, a Jefferson, an Abraham. You could learn a thing or two from the colored. You could learn from everyone.

The screams came faster, piling on top of each other, mounting, mounting, until they crystallized into words. "Me cago en la puta Virgen!" Impossible. She must have said agua, not puta, but agua. Why would she curse the Virgin if she didn't believe in her in the first place? Her accent sometimes mangled things. He hurried to the kitchen for a glass of water. Badinoe entered, rubbing his eyes.

"She needs something to drink," Owen said.

"I thought you were in the shower house."

"She won't mind if I take her this?" Owen held up the glass of water.

"I'll take it," said Badinoe.

"Why can't I go in?"

"There are women who like company and women who like privacy. I advise bowing to their natures." Badinoe looked amused.

"What's so funny?" asked Owen.

"Nothing. I just never imagined I'd be delivering your child."

Owen frowned. Why not? He was a doctor. And what was so funny about it? But Badinoe laughed at things that weren't funny. Always had. Owen remembered him in school, giggling and sputtering, unable to control his tongue. Owen turned on his heels. He could take his own wife water.

"Owen, wait! You need to boil water for the sheets."

Owen knew that boiling water was a ruse to keep nervous husbands occupied. He wasn't nervous, not anymore. The water sloshed as he marched down the hall. He knocked on the door, but didn't wait for an answer. Dolores squirmed on the daybed, her body half-covered in wet, tangled sheets, her face mottled and red.

"Dolores," he said.

She moaned.

"Honey."

"Please," she said. "Get out."

He marched down the driveway. He could not understand. It was perverse. She acted like she was ashamed. She hadn't left the house for months. She'd said that she looked fat. Burgeoning, maybe, taut, satisfying, but not fat. And now, not letting him be there, at the culmination of everything?

He stopped. Something silver glimmered inside the spears of a sotol plant. He leaned down. His framed etching of John Brown. He wiped the dust off the glass. How had it gotten out here?

He brought it to his study. None of Dolores's fancy furniture here, just a good, solid desk, his spine-cracked Emersons, the fossils he picked up on his walks. He propped the etching on a shelf, adjusting the angle so that it faced the painting of his mother. The etching had originally belonged to her. She'd been a great abolitionist. She'd hosted meetings where they burned the Constitution.

He gazed at her steel-gray hair, her intelligent brow, her sharp, sharp eyes. For the ten thousandth time he wished that she could see him now. At this moment, the wish was so big that he could barely swallow. She had died without any grandchildren. Without even a hope for them. He reached into the bowl he kept under her portrait, a glass bowl with layers of differently colored sand. He kept the sand beneath her because she had loved Natural History. When he was a boy, they had walked beaches together, wondering about the vein-streaked cliffs, the shells, the bulbs of seaweed. She would have been amazed at all the colors of the sand out here, the blinding whites, shale blues, clay reds, and more subtle hues too, pale blond stained with green, mustard, rusty peach. Colors that, the first time he had seen them, had made him dismount and scrape up the earth with his bare hands.

Dolores screamed. He closed his fingers into a hard, tight fist. Had his mother screamed like this? Had his father heard? He could only picture him sunk into an armchair clipping a cigar. He wouldn't have had the mettle to bear it. He'd been good for nothing but smoking and evasion.

Owen recalled the look in Ysidro's eyes when he'd brought

him the news. Terror, that's what it was. He'd had to repeat himself twice before Owen realized that the news he was delivering was good.

He hurried away from his study as if he were moving away from the memory of the boy's eyes, down the hallway and out the back door into the cool of the approaching evening. A lizard scuttled across his shadow, a cold-blooded egg layer. Maybe it would be better laying eggs.

Another terrible noise. He walked twenty steps in one direction, twenty steps in the opposite. He saw neither house, nor stables, nor mountains; he saw the dried mud on his boots, the color of blood. This agony could not be natural. The women of Africa popped out their babies, strapped them on their backs, and returned to their squash fields. The toxicities of Civilization had done this to her, reaching all the way out here to the desert. They'd have to study the Africans. Maybe all that squatting and weeding developed some muscle. He should have had Dolores take up gardening. He hadn't thought any of this through.

He headed off to the farthest knob of the hill, then got pulled back. He strode past Casa Grande in the opposite direction and again was pulled back. The house acquired a magnetism, one that reeled him in, then spat him back out. He walked in circles, the house the nucleus, looping around and around, up and down the hill, crisscrossing it from every angle. The sun grew huge and orange, and the clouds rolled into lavender cigars. He made his way to the porch steps and sat there, his exhausted ears receiving her exhausted screams. In the lulls between the screams, the grasshoppers chirred shrilly.

"Happy are the cicadas," his father had said, "for their wives are mute." He could see his father stepping back in mock retreat, his mother glaring. Happy are the cicadas. It was a phrase from one of Badinoe's Greeks, Xenarchos. He could hear his father saying it, delivering that last "chos" in an extravagant, almost tender whisper.

The warmth of the day was gone and he shivered in his suit and still she screamed. He leapt up, rubbing his arms against the cold, then stopped abruptly. He had no right to be comfortable, not with her in such a state. He sat. He shivered. The stars came out and a cloud rolled over the moon. Her screams grew weaker. They didn't sound human or generative. They sounded bad. He marched through the dark, tripping over things. Below him, the lights of Pristina glimmered faintly. He watched the lights go out, one by one, until all but the workings was black. This could not happen. She was too young and brave and free. He had a terrible urge to pray, to grind his knees into the dirt and pray. Never, not even as a child, had he felt such a desire. It took every ounce of his strength not to.

He ran to the stables and felt his way to Generalissimo's stall. He imagined her boot slipping into the stirrup, the graceful, impatient way she pulled herself up. He pressed his face against the salty muzzle. "She will," he whispered. "She will. She will."

It was quiet. Very quiet. Quiet! Owen ran outdoors. The yard was unbearably still. The parlor window seemed to float, unmoored in the dark. "Doe!" he shouted, his voice cracking. A trapezoid of yellow light spread out onto the porch. A figure appeared. Badinoe. Owen ran forward, aware of every break of scrub under his boots. Another figure. Alma. He raced up the steps. "How is she?"

"Very tired," said Badinoe. "But the bleeding has stopped. She should be all right."

He could see her through the window, lying on the daybed, eyes closed, hair everywhere. "Doe," he whispered. He put his hand on the pane. "Doe." She opened her eyes. He smiled, the dust on his cheeks cracking. She raised her hand in a mock military salute. He laughed, wanting once again to get down on his knees. You could thank Nature, couldn't you? Even if she could not hear, could you not thank Nature when good came to pass?

"Mr. Scraperton?" Alma stood behind him, her broad Indian face beaming, her arms wrapped around a bundle of white cotton.

"Congratulations," said Badinoe. "She's all there. Ten fingers and ten toes."

"Huh?"

"The baby."

"Oh, yes. She?" said Owen.

"Yes," said Alma. "You have a daughter."

Owen leaned over the bundle. In between the folds shone a delicate face with long, wet lashes. "A girl? Was she that in the womb?"

"Do you want to hold her, sir?"

"My goodness, those kicks?"

"Shall I take her upstairs?"

"No, give her to me." He reached for her, his hands trembling. She was so small. A tender, tiny breath of flesh. Her heartbeat was alarming. "Her pulse isn't too fast?"

"No, no, everything is as it should be," the doctor said, smiling calmly.

Everything was all right. As it should be. His mother had been a girl too. He kissed her, experimentally, gingerly. She withstood him just fine. He handed her back. Alma readjusted the blanket, cooing tenderly until she noticed the dusting of cinnabar he'd left on the baby's forehead. Her brow puckered. As gently as she could, she tried to brush it away.

S weat pooled between Dolores's breasts, wetted the crooks of her elbows and knees, glued her thighs together. She groaned. She fanned herself. She only got hotter. It was her damn hair; she had too much. She twisted it into a knot and patted around the bed for the barrette. It was a horrid barrette, embossed with a pair of crudely wrought, love-drunk doves, but it was the only one she had left. She lost barrettes. Earrings too. She was always catching herself with one lobe adorned and the other naked. Her sister, Refugio, never had that problem. No wonder, as all Refugio ever did was rock in that chair, hair unmussed, earrings symmetrical. Riding was what did it, Dolores thought, patting her lobes, because now that she wasn't riding—she'd stopped it, no more, never again, she would instead become an expert in riding the bed, a bedwoman—both earrings were in place. Demure little pearls. No point in wearing anything more excessive. Bedwomen looked foolish dressing up.

She found the barrette and fastened her bun, but it didn't help. She flapped the neck of her nightgown, airing her bloated, milk-filled—ugh, she couldn't even look at them. The bun hadn't done any good at all. She was stifling. It wasn't her hair. It was the house, Owen's house. Hot in the summer, drafty in the winter. Why couldn't he have used adobe or brick or something sensible? But he wasn't sensible. People just thought he was because of his voice. When she first met him, his voice confused her too. That was when he still spoke to her in Spanish. He told her she was bonita, and everybody said that, but when he said it, he stretched out the word, pushing it in different directions, enlarging it, making it crackle. God, he had fooled her. He didn't want a woman at all; he wanted an enterprise-sharer. Shopkeepers, he said, had the best marriages because they were immersed in the same enterprise. Did she look like a shopkeeper? Is that what he had seen?

She flopped back on the pillow. The ceiling fan squeaked. The blades needed dusting. She wouldn't tell Alma. Alma would only want to clean them, which would mean that Dolores would have to get out of bed. Absolutely not. She only left the bed to relieve her bladder, an errand that—through an act of enormous will—she had reduced to two, sometimes three times a day. She kept staring at the fan, hoping to hypnotize herself. It spun and spun, a smaller version of a ship's propeller. The house had reminded her of a shipwreck when she first saw it. The way it slanted on its hill, lopsided, like it had slogged on a sandbar. She had had ships on her mind. She rubbed the nape of her neck. Don't think about ships. She closed her eyes and there was the Vera Cruz pier, the throbbing engines, the wet salty winds, the first time, the only time, she had looked upon the Atlantic. Incredible, that water. And at the other side—a whole world.

Don't think about it. But how could she not? She rolled over and searched through the papers on her wobbly bedside table. She had told Owen that she wanted French furniture, and he responded by buying her cheap gilt with spindly, uneven legs. With a house like this, it was just as well that she didn't have guests. She found the envelope, well-worn and postmarked *Paris, France*. Incredible. Some little French functionary had sighed his little French sigh and stamped this very stamp. Some facteur had put it in his bag and driven down rues and boulevards, perhaps the Champs-Elysées itself. She slipped out the letter and frowned at Isabel's neat, obedient handwriting. Dated *14 de octubre de 1898*, the first letter she wrote after Owen canceled the honeymoon. How sorry Isabel was! She would have loved to have seen her. She had been thinking of her just the other day. A friend had invited her on a motorcar excursion! They drove over the Seine and through the countryside, scaring peasants and scattering leaves. She fancied that Dolores would have enjoyed it, although, she had to admit, she found it a bit overexciting. Dolores snorted at the injustice of it, a motorcar being wasted on her cousin. She had written back, asking for more details—the model, the engine, the speed, the sensation—but Isabel couldn't remember, didn't care, was on to talcum powder and the smell of lavender. To be in Paris and be thinking about talcum powder!

The baby stirred. Dolores held her breath. The baby had been a demon this morning, red-faced and howling. Owen never saw her like that. She gurgled practically every time he entered the room, but the moment the baby was left to her—oh, this morning had been indescribably bad. Nothing worked. Nursing and rocking and humming and crooning her name, but you can't calm a baby with a name like Victoria. It's that damn "ict"; you can't coo it. You can't say it gently. It's hard and rocky and unforgiving. "Vic-a-dee, Vic-a-doo"— that's how Owen got around it. Dolores had tried, but when she said Vic-a-dee, she sounded like a frantic bird, and Victoria screamed all the louder. She'd jammed her back in the cradle, too hard. Too hard. Dolores crawled back to the baby, repentant. She had arranged the room so that everything bordered her mattress. The cradle was at the northeast corner, a white cradle with Victoria's name written in red paint, and below, the date of her birth: *April 1, 1900*. The first Fools' Day of the twentieth century. "Sorry," she whispered, touching the air above her, afraid of waking her. Then, because she didn't feel like the English carried any weight, "Lo siento, mi amor." The baby's face twitched. Her hands balled in tight little fists. Dolores rocked the cradle, clucking and humming a lullaby her nurse had sung long ago.

She kept rocking, even after the baby had safely returned to sleep. It was the *creak-creak* of the cradle; it sounded like Refugio's rocking chair. She had never imagined that she would miss Refugio. She had not believed, back in Coahuila, that the world possessed a person more isolated than she. But there had been Refugio, her mother, her father, the vaqueros and their families, the brightly painted wagons delivering piles upon piles of cousins. There had been Indians sitting on the porch, clicking their gums, waiting for someone to dole out a chicken. There had been salesmen and soothsayers. There had been acrobats, button peddlers, men up to no good. Everyone stopped by on their way to Piedras Negras. Here, there was a town of eight hundred, but she might as well have been wrecked on the tip of Tierra del Fuego. No one would talk about anything except for Clarity and Unity and Natural Satisfaction, the Mexicans included. If possible, they were worse than the Anglos, parroting them in stilted English. The peons were probably the same as peons all over, but they were hardly fit for company, and besides, she never saw them. They had no reason to come to Casa Grande. Owen would not give them anything, not even oranges on their saint day. He hated saint days. True religion, he said, was watching an ant wiggle up a cactus thorn. She didn't care much for mass, but his reasoning made no sense. You couldn't confess to an ant.

She reached under the bed and pulled out the sewing basket. Refugio had sent the fabric as a present for having had the baby. It was lovely, white silk with lilac flowers that brought out the color in her hair. It would make a fine dress, something to celebrate her waist returning to normal. She threaded the needle and sewed, stopping now and then to stare at the space in front of her. Her stitchwork was minute and beautiful but, unlike her riding, not known for its rapidity. Not that it mattered when she completed it. No opera. No motoring over the Seine. No getting out of bed for that matter. Well, she'd get out of bed if they were ever invited anywhere. But they wouldn't be. Since she'd arrived, they'd been invited to exactly one party outside of Pristina, a local rancher's barbecue, a veiled attempt by the rancher to get Owen to fund a railroad. Dolores had gone, hoping to make friends. And she could have. There were two perfectly nice ladies she'd invited to tea. But the moment they stepped into her parlor, they glared and sniffed and smoothed their skirts. She didn't even get a chance to ask if they took sugar. She had no idea what had happened until the doctor explained. The picture on the mantle was not of one of Owen's ancestors, but Brown John or John Brown, one of those simplistic Yankee names you could never keep straight—in any case, a great enemy of the South. Even she, who knew nothing, knew that you didn't flaunt a portrait of an abolitionist in a Texas parlor.

The baby screamed. Not a yelp or a whelp or a waking whimper, a full-on furious scream like a knife through the head. Dolores tossed her sewing across the room. The baby's hands and feet moved in tight, quick circles. Dolores took a deep breath. Maybe this time she wasn't screaming simply to torture her. It might be, it should be hunger. She was due for a feeding. Dolores unbuttoned her robe. Another one of Owen's grand ideas. No wet nurse, no bottles. Her role in the improvement of evolution, which seemed a lot more like devolution, turning ladies into barnyard animals. Victoria clamped her mouth around a nipple. Dolores, relieved that she had figured out what to do, leaned against the headboard, feeling rather pleased with herself until she saw her sewing thrown in a heap in the corner of the room. She'd thrown it way too far away, she would never be able to reach it from the bed.

Afterward, sated with milk, Victoria nestled into her, surprising Dolores, for the baby usually pushed away the moment she was through, her tiny arms remarkably strong. Touched, Dolores leaned down and smelled her skin. How wonderful when she was like this, how easy to love every ounce of her. She kissed her tummy, sweet and soft, smooth and perfect, then changed her diaper, laughing at the fat baby legs that wiggled in the air. She wouldn't mind doing the same thing. The problem with being a bedwoman was the crampiness and stiffness. It was no way to live! She rang for Alma. Soon she'd get Otto to construct a garbage chute from her bedroom down to the kitchen. That way she'd be able to toss the soiled rags down the hole without bothering anyone, but for now, she needed Alma. The bell clanged flatly. "Mas como un cencerro que una campanilla de mujer de cama, no?" Victoria kept wiggling her legs. Alma arrived, panting from the stairs. She took Victoria's diaper and opened the shutters.

"Thank you, Alma," Dolores said.

Alma clomped back down. Merde. She'd forgotten to ask her to pick up her sewing. She put Victoria in the cradle, got the pole, and crawled to the northwest corner of the bed. The fabric had hit the wall and slipped down to the baseboard where it lay bunched in silky folds. Dolores leaned over the side, arms stretched, hands clasping the pole. It almost touched the closest fold. She squirmed an inch closer. She had to put a hand on the floor for support. She reached as far as she could—but she didn't have the strength to manipulate the pole with only one hand. She dropped the pole and crawled back to the headboard. But it had felt good to stretch. She mimicked Victoria, rolling back and kicking up her legs. The nightgown slipped, and there they were, not fat and heavy, but long and pale, scissoring through the air. She heard Alma trudging back up the stairs and quickly scooted her legs under the sheet.

"Alma, would you mind getting my sewing? It seems to have slipped."

"Of course, Mrs. Scraperton." Alma pressed her hands to her knees and painfully lowered herself. "Here you are."

"Thank you."

Alma took Victoria away for her bath. Dolores found the needle and returned to her stitching, but she couldn't concentrate. The light was getting low. She turned on the bedside lamp. Perhaps she would write a letter; she owed many—to Isabel, to her mother, to Kern Hook, the Australian ranch hand responsible for getting her into this predicament. No, she got herself into it, or wagging-tongued, jealous cousins, always assuming the worst—they got her into it. That was one good thing about Owen; he didn't care about reputations, ruined or otherwise.

He came back. Dolores felt it before she heard it, a shift in the atmosphere, a crackling alertness. His boots pounded up the stairs, pricking up the beginnings of another headache. He paused at the landing, then started again, not toward her room, toward the bathroom, his tread now softer. Now his voice and Alma's murmured over the splash of water. Dolores imagined Victoria's skin, glistening and slippery wet, Alma holding her underneath the armpit, Owen bending down, letting her squeeze his finger. There would be an expression of awe on his face. The bathroom door creaked, and he strode down the hall, his footfalls back to their normal, general-on-parade *clack-clack-clack*; she pressed her palms to her ears. El jefe glorioso! Striding down the avenue, flowers raining from balconies. The clacking stopped. He stood on the other side of her door. There was silence, a palpable hesitation. When the door opened, he was dark and solid against the warm light of the hall. A mild panic rose in her chest. She stared down at her nightgown, saw a milk stain, covered it up.

"Dolores. Alma has enough to do without bathing Victoria."

Well, what did he expect? Only allowing her one servant. At home, in spite of their scrimping, they still managed to keep some semblance of a household. The springs groaned as he sat on the edge of her bed. He hovered over her. His lean, taut face, his singular eyebrow, the hair almost as thick over the nose as over the eyes.

"Still don't feel any better?"

She shook her head.

His fingers grazed her hip, tentatively. Her body still mystified him; it was, as far as she could make out, her only advantage. And youth. He'd get old soon and when this happened, according to her mother, he'd become more manageable. But not according to Marina—not that man, she'd said, that man and age are playing a different game. She had predicted a disastrous marriage. She was probably right about the age too. He certainly didn't act fifty. Fifty was her father, stooped shoulders, molars ground to stubs, glorifying forgotten forbears. Owen's shoulders were square and his teeth were sharp. Ancestors? Droughts? Locusts? Pah! He smoothed a lock of hair from her forehead.

"Badinoe says you should get out of bed a couple times a day. Exercise. You'll never regain your strength if you stay there the whole day through."

She told him she would as soon as she was able.

"Generalissimo misses you," he said. "He's getting fat. No one to ride him."

"You can ride him."

"Not like you can." He fumbled a kiss. She blinked back hot tears. Bedwomen didn't cry.

♣

The first time that Dr. Badinoe had seen the reduction works he'd been bumping along, bruised and exhausted in the back of the stagecoach. He'd thought he'd gone sleepless too long and was hallucinating. He'd seen plenty of industrial buildings, but in places like Baltimore and Chicago, places with railroads and electricity, not cactus-strewn wildernesses days away from the nearest depot. One condenser alone would have been impressive, but there were eight: towering, faceless brick. And the furnace. And the jaw crusher. How many bricks did that take? How many mule trains trekking how many hundreds of miles over an oasis-less desert? It seemed more likely that the thing had sprung fully formed from Owen's head.

Now, two years later, the works still struck him as strange. He watched a load of ore rumble from the mouth of a jaw crusher, clatter down the chute, and disappear into the open maw of the furnace. On the bottom, two oily-skinned men, shimmering in the heat waves, stoked the fire. Badinoe took off his hat and wiped his forehead. The heat was such that he could barely stand in the shade, doing absolutely nothing other than wait. He watched the fire-stokers, wondering about the composition of the air they were inhaling. Somewhere in that furnace was a leak. He had spent over a year, double-checking and triple-checking his facts, arranging his data into Owen's beloved graphs and charts. Salivations on the rise? Check. Trembling of the extremities? Check. Fetid ulcers? Check. Teeth falling out? Check. Madness? Thankfully, no, at least not yet. But every other symptom of mercury poisoning had been recorded, and the miners who had brought him these symptoms all worked at or near the furnace.

Badinoe had given Owen the report in person. He handed it to him, his only copy, his chest zinging with hope and nerves. "Thank you, Gene. I'll look at it first chance." What a fool. He knew something about human nature. What had he been thinking? That he'd be able to sway him? Owen was enamored, *enamored*. Get him on the subject of mercury, *his* mercury, not any old mercury—he admitted the dangers of the mercuries of Almaden and Konia, but his mercury, Pristinite Mercury, was different. Pristinite Mercury only damaged those whose wills wavered, whose constitutions were somehow corrupt. The good and the virtuous it left alone, or even, somehow, benefited. Look at the health and vigor of almost all of his miners: happy, proud, in better condition than most men that he'd ever seen—the look in his eyes was the look of an adolescent describing his first love, that gleam, that irrevocable faith in its beauty and goodness. What did Badinoe think, some prudent observations and quiet assertions were going to make a dent in that?

The cave girls approached, cheering him somewhat. The cave girls meant that the mule train would be here soon. Up where they lived, up in the hills, the girls could watch the mule train as it crossed the desert and so time their descent to coincide with the train's arrival. They came carrying buckets, some on their heads, some in their hands, some strung from sticks balanced over their shoulders. The best part about them was their voices, mercifully light and free, mocking the humorless drone of the machinery and the English-language laws. Badinoe closed his eyes, the better to listen. He could make out a few words. But for the most part their language was a mystery, a mishmash of Jumano and who knew what else, remarkably musical.

Trailing the group was the silent one, Guillermina Negra. Badinoe recognized her from the way she moved, a smooth glide, the bucket seeming to float on her head. He could not yet see her needle, but he would soon enough. She was famous for the grace with which she simultaneously sewed and walked. Staunch Owenites, people who barely acknowledged that the caves existed, spoke of her approvingly, industry and beauty wrapped into one. He blew a smoke ring and aimed, hoping to give her a tobacco-scented halo. It shimmered toward her and, to Badinoe's amusement, rose over her head. She walked beneath it oblivious, then moved on, her needle flashing in the sun.

The train appeared, eight mules, one driver, and one wagon, creaking under the weight of its burden, a 500-gallon tank, filled almost completely with the muddy water of the Rio Grande. The spent beasts shambled through the dust, too tired to blink away the flies. But the driver, Nueve Dedos, didn't seem the worse for wear. He bounced on his seat, whistling a lewd and cheerful cowboy song. When he got to the girls, he jumped to the ground and stretched, his shirt darkened by moons of sweat.

The girls watched him eagerly, all except for Guillermina, who sat on a dented gasoline canister, her eyes fastened on her needlework. The driver swaggered to the back of the tank, enjoying the girls' eyes and giggles, but once he put his hand on the spigot, the clowning stopped. The water cost ten cents a bucket, and the buckets were rationed. Not a drop was spilled. One by one, the girls floated crosses on the water's surface to keep it from sloshing over the sides, and abandoned their chatter to quietly walk back up the hill.

Last in line was Guillermina. Nueve Dedos got the honor

of balancing the bucket on her head. She scratched a mosquito bite on her calf with her toes, then turned toward the hills, her skirt swaying gently. But now, in a flurry of yelling and confusion, Ysidro Herrida barreled into her. Badinoe groaned along with everyone else as the bucket toppled from her head. He leapt forward as if to catch it. Guillermina got it before he did and tipped it upward.

Ysidro hopped around in front of her, apologizing in English and Spanish and apparently Jumano, promising to buy her another bucketful. She yelled and yelled, silent no longer, her black eyes shining, her fury mounting. Two Anglo kids raced toward them, also yelling Ysidro's name. He took one look at them and sped off. She glared after him, her sewing bunched in one fist, the almost empty bucket in the other.

"Whoa now, it was an accident," said Badinoe, putting his hand on the girl's shaking shoulder. "Let me fill it up for you. It wasn't your fault."

"Thank you," she said stiffly.

He rebalanced the bucket on her head. "De nada," he replied, and watched her resume her trek to the caves, not quite as gracefully, but still sewing.

Badinoe returned to his original errand, but when he got to the spigot, Nueve Dedos gave him a menacing stare. Was it Guillermina? Could Nueve Dedos be angry about that? Badinoe opened his palms in a gesture of peace. You had to be careful with these men. They were so excitable.

Nueve Dedos nodded toward a couple of patrols waiting on the other side of the water tank. "They want you."

"Oh, I see."

They were missing an arm each. Together they made a perfect set. They were the victims of mining accidents—all the patrols were. It was a brilliant maneuver on Owen's part. Give the injured a raise and the right to carry a six-shooter and see if they complained. Badinoe approached, smiling genially, very aware of the flask hidden in his back pocket. But it was empty. If they asked, he would say it was for water. He would show it to them. He had written *Water* on it in preparation for just such a request.

"Good afternoon," he said, wishing that he could recall the younger's name. They'd had a conversation last year about Vermont, where the kid had been born, where he'd had the fortune or misfortune to first hear Owen speak. "How can I help you?"

The kid looked at his feet, as if ashamed. The older one shoved him forward, and the kid unpinned his sleeve, revealing a stump that ended a couple of inches away from his shoulder. Puss oozed from a gash that ran along the side.

"Looks like a knife wound."

"Just a scrape," the kid said, tight-lipped.

"Why didn't you come to me earlier?" Badinoe opened his medical bag—he never went anywhere without it—swabbed the wound with alcohol, and dressed it on the spot. "Come by my office tomorrow."

The pair moved off. Badinoe and Nueve Dedos watched them until they were out of sight. "Cuidado, Doctor," Nueve Dedos said. He made an adjustment to the spigot on the water tank, filled Badinoe's flask, and gravely handed it to him. The doctor held his nose to the rim and inhaled, pausing to enjoy the melting feeling as the vapors tickled his nostrils and throat.

"Magic stuff," said Badinoe.

"Puro, no?" said Nueve Dedos, counting his change.

Badinoe tipped his hat and wandered off, taking care not to look too closely at the other people hanging about the periphery of the reduction works, some of whom would be on the same errand and would not want to be observed. But he wanted to observe. He wanted to know that he had company, that he was not alone in his habits.

He walked down Independence, reflecting on how uncivilized it was, having to smuggle booze from a nine-fingered Mexican, not to mention the indignity of solitary drinking. Why did he put up with this? He, Gene Badinoe, bad-I-know, half-decent doctor, confirmed East Coaster, comfortable with his corruptions. He had no business in this sort of experiment. He would have never come, had he known. Though he should have been suspicious: a town called Pristina. But he hadn't thought about it and the package with the Principles had gotten lost in the mail. Ah hell, even if the package had come, it might not have stopped him. He'd been in such a state, shaking off malaria and grieving for Charles. The invitation had seemed some kind of divine deliverance. A mining town! A Wild West adventure! And so intriguing, to have been asked by Owen. A whole other animal back when he knew him, a kid slouching in a blue sweater, shuffling a pack of cards. Nothing extraordinary; and yet, Owen must have had a seed of something peculiar, something worth investigating, even then. For thirty years later, Badinoe not only remembered his name, but seeing it on the return address had roused his curiosity to a degree that couldn't be explained by the simple desire to know what had become of an old classmate.

He entered into the park, though it was not on his way home, and wandered through the landscaped rocks and cacti, to the pièce de résistance, a small fortune of mercury overflowing from a steel chalice. The two metals were almost the same color, so that the steel looked as if it were simultaneously melting and keeping its shape. There had been mercury fountains in the Roman Empire too. Perhaps that had been what drove the emperors mad, though probably not. In liquid form, mercury wasn't that dangerous, as long as you did not swallow a pint of it. It was the gas you had to be wary of. He pressed his finger into the basin, and the mercury, sun-warmed and pleasant, pressed back. Damn! It was fantastic stuff. A silver droplet wiggled on the palm of his hand. They had called it living silver in the middle ages. Quicksilver now. Silver endowed with the quick of life.

He couldn't blame Owen for his mania. He was fascinated by it too. How could anyone not be? The alchemists had worshipped it. As had the doctors, the whole benighted tribe of seventeenth- and eighteenth-century doctors who prescribed it for practically everything. Dropsy, yellow fever, rheumatism, elephantitus, plague, erysipelas, dysentery, colic, lice and vermin, sore throat, pox. Even now, in its medicinal decline, dentists still used it, and abortionists, to ill effect. He himself used it. Mercuric bichloride to disinfect, mercuric chloride to loosen the bowels. In Cuba, he'd rubbed a trace of pure mercury in chalk and honey to treat crab infestations, and the soldiers had been grateful.

He let the droplet fall back into the fountain and watched it merge into the larger pool. "To poison," he said, and recklessly took a swig of the mescal, right there in public.

If he only knew why mercury affected some and not others, the physiological reasons that some men seemed to be immune. He had compared the incidences of sickness with exposure to the fumes, age, body weight, racial type. The only thing that he could prove beyond a doubt was that furnace men got sicker than the others. But, as Owen was sure to point out, if he ever acknowledged the report, the furnace man who had been stoking the flames the longest was healthy as an ox. Badinoe grunted in frustration. All he wanted, all the report suggested, was that the furnace be overhauled. Yes, that would mean putting the fire out, stopping operations for days, burning through heaps of scarce fuel in order to get the temperature back up to par, but if Owen cared so much about his men, as he said that he did every chance he got, he could at least see if there were indeed leaks. Why hadn't he responded? Had he even read it? He probably read the first sentence then threw it away.

He arrived back at his office, toying with the idea of actually writing a letter of resignation instead of continuously composing one in his head. A man stood on the porch. Not the patrol with the puss-oozing stump, but a slim, mustachioed peon who Badinoe recognized from the Wednesday markets. He had a spot in front of Offitz & Carruthers and a raggedy yellow blanket upon which usually rose a neat pyramid of melons. Badinoe mounted the steps, his consternation giving way to a pleased curiosity. The peons didn't usually come to him, preferring the services of La Herrida. Frankly, Badinoe didn't blame them.

"Buenas tardes," Badinoe said, extending his hand. A gesture that went unmet, for the melon seller was in the process of taking off his hat and clutching it to his chest and had no hands to spare. Badinoe put his hand in his pocket.

In halting Spanish the peon asked if Badinoe could examine his nephew.

"Con placer," said Badinoe, beginning to wonder why the peon hadn't gone to La Herrida, beginning to worry about it. What if he had? What if La Herrida knew that the nephew was a hopeless case and had refused to help? Badinoe would get blamed for whatever happened to the boy. But there was nothing he could do about it now. He'd already said yes. He saddled his horse and followed the man past the reduction works, past Casa Grande, onto a faint desert trail marked with cottonwood stumps and the rusty remains of early mine workings. Not long after sunset, they arrived at a forlorn little jacal. The peon went in to announce their arrival, and Badinoe tethered his horse to a post. To his relief, La Herrida's pointy-eared burro was there too. He tarried by the burro, trying to think of some new way to approach its owner. Maybe out here, away from Pristina, she'd finally talk to him. He didn't want to break into her business, he just wanted to know what she knew. For instance, what had she put in that balm that had fixed Juan José's teeth back in his mouth? It was astounding. He had examined Juan José at the peak of salivation, and his teeth had been loose as marbles. Now he could eat corn on the cob. Badinoe could improve things slightly with a chlorate of potash and myrrh, but he hadn't come anywhere near La Herrida's remedy.

She came out, a tiny, energetic old woman wrapped in a shawl.

"Buenas noches, señora." He doffed his hat.

She gave him her customary glare. He remained still, trying his best to convey a sense of stoicism and respect. She mounted her burro—a move that she did with astounding agility for someone her age—then turned toward him, speaking rapidly and shrilly. Badinoe's heart leapt. But the words weren't for him. The language was incomprehensible. The melon seller ran out of the hut and appeared to be pleading with her. She raised her chin in the air, as imperious with him as she'd been with Badinoe, and clipped off, leaving behind a scent of sage and smoke. Badinoe sighed. She could die any moment, taking with her all her knowledge. It was irresponsible. She had no apprentices, no assistants. She hadn't bequeathed her remedies to anyone. You would think that she'd have some sort of pride of craft.

He entered the hut gingerly, hoping that the disturbance with La Herrida was not on account of him. If it was, the peons were too gracious to let him know. They crowded around, welcoming him warmly. Aside from the melon seller, there were three aunts in black dresses who took turns telling him, showing him, gesturing to him, that the father was off with his goats, the mother was dead, and the boy was sick. Badinoe knelt by the boy's pallet. He was a skinny child, about seven, shivering and sweating, caked over with a pungent plaster that La Herrida must have concocted. There wasn't much to do except give him some quinine, but when Badinoe tried to leave, the boy moaned, and the women looked at him in alarm.

So he remained, sitting on the stamped-earth floor, leaning against a wall that crumbled every time he switched positions. A few inches away, the boy struggled for breath, every now and then reaching out a hand that Badinoe held, then released. He must have dozed off at some point, because he woke with a start, surrounded by blackness and unfamiliar odors and the boy's ragged breath. Louder than the breath, and far more constant, was a steady, piercing *tick-tick-tick*. At first, he thought it was an alarm clock, but a goat herder would not own such a thing. The ticking continued, mechanical and adamant. It sounded like a time bomb, an anarchist's time bomb. But that was just the boy's fever affecting his imagination. The anarchists were in Chicago and St. Louis. Not Pristina. His eyes adjusted to the dark, and he crawled around, avoiding the sleeping forms of the women and the fevered spasms of the boy. At last he discovered its source: a wasp's nest, tucked above the door of the jacal. Moonlit ants streamed up the pale pole and chomped into its papery mass, dismantling it bite by bite.

Just before dawn, the boy's breathing quieted and the flush on his cheeks subsided. The women clasped their hands together and thanked their gods, the virgin, and he, Doctor Badinoe, for the blessing wrought. They made him coffee, which he gratefully drank. As he left, he told them that they could always come to him for help, and he would do what he could, and they would not be charged. But they wanted to pay. The white-haired one ran after him with a basket of eggs, nestled in grass so as not to break.

He took the eggs, it was impossible not to, and carefully set the basket on the triangle formed by the pommel and his thighs. Slowly, carefully, he set off. Sun streamed over the peaks and passes of the Chisos Mountains, tinting the dust on the mesquite pods silver. He passed through an alley of telegraph plants, white tufted, stinking of camphor, and thought that he saw a snake slithering through the stalks. But perhaps not. His horse continued at a placid and unhurried pace, unbothered, and his horse did not like snakes. Badinoe did. Skin shedders. Knowledge whisperers. When the kids chucked rocks at them, he tried to dissuade them. What was it about snakes that caused such enmity? He ought to hire one or two of those kids, get them to capture some snakes for him. He wanted to know whether they were susceptible to mercury poisoning. Birds were. Rats were. Maybe reptiles were too. He could cage a few, rattlers or bull snakes, whatever they found, place them at different sites—at the reduction works, in the mines. Observe.

At the turnoff for Casa Grande he paused, wondering if Owen were home. Probably not, he left for work frightfully early. But even if he were, it would not do to ring the doorbell and ask directly if he had read the report. Badinoe sighed. Perhaps he wasn't being snubbed. Perhaps Owen really and truly hadn't had time to read it. Perhaps he hadn't even looked at the first sentence. He squinted at the roof, noticing for the first time a weathervane. A wrought-iron weathervane, in the shape of a whale, complete with flukes and spout. It shifted in the breeze, and Badinoe fought off a wave of nostalgia. He had grown up with weathervanes like that, fat whales spinning about on peaked roofs.

Up spouted by a whale in air
To express unwieldy joy.

He winced. He had clutched those lines to his heart, feeling as though they'd been written just for him. He had felt such exuberance, such gratitude, that he had sent the poem to Charles. A mistake. Charles had been the most practical of men, no patience for poetry, whales, allusions, what was any of that compared to the scratch of whiskers and grasp of fingers.

Owen came out of the stables. Badinoe's pulse quickened; he never saw the man alone. Always there was at least one other person, usually more. Owen trotted down the hill.

"Morning," he said, his voice brimming with authority and goodwill.

"Good morning," Badinoe replied, involuntarily pulling in his stomach.

"You're out early."

"Yes. I was looking after a patient."

Owen's eyes were deep and glittering, his jaw square. He was not handsome, but he was hard not to look at. Badinoe peered down at his saddle.

"Want some eggs?" Jokingly, he offered the basket to Owen.

"No thanks, we're well stocked." Owen touched his hat brim. "I've got to be off. I'm running late."

"Wait," said Badinoe.

Owen turned back, slightly smiling. "Yes?"

Badinoe had to work hard to get the words out. "My report. Did you get a chance to read it?"

"Ah, yes. Didn't I mention that to you?"

"No."

"Ah."

"Well? What did you think?"

Owen scratched his chin. "I talked to the engineers. The problem's not in the furnace. That's a top-grade piece of equipment." He gazed into Badinoe's eyes. "But you are right. Mercury is escaping, as you so well documented. Very impressive work."

"Thank you," said Badinoe, annoyed at the easy way that Owen's praise warmed him.

"The leak is in the condensers," continued Owen. "You don't get them cold enough, you can't condense all the gas, bits of it seep out. We've got to get those condensers colder. The colder the condensers, the less gas escapes, the more mercury we bottle up."

"And the less sick the men," said Badinoe.

A thought flashed through Owen, whether it was related to the sick men or not Badinoe could not tell. "In any case," Owen said, adjusting his hat, "you'll be pleased to hear that we have a solution."

"You do?"

"Yes. Ice."

"Ice?" repeated Badinoe. The creek was a dry scar, the cisterns empty bowls of rust.

"We're building a factory." Owen smiled at Badinoe's confusion. "An ice factory. Maybe we should name it after you."

"What?"

"It was your report that brought the problem to my attention."

"Yes, but I certainly never intended . . ." Badinoe trailed off, embarrassed.

"Don't be modest, Gene. Just giving credit where credit is due."

Badinoe snorted. "If you need a name, name it after—" He hesitated, unable to think of someone appropriate. "Name it after your daughter. How's she doing?"

Owen's smile shifted to one of pure paternal pride. "She's sitting now, smiling, watching everything, taking note. She's going to get a kick out of that ice, holding it in her fat little hand, feeling it melt. How long since you held an ice cube?"

Badinoe could picture a cube of ice in his palm, but he couldn't bring on the feeling of it, that visceral sense of cold. "A long time," he said.

Owen nodded. "Well, you'll get the opportunity again." He clicked his horse and trotted toward town.

The sun had mounted in the sky and the day was already hot, too hot to imagine ice. But Owen would do it. The peons would be rationed a bucket of water a day, and ice would be made in the desert. No wonder everyone followed him, he worked magic. At least so far he did. Badinoe clucked at his horse and followed in Owen's path, watching his old friend from a distance, the straightness of his back apparent even from here. He started thinking of the ants dismantling the wasps' nest, bite by bite, the clicking of their mandibles on the papery walls so regular and mechanical he had taken the sound for the ticking of a time bomb. He would have liked to tell Owen about it. But it was hard to just casually talk with that man.

1906

O nly a few days after Dolores made an off-hand comment about how a train might benefit Pristina, Owen packed her and Victoria into the stagecoach. "Let's see your train in action," is all he said. Dolores, who had never imagined that he'd take her suggestion seriously, was pleased as could be. They rode up to Marfa—the nearest town on the Southern Pacific, the spot where their own mercury got loaded onto boxcars—checked into the hotel, then headed to the station to watch the afternoon train arrive. Oh, the glory of it! The velvety smoke billowing into the sky, the reverberations of the whistle, the rhythm of the wheels, the astonishing amount of cars, some open and cramped with cattle, others mysteriously closed, bearing who knew what treasures. They met the engineer and the fireman, a gregarious fellow who explained how his boiler worked and let Victoria walk off with a broken coal scoop that turned everything it touched black.

The afternoon had been lively and informative, just the kind of thing that Owen usually loved, but he held himself aloof. Dolores shrugged it off, figuring that he did not approve of the tobacco and jocularity of the fireman. Then the next day, before going home, Owen insisted on hiring a carriage and taking a drive along the Southern Pacific tracks. She could not understand. They would be spending the rest of the day in a stagecoach, not an easy thing to do with a restless creature like Victoria, and now he wanted her to sit in a carriage beforehand? But there was no dissuading him. They went several miles out into the desert until they came to a white bleached mound, wavering in the heat. Victoria hopped to the ground and ran toward it. Owen nodded gravely and offered Dolores his hand, indicating that she too should leave the carriage and inspect the curiosity. They stood by the mound, fanning themselves, or rather Dolores fanned herself as Victoria squatted by the rim of the heap, picking up horns and peering through the eye sockets of skulls.

"What you see here," said Owen, in his grand oratory manner, "are the remains of a pack of antelope. Pronghorn antelopes, the pride of the plains. You know how fast they can run, Victoria? They are the fleetest of creatures, and competitive too. The first time they saw the train, they raced it. They thought it was a game. They ran along beside it, gaining, gaining, aiming to outpace it. They might have too, but the train hit a curve, and the antelopes were going too fast to change direction. Into it they crashed, hitting it with the full force of their speed. The collision swept them off the ground, up into the sky. Two landed on the roof of the train and were carried on to Marfa. The rest dropped to the ground and died of broken spines or perhaps simply shock."

Dolores pictured the antlers and hoofs and bright white tails, flipping like circus acrobats. If you must go, what a way to do it, wind whistling in your antlers, careening into rushing metal! That's what you would remember, your speed, your somersaulting ascent.

"How marvelous," she said.

"I'd call it steel-age wreckage," Owen countered, eying her sternly.

She faltered. How could he expect her to get teary over a pack of antelope? They ate antelope. But clearly he did. They drove back in a crackly, accusatory silence. After a while, she began to understand that it was not the antelope that had upset Owen, it was the train. The trip to Marfa, the viewing of the Southern Pacific, the visitation of the bones, all this was nothing but a very elaborate No to her suggestion.

"But why?" she asked Badinoe, when she got back. "Why take me all the way up there just to say no? Why taunt me with it?"

They were sitting on the doctor's back porch, looking out over his neighbors' laundry lines and the chickens pecking about in the dust. Ice clinked in their cups.

"I doubt that he meant to taunt you. He probably sought to educate you." Badinoe's eyes twinkled. "Can I get you another?"

She nodded. They usually had mescal, but he had received a package from the East and so today he was introducing her to gin and tonic. "A fine invention of the East India Company, I believe. To combat malaria." He handed her a cup.

"Thank you," she said, barely tasting it. "I don't understand. How can Owen be opposed to trains? He loves progress. You should hear him bragging about his ice machine and his automated lifts."

"Believe me, I hear it quite often." He lit his pipe and puffed in that languorous way of his.

"And he hates the mule train. He doesn't have any control over the drivers. They are always getting caught up in suspicious setbacks between here and Marfa. You set down some rails. You get the mercury into a rail car right here instead of having to oversee the whole operation of the unloading and the repacking with a bunch of people you don't trust. How can he be against that?"

"A train might bring things into town that he doesn't want—other people, for example, people with ideas not compatible with his."

"But he says that Pristina is supposed to be an example to

the world. How is that to happen if no one can see it?"

Badinoe sipped at his drink. "Thanks for bringing over the lime. It makes all the difference, you know. A good lime. You really want this train, don't you?"

"I suppose I do."

Badinoe laughed. "I have an idea."

And so an experiment was born, a surreptitious campaign to change Owen's mind and have him lay a feeder line. They called it Project Mercury, for Mercury was, among other things, the god of roads and communication. The newspapers and journals that Badinoe subscribed to made up the bulk of their ammunition. They came weeks and months late, often scuffed and torn, but filled with potential material. Articles about anarchists stockpiling weapons in Idaho, skirmishes in the minefields of Arizona, Colorado, and New Mexico, the proclamations of the ever more formidable Western Federation of Miners. At Casa Grande, over after-dinner coffee, Dolores read the accounts out loud, trusting Victoria to ask the right questions. Why did the workers sabotage the hoist, kill the governor, strangle the scabs? And Dolores answered: Because they didn't know about the Principles, honey. They're warped by money and superstition. They've never heard about merging with the planet. If your father would only share his knowledge! If people could only see Pristina!

But we're not ready, Owen would say. Some day, yes, but not until we've got a full-fledged example up and running.

But Daddy, Victoria would say. Pristina is great! The best!

Pristina was doing well. This much was true. Some genius had figured out a way to turn mercury into electric light, and now all over the country people were installing mercury vapor lamps on streets, in railroad yards and parks. Every day the value of a flask rose higher. Owen had invested their first big gain into a well and an underground piping system so that now each house had a trough filled with fresh potable water. At least half the peons had renounced their faith, moved down from the caves, and sworn allegiance to him. The town had a population of a thousand, Pristina proper that is, good sober people baking bread, breaking rocks, washing and rinsing with abandon. And they were happy, not a whisper of a strike among them. Owen would know. His patrols kept tabs on everything and everyone, except, apparently, her.

For months, as Alma cleared away the dinner plates, Dolores and Victoria started up on the Principles and Owen listened quietly, a big smile wrapped around his face. He loved the praise, of course, but he wouldn't budge. Whenever she got a chance, Dolores would slip off to Badinoe's, and they would discuss his every move and gesture, looking for a clue, a chink, some way to break him down. But all of their arguments and inspirations just led to more of that smug, stubborn, praise-loving smiling. Until one night, as they were going to bed, Owen said, quite out of the blue, "Well. Why not? But you get it up and running. I've got enough on my hands."

Hence her position as Directress of Communications and Transport. After eight months, she had arrived at the point when the first stage of the paperwork was over and true labor began. At this very moment, the railroad crew was grading the bed, or so she hoped. Unfortunately, she could not observe firsthand, for construction began at Marfa. But she'd be there soon enough and, for now, she had the telephone. She hurried her horse along. Pristina only had two telephones, one on the front porch of Offitz & Carruthers and one at company HQ. It would be much more efficient, of course, to have a telephone at Casa Grande. But convincing Owen of that was a project she had not had the time or energy to broach. She arrived at Offitz & Carruthers and saw to her relief that the telephone was unoccupied. She hitched Nickel in front of the store and ran up the steps before somebody else got to it.

"Good day, Mrs. Scraper-tin," said the operator.

"Hello, Gladys. Can you get me Marfa 288, please?"

"I'd be glad to, Mrs. Scraper-tin." The woman loved saying their name. Scraper. Pause. Tin. But not simply Tin. A long, drawn out Teeeeeiiiin.

Dolores listened to the static and did her best to ignore the group of miners loitering about the far end of the porch, observing her. She looked at her cuticles, she looked at her horse patiently swishing away the flies. The telephone line, tied to miles of ranchers' fences, rustled every time the wind blew. In the midst of the rustling came the faint laughter of the ranchers' wives who always listened in on Dolores's conversations, commenting on them without ever once saying anything directly to her. Dolores no longer cared. "Let them cackle," said Badinoe. "It's good for their lungs."

"Mrs. Scraper-teeeeiiiin?"

"Yes?"

"I've got Marfa 288."

"Thank you, Gladys."

She pushed her ear hard against the receiver, trying to make out every note of the foreman's voice, whiskey-rough and Irish, hard enough to understand when they talked face to face.

"Have the men started grading the bed?"

He said something indecipherable. Dolores repeated herself.

"Aye, ma'am. They have begun."

"They have begun?"

"They have begun."

A warm feeling spread through Dolores. She beamed at her horse, waiting placidly, patiently, loyally at the base of the steps. Next she spoke with MacArthur Corkblatt, director of the Stake Driving Ceremony. The lemons had arrived. The band had been hired. The golden stake was locked in the safe at the hotel.

"Very good," said Dolores. "I'll see you tomorrow."

"I look forward to it, Mrs. Scraperton. Have a safe trip."

Dolores smiled so wide that her cheeks hurt. She couldn't believe it. Tomorrow's trip to Marfa was just the beginning. After the Stake Driving Ceremony, Owen, Victoria, and she would board the Southern Pacific and travel all the way to Washington, D.C. She nodded good day to the miners, throwing them into a confused stir of grunting and hat doffing, and trotted down the steps. Washington! She swung up on the saddle. Embassies, streetcars, department stores. None of these dusty-brimmed, awkward miners. Instead, well-bred, well-dressed people speaking of all sorts of things, and not one conversation, not one thought, even, would be about how symbiotic mercury mining could quell socialist uprisings. No one would know, no one would care. She would go shopping. She would buy a mushroom hat. She had so much to do before then!

She galloped back home, thankful that she had the house to herself. It was so much easier getting work done when Owen and Victoria were away. She found the invoice from Monterey Iron & Steel, the California outfit that had forged their rails, and slipped it into her valise. The balance had to be paid before the company would send the final shipment. This was not a problem as the crew would not need more rails for another couple of months and by then the fiscal stuff would be sorted out. The problem was keeping the invoice handy. She had to come up with a better organizing system. It felt like she spent half her life looking for lost scraps of paper.

She had even lost the train tickets, but only for about

five panic-stricken minutes. They had arrived a month ago, cardboard tickets, thick, stiff, and substantial, covered over in bold, cheerful lettering: first class, two adult fares, one child, with transfers at Fort Worth and Chattanooga. She had rubbed, fondled, and worried over them to such an extent that they had taken on the appearance of faded tissue paper. She slipped them into an envelope and put them in her handbag. She tied bows around the presents. She'd ordered a tie for Owen's uncle and honey soap for his aunt. Hardly original, but Owen wouldn't tell her what his aunt and uncle were like. They were people typical of their class, that's what he said. When she asked what that meant, he said that they were Virginians. Virginians. Useful. She hadn't even known of their existence until planning the trip to Washington. Owen, blanching as he did whenever he had to spend money, had contacted them when he found out the price of hotels.

The only person in Owen's family that Dolores knew about was his mother, and she knew too much about her. She had been drilled on her favorite proverbs, her political opinions, her newspaper preferences, her outstanding thrift and unshakeable morality. And her death. Owen had told and retold and retold the story, drawing it out, the wobbly stool he had sat upon, her blue-veined hand upon which he could feel every pulse and tremor, her request that he open the window, his difficulty opening it, the children playing outside, his hope that she could hear their laughter, his return to her bedside, his discovery that she had stopped breathing, that she had not heard the children's laughter, that he had been deprived of touching her flesh at that moment she passed from life into death.

Dolores didn't even know the name of Owen's father, only that he too was dead. "Enough, Dolores. My father is dead." Maybe his mother had killed him. It had to be something unsavory, the way he avoided the topic. It wouldn't shock her, though. Her family might have produced Xavier Gonzalez and his noble martyrdom, but it had its share of shoddy, venal, underhanded deaths as well. She didn't understand how he could be so silent when it came to his family, he who was so damn vocal about everything else. Maybe that was it: the ranting and raving normally applied to the family he had re-routed to industrial relations, the hypocrisy of priests, the necessity of forming a brand-new race. Maybe she could un-derstand that. But it was awfully frustrating. How can you know someone if you don't know where they come from?

Last night, she had again pressed Owen for information, and instead of brushing her aside, he had said, "Dolores, you know everything about my family. You are it. You and Victo-ria. You are all a man could ever need and want." She sighed. He had said this quietly, his gaze direct, and she had felt badly about every joke she and Badinoe had ever made.

A horse appeared on the road. Dolores squinted to see if there were two people on it, in which case it would be Owen and Victoria returning from their Sunday picnic. Owen didn't call them picnics; he called them field trips. It's true that Victoria invariably picked up fossils, pebbles, bones, and a storehouse of impressive words: *cretaceous marl, invertebrates, survival of the fittest*. But they were also picnics. Dolores packed them roasted chickens, hard-boiled eggs, lemonade, and corn cakes. They ate them outdoors, a blanket spread beneath them.

Only one person on the horse. Not them. She eyed her rid-ing boots. They stood in the corner, in easy reach. It wouldn't be hard to catch up with them. Her eyes wandered back to her riding boots. She shouldn't. Victoria liked time alone with her father. She shifted piles and organized. She didn't, actually, have that much left to do. The house could be left a mess. Alma would clean up. Her eyes kept wandering back to her boots; they leaned against each other, impatient, waiting for something. They would have already finished the picnic. Still, she could ride back with them.

She galloped. The wind scoured her face, sending wind-tears down her cheeks and blurring the mesa. How good it was to go fast! Within a few moments, she forgot about her immediate object, forgot about everything really, even the train, so swept up was she in the rhythm of the hooves and the wind blowing her skirts, her ears, her hair. When she reached the box canyon, she felt that she had gotten there altogether too fast. Where were they? The place looked empty. She dismounted, feeling diminished as her feet landed on the flat, still earth. Nickel wandered over to the cistern, and she uncapped her canteen. They told her the canyon with the W marked in the cistern; there couldn't be another, she knew every cistern within riding distance. She arched her back and gazed at the stains of rust and lichen on the rock walls, the tufts of grass on top. Nothing remarkable about the place save for a tree that grew straight out of side of the cliff. By rights, it should have bent up or fallen down, but it stuck out horizontally, parallel to the ground below. She didn't know if it could truly be called a tree, it was more like a scrawny twist of bark, gallantly holding on. Nickel stood absolutely still; he had stopped drinking. He didn't look like himself. His neck was in a strange position, not up, not down, stretched as if he were straining for something but had forgotten what it was that he desired. He looked like a crazy, paralyzed mule. He looked like what she'd felt like until she befriended Badinoe. Lonely.

She peered around the canyon one last time. Pain bloomed in her chest. Maybe they never came. Maybe they just told her they did. She was being foolish. It was just that, well, Victoria was so enamored of her father. Dolores sometimes felt ignored—but she shouldn't complain. She and Victoria had good times together. Just last week, they had invented their own dance. Sunday night they had put on the gramophone and performed it for Owen, earning a standing ovation, though she could detect a stiffness hidden under his enthusiasm. Dancing was allowed, thank goodness, a perfectly legal pastime, but it was just a little too . . . purposeless to make him completely happy. Victoria seemed to sense it too. After they performed, she hadn't wanted to dance again.

Dolores had heard it said that daughters often loved their fathers more. She was not the first woman who this had happened to. Still, it was not pleasant, this feeling that sometimes overtook her, as if she were a bereft suitor. If only she could have a son who would love her more, but her womb remained stubbornly empty.

She came to a lopsided fire circle left over from cowboys or freighters. A scorpion, transparent and nervous, scrambled in the ashes. Dolores crushed it under her boot. She scraped the carapace on a rock, feeling better. Daughters ought to like their fathers better, according to Badinoe. He had all sorts of theories about balance in the universe, alchemy, male and female principles. But unlike Owen, he didn't take himself seriously; he'd make a pronouncement in a ponderous tone, then grin if she started to argue.

She'd never met anyone like Badinoe. Her father also had a passion for the past, but his was wrapped up in Don Xavier and the sword the Pope had blessed a thousand years ago. It had nothing to do with the present. Badinoe's past and present were so mixed up he talked about Pliny like he played checkers with him at the athenaeum. She wondered what would have happened if they had married. She wouldn't have been the Directress of Transport & Communications, but then again, a train wouldn't have been so necessary. She'd wander around, drunk on mescal, laughing at jokes she thought were funny but couldn't explain.

But they wouldn't have married. He wouldn't have asked. He didn't treat her like men normally did. The way he talked about war or clipped his nails, he didn't seem aware that she was a woman. It was better that way. The other way screwed things up, made you want things you couldn't name. Huge, vast, unreasonable things. She couldn't blame Owen for that; it had been her fault too. She remembered their wedding night, staring up at the ceiling. His power within her had felt so monumental, and yet as soon as her breathing returned to normal, she found that nothing had changed. She was still there, exactly as she had been before. What had she wanted? To be obliterated? And Owen, lying by her side, shaking like a leaf in a storm. Some obliterator. Toward dawn, he had slipped off the bed, kneeled in the gray light, put his head in her lap. She hadn't said anything. She had stroked him, as if comforting him, but she didn't know what she was comforting him for. His back had been wet and strangely cool.

Nickel snorted. "Okay, boy." She put her foot in the stirrup and swung up into the saddle. She left the canyon, still thinking about her and Owen's wedding night, her smile slightly rueful. He had not knelt before her since.

The shadows were long, but she was making good time, and soon arrived at the old stone chimney, a relic from an early rancher who'd had the good sense to move on to California. She turned onto the Comanche road. Badinoe had discovered that it was the Comanches who had first found the mercury. The Indians didn't care about mercury per se; it was the ore, the cinnabar, they were after. They used it for war paint. On the first full moon of September, the braves streaked themselves red and set off on their yearly raid, galloping down this very road, crashing deep into Mexico, and then back with horses, slaves, cattle, leaving ashes in their wake. They had been teetotalers too, like Owen.

Her horse buckled back, whinnying, pawing the air with his two front hooves. She barely missed being thrown. When she got him back on the ground, he bulged with tension and wouldn't budge. She looked around for a clue. Nothing. No Comanches. No patrols. Not even a vulture. The earth rolled outward, dotted with prickly pears and purple thistles. The sky was unsullied, a placid blue. She urged and cajoled and rubbed his stiff neck. He held his ground. No millipede in his path, no tarantula, nothing except for the bleached ruts of the road. He rarely behaved so. He was a good horse, not her favorite, but fleet and strong, and generally solid.

She slipped off the saddle, planted one boot in front of the other, entered the space the horse did not dare enter. No shift in atmosphere, no crack in the earth. Maybe it was Zizima, rising invisibly. Dolores cracked a smile. Zizima was Badinoe's latest discovery, the old Phrygian goddess of the mines. He wanted to resuscitate her, engage her in battle with Owen's Puritanism. They had poured some sacred gin in her honor, invoked her with a drinking song.

"Easy, Nickel," she said, dragging his reins. Nickel because he was the color of a nickel, but nickels were dependable, didn't spook. "Easy, Nickel." Clucking, pulling at the reins, the diffident sky all around them. He lifted a hoof, brought it down. One step into the bad patch. She murmured encouragement. She denied the possibility of evil, or even mischief, in the air. The horse shuddered. He picked along the road as if he were picking his way across the aftermath of a battle—a battle deprived of its clean-up commission, a field of stiff, splayed, half-clad mummies, fingers still twisted around heaven-stabbing bayonets, jaws slack, exposing gigantic tooth roots, puttees bunched around tibias and fibulas, matted colorless hair, paper-thin skin stretched over pelvic bones. She had been infected by Badinoe. He and his gore.

She dragged at the reins. Such a powerful head, what was he afraid of? She thought of the scorpion skittering in the ashes, afraid too. Everyone was scared of something. The patrols scared her, and chaos scared Owen. She wondered what frightened Victoria. She seemed oddly unfrightened for a little girl, but there had to be something other than, say, lack of Owen. Nickel picked along. Perhaps he picked through a field of dead horses. Pack horses, wild horses, gringo horses, Apache horses, Mexican horses, froth dry on the mouth, done in by loco weed. Perhaps cattle too, ribs breaking through their hides, pleading for water. And deer, panther-gashed bucks. And antelopes dropping out of the sky, heady with the rush of speeding metal.

♠

Victoria rode in the vee of Owen's legs, her hands resting lightly on the pommel, her arms settled inside his. Those arms. Even with the scrapes and bruises, her skin had a buttery smoothness that took his breath away. He loved the way its soft newness contrasted with the faded old black of his sleeves. It would make a good metaphor for something. Youth sheltered in the black wings of experience? He chewed it over, wondering if he should try it out on Victoria. But these days she buckled if anyone called her young. He grinned. She was six. What about . . . promise . . . promise sheltered in the black wings of experience . . . But should experience be black?

She tugged on his sleeve. They'd reached the site of the future train station, and she wanted to watch the mortar being mixed. He drew in the reins. The ticket booth and waiting area were still lime lines and orange flags and piles of bricks and lumber, but they had a fully erected clock tower. It rose three stories high, Pristina's tallest nonindustrial building, with a clock facing each of the four directions. The dials were for the most part classical white discs marked with black Roman numerals, but at Victoria's request the hands were red and tipped with curlicue arrows.

"Your clock looks good, Vic."

She didn't answer. She watched the workmen mix the mortar, a grave expression on her face.

"Everything okay?"

She nodded, but her forehead was still puckered. Owen wished he knew what she was thinking. This was new, this reticence.

She cheered up at the reduction works, no surprise there, she loved the gear-groaning, wheel-turning, seam-busting vitality of it. She raced ahead of him, tan legs and checkered skirt nimbly darting by knobby mule legs and dusty dungarees. "Stay close, Vic. This will only take a second."

She'd disappeared by the time he finished his business, but he knew where to find her. The whistle had blown, indicating a fuel feed. He found her standing a little too close to the open mouth of the furnace.

"Stand back, Vic."

The coals were red as snake tongues. She looked away for just a second. "580° Celsius, 1076° Fahrenheit. Less if you use lime."

"Exactly," said Owen. "So stand back."

"But look how close they are." She pointed at the men shoveling out slag.

"They're miners. That's their job."

"So? I'm going to be a miner too."

"Not for a while."

Victoria didn't lose interest until the men hooked their rods into the burning metal doors and dragged them shut. Then she smiled at Owen. "Look what I found." She took a rock out of her pocket. "It was in the tailings, but feel how heavy it is. I think it's still got ore in it."

He weighed it in his palm. It was heavy, not to mention red-streaked and free of burn marks. "You're right, sweetheart," he said. "It managed to escape the furnace. Why don't you put it over with the fresh ore?" He watched her run to the proper pile and toss it in. He had no regrets about not having a son. Quicksilver ran in her veins.

* * *

They clopped past the trail to the caves, then up to the white picket fence of the cemetery. Owen unbuttoned the top of his shirt and breathed in the cleaner air of the hills. "What a beautiful day," he said, squeezing Victoria's legs with his. She twisted back and eyed him suspiciously.

"Where are we going? This isn't the way to the box canyon."

"Don't you remember? I told you I'd show you these hadrosaur prints."

"Oh."

"What's wrong?"

"I wanted to see the ammonite." The ammonite was a glossy purple fossil embedded in the wall of the box canyon. "I wanted to touch it."

"We'll go there next time."

"But we'll be in Washington."

"It'll be there when we get back."

She edged away from him.

"We always go to the box canyon, Vic. Sometimes you have to try new places. If not you get crusty."

"But I like the ammonite."

"It's like the train. We have to explore new things, follow strange paths, push frontiers. That's how we discover fresh ore veins, right? If we just stuck with one, we'd dry up."

The horse reached the top of the hill, and the mountains, dark blue against the light blue, rose magnificently into view. Nearer, purple persimmons hung ripe on the trees, and the grasses, pale gold, swished as they passed through them. Owen hummed a song from his childhood.

"Look!" Victoria shouted. A butterfly fluttered around the swords of an agave. She turned back to him, grinning. "You remember the butterfly?"

"Hmm?"

"The butterfly I caught with my net?"

"Yes. A monarch."

"From Mexico," she said, "just like mother. When I stuck the needle through it, it went"—she made a dry, crisp noise with her lips—"but it didn't bleed." She settled back against his chest. "Father, why do we have to go to Washington?"

"I thought that you wanted to go. You don't want us to leave you behind, do you?"

"No."

"Sometimes you've got to make sacrifices, Vic-a-dee. If we want our train, we've got to go and shake some hands and rustle up some money. And we want that train, no? We've got to get our mercury out into the world. It's the best way to distribute it, get it to do what it was meant to do: light lights, oscillate oscillators, disinfect, fulminate, tell the temperature . . . And think of the people we'll meet, the new blood and new talents that will come to us if we only make the trip a little easier. We'll finally get that athenaeum up and running. Wouldn't you like to hear some good lecturers?"

"You're a good lecturer."

"Yes. But believe it or not, Miss Vic, there are things that I do not know. We'll invite men with magic lanterns who can show us pictures of all the places our mercury goes: San Francisco, Peru, the Celestial Empire. Men with Magnet-O-Scopes. Men with X-ray machines who can show us the anatomy of our own bodies. Picture that, Vic."

He squeezed her, excited by those X-ray machines. When he first heard about them, he'd wanted to see if he could apply them to the land, see straight down to the underground structure, but now he was just as eager to look inside himself. Age hadn't sapped his energy, but it had played havoc with his exterior. His skin was sucked dry and stretched tight and visited by unpredictable moles and outlandishly long hairs growing from places they'd never grown before. He wanted to be able to see beneath this confusion, ensure that his skeleton at least was still orderly and symmetrical.

"Will they have X-ray machines in Washington?"

"Yes. And streetcars and expositions—"

"And embassies. What will you say to the French ambassador?"

"Hmm. I'll say, *Howdy, sir, please pass the escargot.* Don't you worry, Vic-a-dee. We won't be dabbling much with those Frenchies, that's your mother's domain. We'll be funding our train and scattering Pristinian seeds to the winds. Then we'll choo-choo out of there and say hi to your ammonite. We'll never have to leave Pristina again. After this, people can come down and see us."

The goat bells rang, plangent and pure, growing louder as they crossed the meadow. Now the animals came into view, horned and shaggy-stomached, half hidden by the grass. The goat herder, a knobby-kneed boy not much older than Victoria, shaded his eyes with his hand to watch them pass. Victoria stuck out her tongue at him, wiggling the tip, one of her less enchanting tricks.

"Stop that this instant," Owen said.

"What?"

"You know what. Don't point your tongue at people."

"Why not?"

"If you want people to respect you, you have to show respect for them."

"But he was staring at me."

"And you weren't staring at him?"

"He has something funny on his face."

Owen glanced as casually as possible at the boy. A large pale splotch marred his cheek. "It's a birthmark, that's all, some fault in pigmentation."

"It looks like he's being grabbed by a white hand, or the hand is coming up from inside him, trying to get out."

He spurred Salt on.

"I don't see why I can't look, it's interesting."

"It's a question of manners."

"But I can look at you." She arched her head back, tipping off her hat, and her dark brown eyes sparkled up at him. They were his eyes, large and widely spaced, crowned with a single eyebrow. She had his hair color too, but everything else was Dolores's. Her lovely nose and mouth and chin. An accessible Dolores. He smiled down at her. Salt stumbled, and Owen turned his attention back toward the trail, but Victoria kept looking at him. He could feel her eyes peering into his nose.

"Not my nostrils," he said, pushing her away. Her hat slipped into the space between them. He put it back on her head. He tried to do this gently, but at the critical moment, the horse jerked, and he ended up jamming the brim down over her braids. She pulled away from him, stiffly. He reached into the pannier. "Here," he said, and offered her an egg. She shook her head. "Come on, you must be hungry."

She took it grudgingly, then peeled it with great attention, managing to get the shell off in one piece. She held it up for his inspection. The sun leaked through the cracks, turning the membrane pale yellow. With an extravagant gesture, she tossed the shell over her shoulder and popped the entire egg into her mouth.

"Water?" he asked.

"Thanks."

They turned away from the mountains, and descended into the mudflat. The ground grew sparse and dry, scarred by arroyos, bleached bones, shoots of clammy weed.

"When are we going to get there?" Victoria asked.

"In time."

She squirmed on the saddle.

"What's that?" he asked, pointing at a Lucifer hummingbird.

She squinted for a moment, then identified it correctly.

"Good for you. In Latin, *Calothorax lucifer*."

"Lucifer's another word for the devil."

"Who told you that?"

"Mr. MacIntosh. We had a lesson on mythology."

"Did he talk about the difference between science and myth?"

"Myths are the stories people tell when they are too ignorant or lazy to think for themselves. Science is the pursuit of knowledge and the natural laws that govern the universe."

"Good."

She paused, then asked if *The Little Matchgirl* was a myth. The matchgirl was her favorite story. "It's more of a parable," he said. "An illustration of what happens in cities. All that blindness and money-scrambling, it leads to people like your matchgirl freezing on the street."

"It's bear's favorite story," she said. "But bear has too much fur to freeze to death."

He scratched his jaw. She was overly attached to that bear. And the little matchgirl too. "Do you ever look at that atlas I gave you? Now that's a useful book."

"Lots of maps," she said. "But there's a big blank space where Pristina should be."

"That'll change with the train."

"I hope they give us a good dot," Victoria said. "Not a little one like Marfa's. Pristina deserves to be marked by more than a circle. It should get a star."

"Star's are only for capitals."

"Then it should get a spiral."

* * *

They arrived at the place where the footprints were, a barren stretch of cracked brown earth. Off on the horizon, a fine haze blurred the mountains, making them look a hundred miles away—impossible that they were just in the foothills, surrounded by grasses and persimmon trees. Victoria held out her arms. He swung her from the saddle, then felt a twinge in his back.

"Don't put me down!" she shouted. "I want to ride on your shoulders."

He told her she was too big for that. She marched away from him, swinging her arms like a toy soldier, tiny against the great blue sky.

"Come here," he said. "Look." The footprints weren't that distinct, but you could still make out three toes and get a feeling for the enormity of the beast. "If we were back in the Cretaceous, we would be sinking on the banks of a swampy lake. The air would be thick and humid, filled with insects, and the hadrosaur, a gigantic lizard some forty feet tall, would be lurching down to the shore to drink."

Victoria squatted next to him, drawing her finger to her nose, trying to go cross-eyed.

"Imagine, Vic, a forty-foot lizard." He drew a line in the sand, walked forty paces, and drew another. "With a duck's bill for a mouth!" He returned and squatted beside her. She kept moving her finger back and forth, intent on her cross-eyed game. "Guess how many teeth?" he asked. She didn't answer. "Guess." No response. "Two thousand!" he said. She tried to poke her finger in his mouth. He swatted her away. "Cut that out. You've got the intellect of a girl twice your age, and you're playing toddler games."

"Why won't you carry me on your shoulders?" she asked. "When we go to the box canyon, you carry me on your shoulders."

"That's so you can touch the ammonite."

She turned away. He tugged on her braid.

"The ammonite's nicer," she said. "It's a spiral. This just looks like a crummy hole in the rock." She sounded miserable. He agreed that the ammonite was beautiful.

"Come here," he said. She lay down and put her head on his lap. He smoothed a damp lock from her forehead. "We've got to try new things. We can't always be going back to admire what we know to be beautiful."

"Was the hadrosaur beautiful?"

"Well. It had a backbone. And the backbone is a beautiful thing. Your ammonite's a mollusk. It had a nice shell, but its interior was flaccid and vague."

"And you need a backbone," Victoria said, "to win Life's race."

"I don't know that Life's a race. It's an experiment or a puzzle."

"But the book says—"

"Yes," said Owen. "I shouldn't have used that phrase. When you really think about it, Vic, when you really sense it, it's not a race, it's an unfolding. It's beautiful."

"But why did the hadrosaurs die?"

"Well," he answered, "it's because you need more than a backbone. You also need mammary glands. That's the lovely thing about mammals. The mothers nurse their young, and teach them to share and cooperate. You can't get any advanced order made up of a bunch of individuals running around eating each other's eggs."

They clopped back at an easy gait, sun-sleepy and content. The sky became dotted with oddly shaped clouds and Victoria, who had been dozing against Owen's chest, roused herself to point out ones that looked like whales and armadillos and

noses. Owen barely heard her, caught up in the rich glowing colors: they were everywhere in the sky, in the rocks, in
the sand. He sucked in his breath, wishing that he could in-
hale them, bring them with him to Washington. At times like
these, he felt a tremor of what he'd experienced the first time
he came out here . . . stumbling off his horse, agog at the
hues and tints, kissing the ground like Columbus kissing the
shores of Hispaniola.

"Don't you see, Vic?" he said. "Talking about Pristina to
people who have never been here, why, it's like offering them
a cup, but no water to fill it. It's an empty vessel."

Victoria didn't answer. They had come to an arroyo, and
she was peering at a dry white branch that stuck up from a
pile of rocks. A scratch of pink cloth drooped from one of its
twigs. "What's that?" she asked.

"It looks like a piece of material."

"Maybe it ripped off in a flood," she said. "Remember the
flood?"

Owen shuddered. They'd been stopped by a flash flood a
few months ago, great big boulders crashing into one another
and thunder cracking like a whip. Dolores had been furious
when they got back, said he'd been reckless having Victoria
out in that, and she was right.

"Remember the bull?" Victoria said. In the lightning,
among the boulders and trees crashing through the froth,
they had seen the carcass of a tremendous bull, its horns
twisting out of the black water. Owen had been appalled. He
shouldn't have been. He knew the merciless force of Nature;
but all the same, the bull, bloated and bobbing in the black
water, had shaken him. "Its eyes looked like bloody bubbles
of milk," she said.

"I suppose so," he replied, impressed at her lack of
squeamishness.

* * *

A dark navy blue spread across the sky, and Victoria's stomach growled louder than you would believe a small girl's stomach capable. Ahead they could see the lights of Casa Grande twinkling faintly on the black swell of hilltop, but they didn't seem to be getting any closer. It was the desert—its thin air could bring clarity, but it could also warp light and change distances on you. Victoria twisted uncomfortably. "We're almost there," he said. But it took close to an hour before they arrived.

"We're famished, Alma," Owen said as the woman poked her head from the kitchen. "What's that you're cooking?"

"Antelope, sir. It's ready whenever you want."

"Very good, what about now? Doe!" he shouted up the stairs.

"She's not here, sir."

"What? Where did she run off to?"

Alma shrugged. "Shall I set the table for two?"

"No. We'll wait."

"But father . . ."

"Fine," said Owen. "Eat in the kitchen. I'm waiting for your mother."

He climbed to the roof, thinking that Dolores might be up there. She wasn't. He looked over the landscape. The reduction works glowed from behind a veil of smoke. The night was black, too dark to see her on the road. He wandered downstairs, stood in doorways, looked into rooms that were dim and unnaturally calm. In the kitchen, Victoria hung a spoon from her nose, and Alma ladled stew onto a plate. He grabbed a handful of crackers, popped them into his mouth, and headed to his study. The desktop glowed under the lamp, its surface cleared of bills and notices. He felt his mother's eyes on him. He turned, reluctantly, and faced her portrait.

He had sworn on her grave that he would never go back. That he would start anew, leave all that behind. But he had meant that he would never go back to Boston. Not Washington. Washington hadn't figured into his considerations. Her gaze was stern and implacable.

He touched the frame, not daring to touch her face. He had killed her. Not intentionally, of course. He had come home late, angry, fouled up by storm-induced traffic. He had been stamping the snow off his boots and cursing the butler for accepting a delivery of the wrong make of scotch when she came out of her room, her finger raised in remonstration. She abhorred foul language. "Owen," she said sharply, standing at the top of the stairway, her back straight, her voice clear, and then—then she fell. All that tremendous power turned into a smudge, a smudge of gray, gray hair breaking out of her bun, gray dress whirling down the red-carpeted steps. She landed with a crack, faceup on the black-and-white tiles. He had noted every detail of her fall, and yet the thought in his head had been the butler signing for the wrong type of scotch. And when her head had cracked so resoundingly on the tiles, and her body had lain still, he had not immediately rushed forth, but had remained on the mat, feeling the cold joints of his toes, flexing and scrunching them in his boots. He had not always been like that. As a boy he had felt the throb and pulse of Nature, the great cataclysms of its endings and beginnings. But not then. Then he stood coldly watching the blood stain her hair and pool on the tiles. A drop of melted snow had fallen from him and landed on a wrinkle in her cheek. He had knelt to wipe it off. Her eyes had been open, steel blue with a pinkness around the edges. They had told him nothing. He had opened his mouth, but was not able to speak.

Yet now he could. And not with the strangled voice of his Boston years. He had been given a new voice, his boyhood voice, deepened and tempered by the desert. He was not the man who had left.

Her portrait stared back. She had been suspicious of every project, even projects dear to her, always keen to darker motives. But there was no darkness here. The train was absolutely necessary, a conduit to spread what she, after all, had taught him. Knowledge that he had to spread, knowledge that was bursting within him. He'd be hoarding it if he didn't share it. He turned from her portrait, his back bristling, as if she had been counseling him to hoard it. She had not been immune to parsimony, that woman. His water cup rested on a sheaf of papers in the corner. It should have been packed. He always drank from it before giving a speech. He rubbed it fondly, glad that he'd found it before they left. Every great speech he'd ever made, he'd always had it by his side, an old, thick-bottomed ship's cup with milky glass panels and a pleasing heft. A present from the sailor on his mother's abolition committee. He'd been fascinated by that sailor, the edge of a whale tattoo peaking from under his cuff, the roughest man to whom he had ever been introduced. Ships' cups were what you wanted, the sailor had said, because they didn't tip over. And they didn't break. Owen had had the cup since 1859.

He went out to the porch, where their luggage was piled high, and gently put the ship's cup in his valise, padding it with a pair of old socks. He leaned over the rail. Still no sign of Dolores. That's why he was so fidgety—her absence. He had to get back to work. Concentrate.

He returned to his study and read through Bailey's patrol log.

<u>1 October, 1906</u>

Item: Old woman Herrida says buenos dias.

The old woman always said buenos días, and Bailey always wrote it down. Owen once asked him why he bothered. "Because, sir," Bailey had answered, "when she finally says *good morning*, I'll have to report her progress, but it won't make any sense unless you know that she's been saying *buenos días* for the past hundred years."

Item: Nat Plank & sons go dear hunting (no permit). Hatty Plank uses this time to bake Jimmy MacIntosh a cake (saffron).
Item: Baseball practice. Archibald Biscot 15 min. late. Caleb Pollen dont show at all.
Item: Tobacco
   <u>cigarets</u>*: old woman Herrida, Caleb Pollen, Ed Beanright, Jesus Rivera, Jefferson Willits, Juan Sanchez, Horse Benson, Kitty Benson, Pat Erstwhile, Emilio Gonzalez, DB Clark, Jet MacGuire.*
   <u>pipes</u>*: Jeb Hartwell, Samedi Jones, Jason South, Fred Navidad, Matt Smitt, Carlito Quintana, Jesus, José, and Jorge Navarro.*
Item: (Rumor) Nuria Jimenez (caves) says Nueve Dedos (Nine Fingers) told her husband he wood poison the water supply. Posible causes: malcontent, a mean streak, and idleness. He aint got no business now that we got the water system.

Who was Nine Fingers? Owen unlocked the personnel cabinet, pleased that he had thought to move it to his house instead of leaving it at Pristina HQ. He found the file, and frowned upon reviewing it. Unemployed. Mooching off the remainders in the caves. No family. A record of drinking that took over three pages. He flipped to the beginning of the man's history. He had been a water freighter, worked the Rio Grande route. No sign that he had applied for work once they cut his services. Even when he had practiced labor, it didn't seem as if it had done him much good. He had been caught smuggling mescal underneath the water tank. And he had given away free buckets to Guillermina Negra, the youngest Negra daughter. Owen reread that last part. Nine Fingers had given the girl free buckets of water, not free buckets of mescal, but still, signs of favoritism rankled the community.

He rubbed his jaw, thinking about the water supply. It worked beautifully, but it was impossible to protect. In the interest of economy, instead of piping water directly into the houses, they'd piped it into open troughs set up in the front yard of each household. A saboteur had only to poison one trough, and the whole system would be infected. He jotted a vaguely worded note to the chief of patrols and yelled for Victoria to get the stable boy.

The stable boy soon arrived panting.

"Take this to Van Sickle," Owen said.

2 October, 1906

Item: Old woman Herrida says buenos dias.

Item: Breechkropf household is a mess.

Item: Mario Rivera (the elder) says Nueve Dedos is all talk. Too lazy to crush a fly in a drop of honey.

Owen pondered the entry, wondering if he should rescind the order, but he decided against it. If the man didn't actually poison the water, he still poisoned morale with his sniping. He was better gone.

Item: Gracie Johnson organizes Bunting Committee (for both the Marfa Stake Driving and the appr. Pristina Railroad Festival):

Mary Lou Henderson, Kitty Benson, Birdy Biscot. Jimmy MacIntosh sched. to speek. (Don't know if this is such a fine idea, see following)

Item: *Jimmy MacIntosh to Hatty Plank:*

If (Mr.) Scraperton cared a wit about education, hed have torn down that school house long ago. (Same old thing about not being able to hear himself over the jaw crusher, his laringitus, etc.)

Complaints about the students, how he would like to strangle them—how they do not posess their words, but voice them—and that they will grow up to be just like their parents.

Talking about the athenayum: The only way (Mr.) Scrapertons going to fill it up is by booking cockfights, weeping virgins, and geetarists.

He said that theres nothing wrong with having a toilet and voting in the elections. He would be content to be part of an asendant and prosperous nation instead of trying to start a new one with a population of barefoot 1/2 breeds.

He said the women of Pristina were dried up ninnys, everyone except Mrs. Plank.

Mrs. Plank gave sympathy and made him stay for an extra cup of tea.

Owen raised his eyebrows, more interested in the developing friendship between Mrs. Plank and Mr. MacIntosh than the content of MacIntosh's conversation. Bailey didn't like MacIntosh, and had misquoted him plenty of times before, but Owen didn't think he'd implicate Hattie in anything suspicious unless there were grounds for it.

Item: Fray Rodrigo in Oblaba: 27 women and children from the caves, but no one from Pristina proper at the river crossing.

Item: Ivor Magruder will compose a song comemorating the train. Sarah Carruthers will do the lyrics.

Item: Birthday Party for Pip Hartwell. Good spirits. A toast to the continuing prosperity and growth of Pristina.

Item: Caleb Pollen, Archibald Biscot, Jorge Jimenez went to Dr. Badinoes to play cards (no money) and take a "prescription." None of them are sick.

Owen sighed. He should have given Badinoe his walking papers long ago. But he had delivered Victoria. And he had saved her from a terrifying bout of brain fever. Perhaps even more importantly, there were moments when the sheen of skepticism that coated Badinoe's face would lift, when he seemed so close to understanding, to truly understanding what Owen had to say. How could he throw him out when he felt that spark of potential? And Dolores would be miserable without him. They liked each other and worked so well together, formulating hygiene programs for the children.

Where was she?

Owen found himself before her door, his hand on the knob. He turned it, flicked on the light, sat on her bed. An open valise lay on the floor with an assortment of silky things, tossed in, unfolded. On the bedside table, a single glove lay crumpled on a stack of old *Railway Age* magazines. He caressed the calfskin between his fingers.

He was flipping through the top magazine, admiring the engines, when downstairs, the front door opened. He threw the glove back. Dolores's room was strictly hers, not to be entered unless invited. He heard her voice, hurried and gay, saying something to Victoria, then her footsteps on the stairs. He wavered in between the bed and the door. She ran into the room, and stopped when she saw him. He could see her pause, a question forming. How would he answer? It was his house after all. She did not put forth the question. Her breathing was heavy. Her eyes shimmered.

"I'm sorry I'm late," she said, brushing her skirt. "Nickel had an awful scare. I walked for miles, dragging him by the bit." The top button of her shirt had come undone, and a shadow moved inside the hollow of her neck. "Owen?"

He grabbed for a reason to be there. "I meant to ask you if you paid Alma." His words came out stiff and quick, and he regretted them immediately.

She stepped past him, the coarse fabric of her skirt grazing the back of his hand. She opened a drawer of her dresser and rummaged through it.

"She has to get her chits before we leave."

"I'm aware of that."

"I'll pay her," he said, leaving the room.

"I will do it, Owen. I was planning on paying her tomorrow."

She shut the door behind him. He stood at the end of the hall, facing the window, unable to see outdoors, only the light reflected from the lamp and his own shadowy features. He had to finish Bailey's report, but he could do that on the train. He ought to go over and talk to the patrols about Nine Fingers. They didn't have to be overzealous. They only had to make sure the man never set foot in town again.

He leaned his thighs against the windowsill. He should have said that she looked beautiful. Not that she looked beautiful, that she *was* beautiful. It was the way her eyes had been shining. They had not been one color. They had been like the ocean. Like the sun hitting the Atlantic. A liquid metal shimmer floating around the soft troughs, too much light for the water to absorb.

He marched back to her room, knocked. "Dolores," he said.

"I'll pay her tomorrow."

The door remained shut. There were fingerprints on the white paint. "Hey, beautiful," he said. "Let me see your eyes." He heard a soft laugh and footsteps.

She peeked through the crack. "Come in."

♥

Women swayed their hips, tubas pumped, lemonade splashed. Marfa was having a party. Ysidro had seen parties. He'd been to El Paso and Juárez. He'd been clear up to Detroit, to the Gulf and to the Pacific. He'd been to parties where women in wings played the harp, and girls stood on one leg, like flamingoes, holding the other leg stretched up so that their ankles touched their ears while men in top hats crawled around on all fours, snapping their garters. He hadn't been a guest at these parties, but he'd seen them. He wouldn't want to be a guest even if they'd allow someone like him—they'd put collars on you if you were a man, lead you around on a leash. Much better to be at a stake driving, standing up on two feet with your thumb hooked into the pocket of your dungarees, the sun warm on your skin, and the tinny off-beat band making you want to whistle. He even had a companion, a flat-faced Delawarean—a traveling engineer—who had attached himself to Ysidro a few minutes ago and was saying something incomprehensible. A lady with fruit on her bonnet bumped into them, sloshing her drink.

"Whoops!" she giggled.

Ysidro grinned. Scraperton had provided the lemonade free of charge, possibly the first thing he'd ever given away in his life. And, as if to prove that justice was not entirely mythical, someone had spiked it. The traveling engineer hiccupped and tugged on his sleeve.

"Yay, brother?" Ysidro managed, not too lucid with his own tongue.

His companion's face swam forward. "The traveling engineer must have no friends," he said, spraying Ysidro's mouth and cheeks with a fragrant spittle. "He must understand that he is not employed to make excuses for men who were cut out, and by God intended, for some other vocation besides railroading."

Ysidro wiped his face. "That's noble, brother." The man did not look amused. What was he doing calling this man brother anyhow? But there they were, greasers, the good citizens of Marfa, Scraperton's lackeys up from Pristina, all joined in fraternal bon-hom-mie. "Don't believe I have a vocation myself, though I sure as hell have an antivocation."

He'd only been in Shaft 8 once, but that was enough. He'd had nightmares about that rat stumbling out of the cardboard box, that ghost burro. Abuela had explained that the animals were telling him things, that's why they'd affected him so forcefully. She said animals could talk to you if you knew how to listen, and these animals were telling him not to work underground. He didn't need animals telling him what to do. He had known the moment that he saw Mr. Scraperton, the red sweat beading, as if he were sweating cinnabar straight out of his skin. He had known right then. No heat that didn't come from the sun. No cinnabar sweating out of his skin. Even being here in Marfa was a little too close to those mines. But he wasn't ready to leave yet, not until he figured out some way of seeing Guillermina.

His father! Ysidro jumped behind the traveling engineer, suddenly alert and sober, his eyes as sharp as nails. His father was standing across the street. The engineer tried to turn around but Ysidro grabbed his elbow. "Por favor, stay still a moment." How had his father gotten out of his shift? Scraperton never declared holidays. But his father, in a shirt so white it made you blink, stood there clear as day, clapping in time to the music. Ysidro dropped down to his hands and knees. Quietly, steadily, he crawled between polished lace-ups and dirty cowboy boots, toward the alley that led to his boarding house.

"Oooh, Ysidro! Helloooo!" It was the postmaster's wife, after him all week, some kind of story about a broken banister.

"Shhh!"

He nosed past her skirt. She shifted it, exposing a finely dimpled knee.

"What are you doing down there?"

"Later," he said, getting to his feet and running. Just as he reached the alley, he looked back, wanting to make sure that his father hadn't seen. But in that moment, his father saw. Why had he done that? Just like in the story, except looking back hadn't returned his father to the underworld. He watched numbly as his father and Van Sickle extricated themselves from the crowd and ran toward him.

"Son!" Cleofas cried. His arms were open wide, his eyes wet with emotion. The moment they touched, Ysidro gave way, melting into those shoulders, so strong and familiar. His father pushed him back so he could look into his face. "When did you get here? I didn't even know! How happy I am to see you!"

"And I, Father, how good it is to see you. I have missed you." Which was not a lie. He'd never met a man with eyes as kind as his father's.

"Do you remember," Cleofas said, ushering Ysidro into the middle of the ironed shirts and clear eyes of the Pristina crowd, "how you used to translate for me? Everyone listened to you. The men would crowd round, you were the best one there, and only ten!"

"You don't need me now. Listen to your English! It is very good."

"It is all right," Cleofas shrugged. Then he smiled at his son. "Thank you for your letters. How many times I wished that I could write back to you."

"There would have been no point, Father. Your letters would not have gotten to me. I've been moving around."

Van Sickle elbowed up beside Ysidro. "I hear you've been making a name for yourself in carpentry."

Ysidro nodded, wishing that he had the guts to tell him he'd built a bordello.

"Cleofas is very proud of you. He shows your letters to everyone."

He didn't like Van Sickle's tone. Was he making fun of Cleofas for not being able to read? Ysidro shot his father an inquisitive glance, but Cleofas just beamed at him and Van Sickle as if they were all part of the same beloved family. How had he ever had the strength to leave? His father had only him, no other children, no wife, just Abuela with her curses and maledictions.

But he had the mine. You didn't need so much family if you loved the mine the way his father loved the mine.

A wave of hollering and whistling swept through the crowd. Scraperton had arrived. Ysidro caught himself rising to his tiptoes as determined to see him as everyone else. The same five-button suit. The same flat-brimmed hat. Scraperton put a hand on the edge of the stage that Ysidro had helped to build, and easily swung himself up. Ysidro felt like he had never left, standing next to his father, watching Scraperton position himself behind the podium, those black eyes shining so strong they seemed to be looking at you even if you were fifty feet away. All around people roared with enthusiasm. Behind Scraperton a bunch of bigwigs sat on wooden chairs, paunched and pleased with themselves. They were from Marfa. They didn't yet know that their purpose was to serve as wallpaper. Scraperton opened his mouth. He didn't say anything, just wetted his lips, and the people fell silent.

"Friends," he said, pausing to let the word linger. "A day like today is the wine of Nature." His voice was sonorous and certain and struck into the heart instead of the brain. Ysidro wanted to plug his ears with cotton. His abuela was the only one he'd ever met unaffected by Scraperton's tongue. It wasn't because she didn't, or at least pretended that she didn't, understand English. Plenty of cave people who could barely muster a hello melted when he opened his mouth. But not Abuela, she'd stab her stick in the ground and mutter about how he'd murdered the alamos. She'd never forgive him for cutting down those trees.

Father coughed. He cleared his throat, but the coughs came back, shaking his whole body. Ysidro slapped him on the back and Van Sickle handed him a canteen of water and still he coughed. Finally he got some water down and wiped his mouth, apologizing for having disturbed the speech.

"Don't apologize," Ysidro said hotly. "Are you okay?"

Father gave him a stern look and returned his attention to Mr. Scraperton. Soon he was mouthing the words along with his boss. Ysidro stared at the ground, focusing on the wrinkles in his boots, the clumps of dirt and dead weeds, in an attempt to cut off his sense of hearing. With much effort he succeeded in making Mr. Scraperton's voice a river of noise. The words became indiscernible and the phrases no longer bothered him. He was elated. He had never blocked out that voice before. But there was no one to brag to; they were all spellbound, nodding away with the man who put them underground the entire stretch of daylight.

He rubbed the spool of thread in his pocket. Red #4, a

color you couldn't get at Offitz & Carruthers, though what
the hell could you get there except moldy queso and size-
eight boots? Red #4 was the color of blood. He had bought
it for Guillermina. He had a piece of her embroidery back at
the boarding house, a picture of Jesus looking like he'd just
knocked the brains out of everyone in a brawl and was rising
to his feet, gulping in the air, triumphant and furious. Real.
The thing looked real. How had she done that? With only
thread and a needle? Her eyes, as she had shown him this,
had been so calm and thoughtful, the reverse of the picture,
so bloody and fierce—confusing him utterly. He hadn't been
able to do anything but nod like a moron and say, *Bueno*. Yet
somehow she had understood, her eyes softening as if he'd
given her the most eloquent of compliments. If his father was
going to drag him back down to Pristina, at least he'd be able
to see her. He'd been thinking that he could somehow sneak
over to the caves without anyone finding out. But how? This
way he could call on her openly. He imagined walking with
her down by the mercury fountain. Once, as children, they
had played in it together. They were very small, maybe four
or five, the moonlight shining down on them. How could that
have been? No patrols around to stop them? No adults? Perhaps it had been a dream. Yet he remembered so well the sensation of holding hands with her, balancing on the surface,
the slick, jiggly feeling of the quicksilver moving beneath
their feet.

Father began pounding his palms together. The speech
had ended. Everyone clapped and hooted, a gigantic pack of
sheep bleating and baaing in deranged ovine appreciation.
People patted him on the back and he smiled back, not wishing to insult. The tubas and trumpets piped up, and the press
of swaying bodies got tighter. Ysidro was pushed this way
and that as the crowd moved to the fresh ties and glittering

rail that marked the beginning of the feeder line. There was more pushing and shoving as an aisle formed.

Ysidro found himself at the very front, looking straight at Victoria, who he hadn't seen since she was three or four. The two of them outside, sitting in the sun on the steps behind Casa Grande. He was shaping river clay into figurines. She was squashing each figurine as quickly as it came. Now she was a skinny little girl, solemnly holding a red velvet pillow out in front of her, the bearer of the golden stake. She didn't see him, too focused on her task. The stationmaster took the stake from the pillow and positioned it on the first tie. Scraperton cast the first blow and the crowd burst into applause. He offered the mallet to his wife. Ysidro craned his neck, the better to see her.

She was still beautiful, even after all of the other beautiful women he had seen. Her curls were no longer as mysterious, he'd seen hairstyles like that in his travels, but none fit their bearers so well. She shook her head at the proffered mallet, the ringlets bobbing around her face. The crowd roared for her to reconsider. You could see that she wanted to, that she was just saying no for manner's sake. Mr. Scraperton nudged her. She gave him a look then took the mallet, handling it with surprising ease considering her slender arms. She swung it high, then slammed it to the stake with perfect aim. Great cheers rose up. She handed the hammer back to her husband. As he took the handle, she pulled him toward her, and kissed him on the lips.

After the ceremony, the Pristina crowd set up long outdoor tables and ate from plates piled high with roasted pig, peppers, chili, and corncakes. Ysidro forked the food into his mouth—he hadn't had such a feast in ages—and pummeled his father with questions about the people back home. His father chewed thoughtfully, considering each response with great thoroughness, before answering, "Gwenn is doing good. Rodo is good. Jorge is not so good."

Van Sickle leaned over them. He'd found a space for Ysidro on one of the stagecoaches taking people back.

"Thank you, sir," said Ysidro.

"It will be good to have you with us again. We may even have a position for you in Shaft 8."

Cleofas broke into his widest smile, his face folding into good-natured wrinkles. Ysidro's stomach twisted. He pushed aside his plate. Words began to flow out of him, unbidden, un-planned. He told his father that he had a job waiting for him in Boise, an important position helping the engineer. The old man listened carefully, his worn brown eyes never leaving Ysidro's.

Later that night, Ysidro watched his father's stagecoach roll off, waving like he was a good son. In the morning, to miti-gate the lie he'd told, he bought a ticket for Boise. Somewhere between Kansas City and Denver, he dreamed about the fish-ing spot past Casa Grande where the creek ran through the boulders and the long-whiskered catfish and bullfish circled round the pool. There had been a big cottonwood stump with a crack in it where he'd hid his fishing spear. In the dream, he reached into the crack of the stump, but instead of his fishing spear, he got the bony hand of his abuela. He pulled her out, and she embraced him, her body at once rickety and strong, her skin warm, her hair smelling of tobacco and sage. He awoke feeling good. Abuela would forgive the lie. She'd wanted him to leave. She'd given him a can full of coins and old bills when he first set off, almost a hundred dollars, and told him he was brave and good, not the kind of words that usually came from her mouth. He rubbed a finger on his palm, recalling the dream feeling of her bony hand, the pulse still strong and urgent.

◆

In her hurry to get outside, Victoria buttoned her coat lopsided. "Wait, sweetheart," Dolores said, leaning down to correct the mistake, but at that moment, the butler opened the front door, letting in a gust of crisp leafy air, and Victoria bolted onto the front lawn. Dolores, laughing, started after her.

"Dolores!" Clara stood on the front stoop. "You're not leaving now?" Her gay, warm voice with the iron underneath. "The ladies will be arriving for bridge any moment."

Dolores smiled stupidly. "Oh, yes. Of course."

And so they were directed to the second sitting room, a dim cave with a heavy chandelier straining from its chain. It smelled of windows never opened. It smelled of Clara, her powder and breath, a certain sticky watchful scent caught in carpets, cushions, knickknacks, the silk brocade that lined the walls. Dolores shook her head as if there were water in her ear. The first day in Clara's house had been so different, a true intoxication. Hot water straight from the faucets! Electricity! A telephone on each floor, with an armchair next to it where you could sit, and a door if you wanted privacy! But Clara lost no time in souring it, her doughy head poking around doorways, her eyes bulging, her nose twitching, her comments, her suggestions, and worse, the virtue with which she spoke to Dolores, her obvious pride at her own liberality, treating her like a full-born American.

Dolores picked up the newspaper and flipped through the business and society pages. Mrs. Bottomley-Oakes would be presiding over this year's Christmas ball. Perhaps she was related to Les Bottomley, the gentleman who had taken the senator's place as Dolores and Owen's chief financial hope. Owen was meeting him right now. Dolores sighed, wishing that she were there. Owen's manners were too brusque, and on top of that, he'd come down with a throat infection that made him barely audible. Next time, she'd insist that she go with him, help him out with the talking.

But for now, she was here. She eyed the liquor cabinet, amusing herself by the thought of greeting the bridge ladies with whiskey on her breath. Clara not only didn't drink, she didn't "countenance drinkers of any ilk." That's why they'd elected her chair of the local Women's Christian Temperance Union. ("Do you belong to any committees? In America we like to do our part.") The liquor cabinet belonged to her husband. Every evening at six o'clock, he opened its mahogany doors and swayed back and forth, surveying the decanters and scratching his belly as if he didn't know exactly what he was in the mood for. Port, always port. Clara would purse her lips and plunk brown sugar into her tea and mutter about gout and liver ailments. Benjamin didn't seem to notice, and often helped himself to a second glass. Owen said that they were a living example of checks and balances.

She'd felt an affinity for Benjamin, but never managed a moment alone with him until the other night. Owen and Clara were going on and on about whether the Fijians should or should not toss the missionaries into cauldrons of boiling broth, and Dolores was trying to think of some reason to excuse herself from the table, when Benjamin tapped her on the knee. Did she want a tour of his decanter collection? They sneaked out of the dining room like a couple of kids. Each decanter had a "unique and storied" stopper. One was an imperial eagle retrieved from the wreck of a pirate ship; one a Liberty Bell, rare because the caster forgot to put the crack in; the one for the port, a golden pyramid, which was given to Benjamin by a "gentleman of high influence" and an initiate of certain mysterious rites. He told a joke about the power of pyramids versus the power of port, then broke into a wheezy laugh. She laughed too, not at the joke but because he reminded her of her cousin Agosto. Then he unstopped one of the more modest decanters, and poured himself a digestive. She watched. He didn't even ask if she wanted a sip. Of course, if he had, she wouldn't have been able to accept, not with Owen in the next room. But she'd been disappointed. Somehow she'd thought that he'd understood something about her, but apparently he hadn't. She was just Owen's wife.

Something creaked that shouldn't have. Dolores glanced up to find Victoria scrambling along the high shelves of a floor-to-ceiling bookcase. She'd made it halfway up, about six feet from the ground. "Victoria!" Dolores sprung up and checked the hallway to make sure Clara hadn't seen.

"What?"

"Get down."

"But Mother—"

"Get down!"

"But look," she said, pointing at the very top of the case. "Figurines."

"Sweetheart, there are plenty of figurines down here."

"It's the blind leading the blind."

"Get down."

Victoria got down. Dolores examined the shelves for footprints or a collapse in the orderly lines of books. "You're going to practice sitting still," she said. "Absolutely still for ten minutes."

Dolores peered up at the figurines. Could it really be the blind leading the blind? No. It was a medieval parade, Chaucer's pilgrims or something like that. She hated these figurines. They were everywhere. On the table in front of her stood Daphne, imprisoned in her tree, and Apollo, the brute, still free to do what he wished. Horrid stuff. And next to them—ugh—a bowl of saltwater taffies. That's what the house smelled like—stale candy. They were everywhere, sticky ribbons, butterscotches that gave you tongue splinters, bleeding peppermints, and these obscene purple and green taffies. Victoria looked at them hungrily.

"No," Dolores said.

Victoria tried an expression of wounded innocence. Dolores told her to go to her room and get something to play with. The girl bounced from her chair and ran up the stairs. She returned a couple minutes later with her bear and *The Little Matchgirl*.

"You want to read *The Little Matchgirl* to me?" Dolores asked.

She had heard it at least a hundred times. A beggar's daughter, selling matches on Christmas Eve, freezes to death while the rest of the world sits by the fireplace, eating plum pudding. Why did children love hearing the same thing over and over and over again—and how did they select their peculiar obsessions? Last winter, in the middle of a hailstorm, Victoria had taken off her jacket and boots, filched a couple of kitchen matches, and slipped out the back door to reenact the whole thing. When they found her, she was blue in the face, in a weird kind of ecstasy.

"Bear!" Victoria chided, and slapped his paw.

"What did he do?" Dolores asked.

"Stuck out his tongue," Victoria replied primly. Then she stuck her tongue out at Bear, her ridiculously long tongue, so long people were startled when they saw it. Dolores resisted saying anything. Victoria was proud of the effect of her tongue. The more they chided her, the more proud. She looked directly at her mother, her eyes shining boldly.

"Shall we play checkers?"

"No," said Victoria. "How about bridge? How do you play bridge?"

"You don't want to know," Dolores said.

"Who's coming?"

"Mrs. Wildebeest, Mrs. Gumhatchet."

"It's not Gumhatchet. You're saying it wrong."

If only they bet, then she could have excused herself on the grounds that Owen forbid gambling. But they didn't. They sucked butterscotches and swapped stories about impertinent help.

"You never say anything right."

"That's absurd. My grammar's far better than Mr. MacIntosh's."

Victoria started to say something but stopped. She repositioned Bear on her lap, then, in a kinder voice, asked her mother what she was reading. Dolores glanced at her paper.

"Well," she said, "here's an article on that cat killing Aunt Clara was talking about." It had happened in the neighborhood. Mrs. Winnie's white angora had been found in a nearby alley, sliced up most cruelly. There were two puzzling things about the case, according to the journalist. First, the gory way the animal had been killed, and second, the fact that the perpetrator had neglected to remove the identification chain, a thing of some value, made of silver and semiprecious gems. Could this be a case of animal sacrifice? the journalist asked. An infamous Negro witch doctor had recently arrived in town. Perhaps there was a connection. Dolores ripped out the article. A witch doctor. She'd send it to Badinoe; he loved witch doctors. And witches too. He had a story about a cat in Baltimore, some matted-fur, fishy-breathed wretch that had followed him as he drunkenly wove through the alleys.

She started folding the article, then saw the picture on the other side. It was an elephant carcass chained to the trunk of a gorgeous black automobile. A Reo the Fifth. The driver, a mustachioed man in safari gear, leaned against the car, grinning at the camera. *You can do it with a Reo!* the caption said.

"That's what we need, sweetheart. We need a Reo." She looked up to catch Victoria stashing a handful of saltwater taffies into the hole in Bear's leg. Her cheeks were bulging. "Hey!"

Victoria covered her mouth with her hands.

"Your teeth are going to fall out eating that stuff." She didn't know what to do with her. They should have been at the zoo. "Walk around the room," she said. "Pretend to be an elephant."

Victoria circled the room, chewing discretely. She stopped by the window, drew aside the inner gauze curtain, and pressed her hands directly against the glass. You could see the fingerprints across the room. Dolores pushed herself up off the sofa. She'd help out; they'd go into each room, smearing mother and daughter fingerprints on every windowpane and mirror.

"There's someone outside," Victoria said.

The bridge partners were finally arriving.

But it wasn't them. A man in a leather jacket and a crumpled khaki fishing hat walked up the path. Parked on the street behind him was an elegant white sedan with mud spattered around the wheels.

"Who is it?" whispered Victoria.

"I don't know," Dolores answered, staring at the motorcar.

The bell rung. There was a hubbub in the foyer, the butler sounding more cheerful than usual. Then the parlor door swung open, and the man from outside entered. The butler had taken the leather jacket, but the fishing hat remained. He reminded Dolores of the man in the Reo ad. His tweed suit was of extremely fine quality, yet it looked as if he had slept in it. Victoria slipped her hand into her mother's.

The man studied them without removing his hat. "You're not Owen's wife?" She told him she was. He stuck his hands in his pockets and rocked back on his heels. He had been expecting someone duskier, he said, maybe in a serape. "You know Mother."

He was James, Clara and Benjamin's son. She'd only recently learned that a son existed. No one had informed her; she'd inferred it from conversations. She looked at him, not knowing what to say. He stared back. He had triangular eyes with creases at the corners. They were not unfriendly. He walked over to them, the tackle on his hat faintly jingling.

"Nice hat," she said.

He grinned and poked the bent brim up with his pointer finger. "You like it? It's my driving hat."

"You must be James," she finally said.

He nodded reluctantly, then leaned down to Victoria. "And you," he said, "are my cousin. Fancy that." Victoria told him she had three cousins in Mexico. "You do?"

"Yes. Rodrigo, Agosto, and Nacho."

"What are they like?"

Victoria made a face.

"She's never met them," Dolores said.

"She looks like Owen," he said.

"I know," she said.

He looked at her, his eyes direct and questioning, then shifted his attention to the room. She watched him, finding herself at a happy loss for words. "Is that your car?" she asked.

He nodded, affecting a bored manner.

"It's not a Reo," she said.

"No," he replied, lighting a cigarette. "It's a French Darracq."

Daa-rracq, the porch swing creaked, *Daa-rracq, Daa-rracq*. Dolores hadn't needed James to explain what a Darracq was. She knew Darracqs. Americans made solid, practical cars, but they could only go about twenty-five miles an hour. The French understood speed. And of all the French makes, Darracqs were the fastest; a Darracq won last year's Vanderbilt Cup and would probably take this one's too. James might even be driving it, although he'd have a better chance if he ordered a simpler model. His present one was loaded with weight-adding features, most egregiously the rear seat, raised on a revolving axle so the passengers could spin around. It bothered Dolores's sense of forwardness, but it had served a purpose. When James took her and Victoria on their initial trip, Victoria insisted on sitting in the back, then made James stop every five minutes to spin the seat. She ended up getting so dizzy that she vomited in the gutter, and refused to go driving with them again.

Victoria elbowed her in the ribs. "Ho!" she yelled.

"Ho!" Dolores yelled back, jabbing her foot at the rail.

They were playing a game where every third swing, they kicked off from the porch rail, making sure that their feet touched the wood at exactly the same moment and shouting *Ho!* But now Dolores broke the rhythm. The swing lost its equilibrium and wove spasmodically.

"Mother!"

"It's all right, I'll get us back on course."

Ho! Creak-creak-Ho! They gained speed. Dolores loved that moment right before the end of each swing when it felt as if she would continue to be lifted higher and higher. *Ho! Ho! Ho!* Their voices rose exuberantly until Dolores remembered Owen.

He was upstairs in bed, with a green and yellow scarf wrapped around his neck, refusing to take Clara's medicine. His throat had erupted, reducing him to barely audible rasps; all his speaking engagements had been cancelled. Progress on the railroad had ground to a halt. Dolores no longer cared. Indeed, she treasured the delays; they kept her in Washington, kept her from having to think about what to do, what to do.

"We have to be quieter, honey, your father needs his rest."

Victoria shook her head. "Ho!" she shouted, even louder.

"Victoria!"

"But he's not resting."

"Yes, he is."

"No, he's not. He went to meet the man from the Interstate Commerce Commission."

"What?" He was in no condition to see anyone. "Did he take off that scarf?" He tied it so tightly that the ends stuck out like the bow on a Christmas present. The "firm structure" was supposed to be key, but he looked ridiculous.

"Nope."

"He should have. He's never going to make any headway bundled up in that rag."

"He needs to get his voice back, Mother. It's for his health."

"If he wanted to be healthy, he'd take his medicine and stay in bed."

Victoria got off the swing, as if to reprove her. Dolores snorted. Victoria could not fool her. She was delighted with Owen's condition. He'd appointed her his spokesman at dinner. She kept them there ten minutes longer than usual discoursing on mercury production and desert flora.

Victoria looked hurt. "I do want him to get better," she said in a plaintive voice.

Dolores patted her head. "I know, sweetheart. I have an idea. Let's do the bittersweet." Yesterday Victoria had discovered a bittersweet vine growing on the fence of an abandoned lot, and they'd decided to make Owen a get-well autumn bouquet. Victoria went to fetch the vase and carefully set it on top of the porch steps. It was an Oriental vase, yellow with flying fire-breathing dragons. They had bought it especially for the dragons; the flames coming out of their mouths were the same red as the berries. Dolores gathered the tangle of cuttings from the backyard and sat on the steps across from Victoria. They took turns poking the branches into the vase. The leaves rustled dryly, and dislodged berries dropped down and rolled on the uneven porch planks.

"They look like pills," Victoria said. "Maybe they can make your throat better."

"Probably work better than that scarf."

Victoria squeezed a berry between her fingertips, studying it as if it were a puzzle. "James is going to take me to see the tallest woman in the world."

"I thought you didn't approve of James."

"Eight feet tall and 345 pounds, a Tyrolean peasant. They have her on display at the Hippodrome."

"I thought you said he was a bad influence."

"He's a journalist," Victoria said after a time. "Father says that it's good to befriend journalists."

"He doesn't write about mercury mining. He writes about automobiles."

"He's very interested in Pristina. I'm not always lecturing him. He asks me questions."

True enough. He kept her going for hours, grilling her on Internal Knowledge, mestizo physiognomy, Unity and the penal code, drinking, gambling, God. Especially gambling.

"Why so much about gambling?" Dolores had asked him when they were alone.

"Because, my dear, old Uncle Stephen was a great one for games."

"Uncle Stephen?"

"Owen's father."

"Ah."

"And Owen inherited his skills."

"What?"

"You didn't know that? Owen *won* that land out there in college. We used to joke about how he could use the mercury for weighing dice."

Owen had won Pristina on a bet, he who was so opposed to gambling. She would never understand that man. She would love to tease Owen about it, but she couldn't, not with that scarf tied so tightly around his throat. She stuck a bittersweet stem into the vase and smirked at herself. The truth was, kindness had nothing to do with it. Even with the scarf and looking ridiculous and a line of failed investors a block long, Owen still had the power to check her. He could check James too. James hadn't made one knowing comment, not to his face.

Victoria got up, stepped back a couple paces, and frowned at the bouquet. "It's not balanced right." Dolores stuck another vine in, trying to help. Victoria groaned. "No. No. No." She tugged at the central branch then twisted it thirty degrees. "There." She looked a little more satisfied.

"Owen will love it," Dolores said.

Victoria, palms pressed together as if praying, but certainly not praying, nodded. She picked up the vase, quite heavy but she liked to show off her strength, and said she'd take it up to Father's room.

It wasn't just his room. Dolores stayed there too. The two of them together in a big double bed with plump cherubs and grapes bulging out of the headboard. It was a perfectly comfortable bed, but she couldn't sleep on it. Whenever she lay on the mattress she felt the vibrations of the Darracq below her, then she'd be wide awake, clenching and unclenching her toes. Last night, Owen had offered her compresses. When that didn't work, he started in on the city, a half-whispered, half-gestured rant about the bigotry of the Washingtonians. He thought she was agitated because of the proposal to segregate streetcars.

A leaf blew onto her lap. A brown, curled-up oak leaf. She brushed it off and adjusted her shawl. It was getting cold. Clara would be calling them indoors soon. It would be smarter to go before Clara called. The woman got annoyed at having to tell them everything.

Victoria returned, the vase gone, in its stead a small burlap bag containing her jacks. Dolores suggested they go inside. Victoria begged to stay out a little longer and without waiting for a reply scattered the jacks all over the porch. "Please," Victoria said. "Just one game."

Dolores shrugged. She didn't want to go in either. She returned to the swing and rocked back and forth, fondling the rope it swung from, a thick hemp rope that should have been coiled on a pier somewhere, but it might have only been the seagulls that made her feel that way, swooping above the rooftops and leafless trees, exploring inland. She closed her eyes and listened to the bounce of the ball, the clink of the jacks. Over and over, bounce, clink, bounce, clink, counterbalancing the creaking of the swing. There was a pause. She half opened an eye. Victoria scooped up the jacks then quickly and furtively rescattered them. So much for just one game.

Dolores smiled to herself, thinking how nice it would be

if you could avoid every difficulty with jacks. The sessions in the second sitting room were inevitable. Owen and his scarf, Clara and her tea, Benjamin and his port (it no longer bothered her that he never offered a glass; better if he couldn't fathom her having tastes of her own). James slouching in the mossy green armchair, clinking the ice in his scotch. She would try not to look at him. And fail. She half twisted herself so she could see his oak. It grew in the center of the yard, muscular and knotty with a mulchy black hollow in the trunk where he had stored treasure as a kid. "What kind of treasure?" she'd asked. "Spent bullets and old keys," he said. And some real treasure too: a gold tooth, a silver butter knife, a doubloon. She'd had a similar tree on her hacienda, a live oak, festooned with old man's beard, in which she'd hidden her baby ring.

She laughed out loud, unable to contain the upwelling inside of her. A feeling that she had not really believed existed, had taken for a fantasy dreamed up by books and bored, silly women. She had been giddy with Kern, yes, but the delight was more that of mischief, of discovery, of figuring things out. This was as if her very soul had doubled. He'd look at her and she'd get so jumbled that she could barely speak, and yet the jumble was not one of nerves but of elation. How could it be that the presence of a man, simply a man, flawed through and through—she had no illusion in that regard—how could he do this?

"Mother!" Victoria shouted. Dolores jumped. "Get the ball!"

The little pink ball rolled toward her, its course erratic due to the warped planks of the porch. Her leg shot out.

"Got it," she said, pleased at her reflexes.

"Can I have it?" Victoria asked.

"Maybe." She rolled it under her shoe.

"Please."

She nudged the ball back over. Victoria caught it and returned to her game. The church bell at the end of the block clanged. The screen door banged open. Clara, summoning them to the second sitting room. But she didn't. She edged her bulk to the middle of the porch and rubbed her arms.

"Brrrr, it's brisk," she said, surprising Dolores with an amiable smile.

Dolores nodded in agreement and said they'd come in as soon as Victoria finished up her game.

"Oh, don't bother," said Clara, fluttering a plump hand. She approached, *clomp, clomp, clomp,* shaking the floorboards, and asked if she could sit down.

"Of course," Dolores said, scooting to the side. Clara lowered herself. The bench groaned, and the rusty ceiling hooks creaked, but the swing held. Dolores could barely move, squeezed between the armrest and Clara's huge lap. They watched Victoria scooping up her jacks.

"She's an agile creature," Clara commented.

Dolores nodded. It was one of the nicer things that Clara had said about Victoria. Maybe she'd decided to accept them into the family; maybe that's all this was. It seemed to be the case. Clara, tittering, related her maid's latest mistake. Dolores said, "Oh yes, how very stupid." Clara prattled on. Dolores kept smiling and agreeing with the things Clara said. Victoria shouted. Her ball rolled toward them. Dolores moved her leg to stop it but it veered toward Clara. Clara probably couldn't have moved her foot down fast enough, but she didn't even try. Her feet dangled. The ball rolled under them, through the slats of the railing, and off the porch. Victoria groaned.

"Well, go get it, dear," Clara clucked.

Victoria went down to look for it. Clara watched Victoria thwack through the bushes and mentioned something about being young again. Dolores managed not to snort. She could not imagine Clara young. She wanted to get up and help Victoria find the ball, but she couldn't think of a graceful way to unpry herself from between Clara's lap and the armrest. Another engine rumbled in the alley. She trembled. James. She recognized his engine. How could Clara be his mother? A mystery—or, more likely, a warning. But Dolores had never been able to heed warnings.

"Cousin James!" Victoria shouted, as the back gate swung open.

"Hello, sweetheart."

"Look!" She pointed at a squirrel perched on a low-lying branch of the old oak tree.

"Shall we toss an acorn at it?" He smiled at Dolores. She was already off the swing, moving toward him. She had to stop. She leaned against the post. He climbed the steps and leaned against the opposite post.

"James," said Clara.

"Hmmm?" he said, looking at Dolores.

"Go inside. Your father wants to talk to you."

Still looking at Dolores, he took off his gloves. She had taken off those very same gloves, in the car, their last trip down the canal. Held them to her cheek as if the leather were his skin.

"James, did you hear me?"

"Yes. I always hear you." He bowed to Dolores and blew a kiss to his mother. "And I always obey."

Clara got up with a groan and started to follow James inside, then changed her mind. She sighed, rather dramatically, then drew herself up tall. "He pretends not to be, but at bottom he's a good boy," she said, approaching Dolores. Dolores, confused by the change in Clara's manner, didn't know what to say. Clara looked at her intently, as if to drill a message into her eyes. A warning. "Owen is a good man too," Clara added.

Dolores nodded. She was shaking. Clara stood across from her, all of a sudden impressive and implacable.

"My, it's gotten cold," Dolores said, hoping to disguise the shaking.

"Yes," said Clara.

Dolores turned away from her. "I hope Victoria has her jacket buttoned." She scanned the backyard. Clara continued to watch her. Where was Victoria? Dolores couldn't see her from the porch. She went down the steps, grateful for the distraction. "Victoria!" She looked behind the oak tree, in the bushes, by the birdbath. "Victoria!" she laughed. "Where are you? I give up." No one answered. Clara watched from the porch, her face scrunched up, pale and disapproving. "Victoria! Come on! Time to go inside!" Dolores shouted. "I mean it!"

Wind blew through the leaves, coldly whistling.

Dolores's stomach knotted. "Victoria?"

The gate to the back alley was open. She checked in James's car, under the wheels, in the garage.

"Victoria!" she yelled, frantic now.

The back door slammed open and James's footfalls hurried down the path. "Victoria!" he called. Their eyes met as they waited, hoping that a fresh voice would do the trick. But Victoria did not respond. "Little scamp," said James fondly, shaking his head. He was trying to calm her down. He was right. How far can a child go in five minutes? Less than five minutes.

But Dolores could not shake the feeling. She turned from him and ran, calling her daughter's name. Brick house after brick house. Gas lamp after gas lamp. People looking at her with pity and interest. Then she heard the shrieking.

♠

O wen's water cup was broken. He had opened his suit-case to find shards of glass sticking out of his socks and had been struck by a grief that he knew to be disproportionate. It was a cup, a simple workingman's cup. Yet he could not help thinking that if still he had it, if he could drink water from it, then he could swallow down the inflammation that had taken over his throat. His throat! Such pain! But worse, so much worse, he could not speak, not even whisper. Never could he recall an infection like this. He was certain it arose from Washington's atmosphere, the murky air—the city had been built on a swamp, after all. But he sus-pected that there was more to it, that perhaps it was not just the natural humidity of the place but the corruptions of its dealings that tainted it, for could not men, the combined ef-forts of men, affect the atmosphere? Create an atmosphere that poisoned or buoyed one up? He had to get better! People were pulling out, afraid of the cost, skeptical of the Princi-ples, treating him like a wide-eyed simpleton. He wanted to wring their necks. He wanted to drag them all the way out to Pristina. Forcibly pull back their eyes: make them see. Right now, look in front of you. A cheerful labor force, an intermingling of the races, peaceful and beneficial to all. It is not a dream. I have done it. The fools! And now the Interstate Commerce Commission was on his back. Offi-cially, for a feeder line such as the Pristina Line, you did not need to deal with the Commission, but it turned out that you did. That was Washington in a nutshell: you didn't, but you did.

Owen adjusted his scarf then straightened his suit, preparing himself to enter the 401 Club. Benjamin knew a man on the Commission, and had arranged the meeting. Benjamin had been the model of a good host, uncomplaining as their stay grew ever longer, arranging meetings like these. Owen knew that he should be grateful. He was grateful. But it grated on him, taking these favors from Benjamin. He suspected that Benjamin was taunting him, arranging this meeting here. Owen's father had been a member in good standing. As a boy he had sat in a coach, clutched tightly by his mother, her chest rapidly rising and falling as they waited and waited for him to come out. One time, his father had come out with Benjamin, the two of them with their hats and red sideburns trotting down the marble steps, swinging their arms identically, singing a song that had made his mother go white.

The inside was so smoky that he could barely see, but he didn't need to see. He knew what he would find. He had been a member of clubs like this himself: wood hauled in from every corner of the globe, shined spittoons, silver trays slicing through the murk. The men were pale, interior men half grown into armchairs, or young ones slapping cards on the table. How could anything new and truly productive happen here? Wealth might be piled up, but a new world built? Benjamin's friend, a jowly lawyer with half-closed eyes, shook his hand and showed him to a table. Owen felt for his pencil and wrote: *Hello. I am pleased to meet you.* Dolores had been urging him to mind his manners.

The lawyer laughed. "Pleased to meet you too. How can I help you?"

Owen wrote down his first question and readjusted his scarf.

He had a hard time concentrating. The lawyer's responses seemed as convoluted and inconsequential as everything else he'd heard over the past couple months. He imagined his father, in this very club, slouching at the head of one of the card tables. He'd watched him play when he was a kid. His father had been quiet when the cards were dealt, waiting until the game got going before opening his mouth. Then he'd start. He had a gravely drawl that people said contained a pinch of molasses, just sweet enough to suck you in. He could tell stories of horses and women and Old Virginia, but he didn't need to; he could simply list the names of the cows on his grandmother's tobacco farm, and his listeners would be charmed.

"Do you play golf?" the lawyer asked. "Why don't you play a round or two with Chuck Raspberry. Take him to the Arlington Club. I've got a membership there. I'll work it out for you."

Golf? Owen hadn't played golf for twenty years. The lawyer lit a cigar and advised him on the ins and outs of Mr. Raspberry's game. Owen coughed and rubbed his throat. The young men at the table beside them pushed back their chairs, bragging about the places they had been. One of them, an awkward-looking fellow with a rash of boils on his neck, certainly not a member of the club, someone's guest, probably had a fat wallet, tipped over an ashtray. It crashed to the floor and broke amidst a round of oaths and laughter. An old colored man knelt to clean it up. The youths circled the man, pointing out shards that he had missed, their laughter rising. A tirade rose in Owen's throat, battling against the blockage. No one noticed.

"Mr. Scraperton!" The lawyer tugged at his sleeve.

Owen, startled, turned back to face him.

"Look." The lawyer pointed at the entrance. Benjamin wavered in the doorway, his hands fluttering and waxy in the smoky dark. Something was wrong. Owen jumped from his chair.

Benjamin grasped his elbow. "Victoria—" he said in a low, confidential voice.

A noise, the first noise in weeks, broke out of Owen's throat.

"She got into a scrape, some boys from the neighborhood—don't worry, she'll be fine. She'll be fine."

The hoof beats clattered on the cobblestones. Owen stared at the street ahead, unable to face Benjamin, who sat beside him, inanely muttering: *She'll be fine—it's inconceivable, their uncle is a fine man, a good man—she'll be fine—not to worry, James found them before anything could happen—it was only a scuffle, children can be beasts—she'll be fine—a nick to the tongue, that's all—and to think, just last week we were playing golf together, their uncle and I—she'll be fine—last time I play with him—she'll be fine—just a nick, a very little nick, really.*

The hoof beats felt like they were pounding right into Owen's gut. He should not have brought her here. The place was a cesspool. He had gambled with his own daughter's life. The hooves kept pounding, pounding, pounding until finally they reached the hospital. He leapt out of the carriage before it had stopped and raced into the lobby, shouting, his voice back, hoarse but audible. Somehow people understood and he understood them enough to follow their directions. Up flights of stairs, down a hall, into another wing . . . Now he stood before a door. He steadied his breath. He opened it. The room was quiet. It smelled of vomit, bleach, golf. Dolores leaned against the wainscoting. There was blood all over her dress. Victoria lay on a narrow iron bed with blue sheets. Bandages swathed the lower half of her face. Her nose was fine, but both of her eyes had been punched and a welt swelled on her forehead. A scuffle? That's what they called this? A scuffle? Owen knelt by her bed. He put his hand on her little arm. He blew on the welt. Her eyes opened; they weren't focused.

"Sweetheart," Owen said, gently squeezing her arm. "Are you all right?" Her eyes swam. Then they caught onto his. There she was. There was her glimmer. "Sweetheart," he repeated, his voice cracking.

She looked at him, a lively look, the look of the little girl undaunted by flash floods and bloody bull carcasses. A look that after some moments softened into a question.

"You're in a hospital," he said, stroking her hair. "But don't you worry, not for long."

Dolores knelt down beside him, her shoulder lightly grazing his. Together they peered at their daughter, trying to lighten their expressions, to erase the reflection of her wounds from their eyes. "Mi amor," Dolores said softly, tracing her finger along the dip of Victoria's nose. "Your tongue will heal, my love. The doctor told us so."

"It was my fault. I should have never brought you here," he said. "It's this place, it's this place."

"It's not your fault," Dolores said, her voice catching. She put her hand on his back. A bolt of electricity ran through it, surprising Owen with its strength, for Dolores looked so pale.

When Victoria closed her eyes, he followed his wife back to the wall and they leaned against it, side by side, watching their daughter, listening to her breath lengthen into sleep. A nurse came in and offered them chairs. Dolores shook her head no. He did too. They would both lean against the wall, a silent sentry watching the rise and fall of Victoria's chest. He put his arm around her.

"She will be all right."

"Yes."

"We should have never come," he said.

"Perhaps you're right," she responded softly.

He pulled her closer, grateful for the sound of her voice. Her hair smelled good and familiar, a tang of desert wind and sun on rock.

The train swerved around a bend and Owen's pen slipped, slashing through the words. But they weren't working anyway. He couldn't write. Every time he looked up, he was confronted with the sight of Victoria, her beautiful face obscured by the tongue splint. Owen had never imagined that you could bandage a tongue, but you could do just about anything with the right kind of harness. Two gauze strips crossed over her cheeks and formed an X at the back of her head, keeping the thing in place. The cast itself was much like any other type, made of plaster and gauze, and coated over with clear shellac because of the moistness. It protruded from her mouth, shockingly white, pointing at you. But she didn't mean to accuse. She'd been a terrific sport. The slightest look of concern and she'd scrawl I AM FINE on her chalkboard. The chalkboard was worse than the splint, dangling from her neck on a white string, reminding Owen of beggar children and amputees. She loved it though. She only let them remove it before she went to bed, and then she insisted on wedging it between the mattress and the wall of her berth.

Dolores sat beside her staring at nothing. He had felt so close to her those long days at the hospital, more dependent on her than he had ever felt, her guiding him along the halls, reminding him that Victoria would heal. But once they boarded the train, everything changed—at least that's what it had felt like. There had been a moment when the city receded from view, when he had turned to her wanting to share his relief and the words had shriveled on his tongue. She looked like a ghost. He had thought that there was a problem with her health, but she wouldn't say what was wrong. He only realized that it was not her health when the conductor knocked, and she perked up and conversed with him in a perfectly ordinary manner. When Victoria wished to communicate with her, her eyes sparkled with softness and care. It was just he who received these dead eyes, this slack face. He could understand if she were mad at him, or perhaps felt guilty alongside him, but why not articulate it? How could he respond if she would not speak her part? He had never completely understood her, but before when he didn't understand her, he felt as if he were involved in a delightful mystery. Now he felt as if he were locked out of his own home.

A bottle rolled against his foot. Bottles, Victoria's empties, were strewn all over the floor. Dolores only picked them up when the urge came. Milk, juice, protein elixir bottles, green glass, clear glass, blue glass, narrow ones and fat, molded and plain, gathering speed when they hit on a diagonal, crashing into corners and knocking against each other. Underneath was a whispered commotion of drinking straws, straws that they'd ordered especially for Victoria, now flattened, used, and stepped on, and drafts of the stockholder letter, crushed into tight inky balls. They shifted with the straws in a paper tide that sometimes cushioned the crashes, sometimes didn't.

He wadded his latest ink-smeared attempt and took out a fresh piece of paper. The problem wasn't returning the money to the stockholders. Obviously they needed to be reimbursed. The problem was that he didn't want them reinvesting their capital in anything that would connect the cities to the country. But there was nothing legal he could do. *Esteemed Gentlemen*, he wrote, starting another draft.

I relate to you an incident that occurred this Sunday past, the 7th of November, 1906, in Washington, D.C. You may have heard of the Bradleys of Baltimore, a fine, old family that fought in the Revolution, established a shipping line, a museum, and a foundling house. Great achievements, indeed, yet these achievements did nothing to shield the Bradleys from the winds of degeneracy that corrode our cities. In such an atmosphere, the most admirable families can and will produce degenerate offspring.

Christopher and Horace Bradley began killing cats when they were nine and eleven years old. They disemboweled them in a wood shed, explaining to anyone who heard that they were conducting scientific experiments. When their pastime was discovered, their parents sent them to Washington. Perhaps they thought that the change in scenery would affect a cure. Perhaps they simply did not want to be confronted by what they had spawned. They were put under the care of their older brother, a promising junior doctor at George Washington University. But in tune with the hedonistic temper of the times, this brother was more interested in his tennis date than familial duty. He left Horace and Christopher in the care of a servant. They broke into his medical case, stole a scalpel each, and left the house.

They crossed my daughter's path on 19th Street.

Owen looked back at Victoria. Her eyelids drooped from painkillers. She was not supposed to have been alone on 19th Street. She was supposed to have been in Clara and Benjamin's backyard. She had been there only moments before, playing jacks on the porch, but the ball bounced out of her reach and rolled into the backyard. She had explained all this on her chalkboard. When she went to fetch the ball, she got interested in a squirrel who led her out the back fence, down the alley, and onto 19th Street. There, a cat frightened the squirrel up a tree. Then the Bradley boys appeared.

My daughter is six; the Bradleys are thirteen and fifteen. When

*she tried to save the cat that they were after, they fell upon her.
She screamed. They forgot about the cat when they saw the length
of her tongue. They express no remorse; they said they wanted to
take it out and study it. The younger of her assailants had forced
down her arms, while the elder straddled her chest and wielded the
scalpel. This took place in full daylight, on the street, my daughter kicking and shrieking, neighbors running out of houses shouting. It wasn't until James grabbed Horace's hair and yanked back
his head, almost breaking his neck, that he dropped the scalpel.
Blood streamed over Victoria's face, soaked her collar, stained the
cobblestones—*

Owen crossed out the last couple of sentences. He hadn't
been there, he didn't have the right, although it seemed to
him that he could see it. They'd slashed her tongue straight
down the *median sulcus* or central groove, about two-thirds of
an inch deep.

He crumpled the letter. It was too graphic, too emotional,
too outraged by the particulars. And its emphasis was false.
The boys didn't slit Victoria's tongue, Washington did. People were not meant to live in cities. Cities twisted them into
horrid mutations. Especially Washington. It was as polluted as
Pristina was pure, pretending to represent the Union, while
at its core, Southern through and through. Lincoln had been
shot there, and now they were segregating streetcars.

Esteemed Gentlemen:

Flee Washington. It is a forked-tongued city.

It had tried to take his daughter. It had put its mark on
her. But she would not be marked forever. He had gotten
hold of the very best doctor, Dr. Thermadore, a heroic-jawed,
sharp-eyed surgeon. He had personally sewn and splinted her

tongue. When the bandages came off, he had assured them, they'd find it whole with only a tiny scar.

They lurched down the corridor. On one side, a worm-colored sky and dead fields of cotton, on the other, scarred mahogany doors. At the dining car, they settled at a window table as the waiters filled salt and pepper shakers and straightened the corners of white table linens. It was best to get here when the car was empty; otherwise people peeked over their menus to stare at Victoria's cast. Their waiter arrived and asked what they wanted. Owen decided to remain silent; Dolores could order. The waiter asked them if they'd like some more time. Owen shook his head. The waiter nodded and looked out the window. A minute or two passed. The waiter wetted his lips. Dolores, not looking the least defeated, smiled.

"My daughter will have the split pea soup, in a fountain glass, if you please."

"Very good, ma'am. And for you?"

"A cup of coffee will be fine."

"She'll have the chicken salad sandwich," Owen said. The waiter turned to him. "Toast the bread. She likes it toasted." A family entered the dining car. "And get me a steak. Rare's fine, just bring it out as fast as possible."

The car had half filled up by the time the waiter came with their food. He put Dolores's sandwich down first. They'd burnt the toast then stabbed it through with miniature American flags. Dolores pushed it aside and helped Victoria with her soup. The vertical shape of the fountain glass made it easier to use with a straw, but it was a lumpy and grayish split pea, not the kind of thing you wanted to look at. Dolores sorted through her bag, found a straw, and inserted it into Victoria's cast. They'd had a special groove put in for this purpose. Owen kept an eye on the people who poured into the dining car. They were better behaved today. Still, an obvious silence fell as the people passed their table, making every scrape of his fork and knife audible. Beyond their immediate periphery, the car hummed with conversation.

Victoria sucked up the last bit of soup. He stared out the window, trying to block out the sound of her straw. They had reached some woods, trees sparse and barren, branches clawing at the sky. Then like a slide at a magic lantern show—they must have changed the lighting—Dolores's face was superimposed over the trees. Not the Dolores across from him. A luminous, serene Dolores floating on the windowpane. His Doe. His impossible D. He had to be patient. Perhaps her emotional state was not so much fury as a delayed reaction to the shock of what had happened. She had been the stronger one at the hospital, murmuring that all would be okay. He had understood that Victoria would recover, but what had agonized him was the understanding that it might not have been, that they had risked her, their only child.

She took Victoria to prepare for bed, leaving him alone at the table with the remnants of their meal. He stared at her chicken sandwich, untouched, the lettuce brown on the sides, the dressing now translucent. He bid a waiter to take it away and ordered a coffee. Then a second. Then a third. Eventually the maitrê d' approached. There was a long line for dinner, might he take his coffee in the smoking car? He wandered the narrow corridors, exchanging good evenings with people, comforted by the sound of his voice, and even better, the sound of other voices responding. He met a scientist this way, and they talked about Wilson's cloud chamber and the Russian troubles until the scientist's wife dragged him off, and Owen was alone again. When he returned to the compartment, the door was shut. He didn't need to open it to know that inside Dolores sat with her back pressed against the seat, her hands listless by her sides, her eyes cast down so that he couldn't look into them, only see the purple pouches beneath. He walked on. He entered the sleeping car. It was ill lit and smelled of strangers snoring behind heavy yellow curtains. Victoria's cast glimmered in the dim surroundings. He crouched down and kissed her.

"Good night, beauty," he whispered.

Her eyes opened. She smiled and touched his cheek.

He returned to the compartment. Dolores, as expected, didn't acknowledge his entrance. It was unacceptably cruel, especially considering that in Washington, even before the accident, they'd shared a bed every night. How affectionate she'd been! Clucking over his throat and kissing him on the temples and whispering scandalous and improbable stories about Clara. She had loved him with unexpected ardor, and he had fallen asleep to the smell of her cream and her hands on his chest. The whistle moaned. He took out a fresh sheet of paper and stared at it.

The bottles rolled and crashed as the train curved around a bend. He shook his pen.

Esteemed Gentlemen:

I regret to inform you that due to unforeseen circumstances, construction of the Pristina branch line has been discontinued. Your investment will be returned in full.

Sincerely yours,
Owen Scraperton

He blew on the ink. He paced. "Dolores?" He stopped in front of her, holding the letter a few inches from her face. "What do you think?"

She didn't respond.

"You have to tell me what you think."

He held the letter in front of her face, resolved to stay in that position until she said something.

"In case you didn't see," he said, "I finished my stockholder letter. I think it's best not to tell them why. Let them figure things out on their own." Her eyes were blank. "*Due to unforeseen circumstances,*" he read, "*construction of the Pristina branch line has been discontinued.*" He looked over the edge of the paper. "*Your investment will be returned in full.*"

The train creaked and shuddered. He got down onto his knees so that he could see her face properly. Her eyes were sunken and dull and didn't blink. He was horrified at their lifelessness. She had never looked like this. He couldn't recall one instance, no matter what their dispute. A bottle rolled into his calf. He was still kneeling and, now that he realized it, extremely uncomfortable.

She made a noise in her throat.

"Dolores?" he whispered.

"To the point," she said.

"What?"

"Your letter . . . makes a succinct point."

"Dolores," he said, grasping the soft muscle at the top of her arm.

She detached his hand. Instead of letting go, she stared at it as if it belonged to a stranger. "I'm tired," she said.

She was. He saw then. She wasn't mad at him; she was exhausted. He remembered himself after his mother died.

"Dolores," he whispered, "it wasn't your fault."

She smiled wanly.

"She's alive, she's well, her bandages will come off in a couple months. It will be as if nothing happened."

"But it has happened," she said. "What has happened I

can't tell you, but it has happened." There was a distance in her voice that he felt incapable of bridging.

He touched her hand. She didn't retract. He stroked his thumb along the line from her wrist to her knuckles. "Doe," he said, "we're going home. It's a good home, a safe home." Her eyes flickered. A light came into them. Not the golden sheen, a quieter sort of light, filled with question and remorse.

That light in her eyes stayed with him deep into the night. He lay in his berth, brushing his fingers against the curtain folds, feeling her across the aisle from him. He felt a strange closeness with her, as if that light were the beginning of a new understanding between them. He laced his fingers across his chest and pictured her as he first saw her, cantering through a field of creosote and cactus. In this way, he fell asleep, a calm sleep that lasted way past daybreak.

He awoke with a shock. He never overslept. The sensation was so alien he was afraid that the previous night had been a dream. But he hadn't been dreaming. When he got to their compartment, the floor had been swept and the bottles re-moved. Dolores, in her green dress, the one with the low collar that she knew he liked, sat across from Victoria. They tossed a ball of orange yarn back and forth. He said good morning and Dolores pitched the yarn at him.

"I'm starving," she said.

"I'm not surprised." She had barely taken anything since the accident but black coffee.

In the dining car, Victoria and he watched Dolores eat three eggs, two biscuits, and a plateful of bacon. You could tell that Victoria was smiling behind the cast. When they got back to the compartment, she stood by the window for hours, pointing at the most common things, and Owen thought it was enchanting just to hear Dolores name them. A windmill. A spotted cow. A big, blue Texas sky.

By late afternoon, the hills were dotted with cattle barons' mansions and smokestacks belched in the distance. They were nearing Fort Worth where they would switch to the Marfa train and be done with cities for good. He and Doe gathered their belongings, checked under seats, bumped heads, and apologized laughing. "Oh, Dolores," he said, wishing for a moment that Victoria weren't there. But she was. They joined her by the window. The sky was dark and getting darker. By the time they crossed the river, it was a violent purple, and fat drops splattered against the pane. Victoria traced her finger along the glass, following the drops as they wriggled upward. The train inched through a shambly part of town filled with sagging bungalows and laundry lines getting wet. In one of the unkempt yards, a man stepped out into the storm carrying a chair. He set the chair down by a crooked fence, then climbed upon it, and from there, climbed onto a fence post. The rain poured down as he squatted on this post, a slim piece of wood that looked like it would snap at any minute. He clutched the sides for balance, then slowly, precariously, rose. People struggling with umbrellas came out of houses and gestured for him to get down, but the fool remained standing, wobbling on his bizarre perch. Then he pulled a metal flask from his greatcoat and flailed it at the crowd.

"Look at the idiot," Owen chuckled.

"But brave," Dolores said quietly.

They rolled into the station, a grandiose Beaux Arts building with an arched red roof under which a multitude jostled and yelled and hawked trashy curios. Owen guided Victoria and Dolores through the crowd, looking for a place where they could sit. Eventually they found a café with a sticky table and overly sweetened hot chocolate. He and Dolores watched people pass by, and Victoria drew a picture of a woman holding a staff.

"Nice," he said.

She wrote that it was a peasant from the Tyrol.

"Wonderful," he said. "See that, Doe? From the Tyrol. She did like that atlas." When he gave it to her for her birthday, Dolores had insisted that she was too young.

Victoria erased her board, replacing the picture with a request to see the mural on the far side of the station. Owen left Dolores to watch their belongings. The mural was a three-panel piece showing first a pony express courier, then a line of telegraph poles, then a steam locomotive. Victoria strolled along the panels, pointing her tongue cast at whatever interested her. At the far side a plaque informed them that the mural was entitled *The Evolution of Communication*. Victoria gave Owen a skeptical look.

"I know," he said. "They got it all wrong. That's what we learned this trip. That's not evolution, it's confusion and pollution."

She opened her arms, and he lifted her onto his shoulders. When they got to their table, Dolores had left. A waiter brought him an envelope. Inside he found a quick scrawl saying she'd be back soon, so they ordered another round of chocolate. Owen sipped, pursing his lips at the sugar, and tried to spot Dolores amidst the milling people. Victoria held her cup in both hands and single-mindedly slurped through her straw. The ladies at the next table nattered on in shrill voices and cast sidelong glances at Victoria.

"Where is your mother? The train's going to board any minute." Owen tapped his spoon on his saucer, as if he could recall her with the sharp *clack clack clack*. A parade of people passed by. Gunslingers, half-wits, peddlers with thick necks and garlicky noses, blanketed Indians, Mexicans with streams of children. No Dolores. The loudspeaker announced that their train was boarding.

After the second boarding announcement, he saw her. Too relieved to be angry, he jumped up waving. She waved back, nearing gracefully in her green dress with the low collar. Something glittered around her neck, a piece of silver dipping down into her cleavage.

A crucifix.

He froze, not believing. But there it hung, the cross, the twisted man, the barbaric nails. What was she thinking? A horrid smile contorted his face. He heard himself roar, felt his hand rise. He hit her on the cheek, hard enough that he knocked her off balance, hard enough that his palm, calloused as it was, stung. The people around them fell silent. He was aware of a circle forming. In the center of this circle, Dolores stood tall and steady, smiling imperiously.

1908

♦

L a Herrida had died. Dolores could not say that she'd known her, but she'd loved the way the woman had jabbed her cane and flicked her ashes, and Dolores had vowed that she'd get a decent funeral. None of this Pristinian fare, some Lucretian sermon about how we were all atoms and vacuity. She would get a real, robed preacher, albeit a fat one with atrocious breath. She didn't care that La Herrida had shown no signs of Catholicism (as Badinoe loved to point out). La Herrida had flaunted Owen's each and every rule. Her funeral ought to carry on in that tradition.

She peeked in the bag, recounted the bottles. Oblaba not only had a visiting priest, it also had a cantina whose proprietor had so far proved himself capable of procuring anything for which she asked. His latest feat was sherry, the same brand her Aunt Marina had used, an amber glass bottle with a red foil cap, *Jerez, España* smeared on the top. There had always been at least a half dozen of these red-capped bottles lining the ledge in Marina's kitchen. Dolores had dreamed recently about that stone kitchen with black hooks coming out of the wall and fireplaces you could stand in. Upon waking, she'd charged down to the pantry and threw everything off the shelves looking for her recipe book. She'd finally found it in the basement, under a box of chipped china and a horrid brass ashtray in the shape of a radish. It was a hand-bound album, the cover neatly stretched with beige cloth and tied with a gold silk ribbon. In the upper-right corner, her mother, in her careful, modest handwriting, had blessed her marriage and her table. It had been a wedding gift.

Dolores realized now the labor her mother must have put into it, writing out each recipe, first in pencil, then in ink. She evidently hadn't been thinking about that earlier. She'd opened the cookbook to find the word *Recetas* underlined and promising at the top of the page, while below, a razed rectangle cut through the meat of the book. Inside the hole lay a tarnished spur. It took her a while to remember that it was the very same spur that had once adorned the heel of her Australian ranch hand.

She had no such souvenir of James. She didn't want reminders.

How could she have ruined her mother's handiwork, and for what, to commemorate what? A mistake she had made at sixteen? She'd thrown the spur away, tossed it unceremoniously into the trash, then sat down at her desk to write for another set of recipes, this time in pencil, on note cards, nothing fancy. A couple of weeks ago, they'd finally arrived. There were a bunch of chilies and egg dishes that didn't require liquor, but the ones that interested her demanded dashes of cognac, dribbles of Madeira, an entire vat of wine for the properly drowned goat.

The church bell clanged. The warped old doors opened, and the congregation straggled out. The majority were from Oblaba, but there were still a good number from the caves. Every third Sunday of the month, the padre did his Oblaba round, and the cave people did their march, the children on burros and the women on foot, trekking a good ten miles along a thankless trail. Owen wouldn't even give them credit for the effort, said they were mindless mules lured on by the padre's "sugared tongue." What nonsense. If anyone heard

Owen and the padre speak they would know which one had the sugared tongue. The padre had a drab, serviceable voice; it did occasionally soar, but generally it clodded and clopped along endless stretches of flat, gray ground.

A cavewoman rushed toward her—a thick-boned mother of twelve—grabbed her hand, and planted a fervent kiss on her knuckles.

"Buenas tardes," Dolores said, pretty sure that the woman's name was Camino, but deciding not to risk it.

The woman rose, beaming, cheap glass earrings jangling back and forth. Dolores had sent a food box to her when Owen docked her husband's pay. In a moment she was joined by many others, whiskered women, eager-faced girls with bows in their hair, shy boys with half-open mouths. Voices called out, blessing Dolores, thanking her for various things; hands pulled at her sleeve, requesting more. They came in such a pack that it would have been difficult to greet them each by name even if she could remember them.

The padre appeared in the doorway of the church, his belly bulging beneath his grease-stained robe, a belly that Dolores wished she could look at without thinking of Owen ranting about priests growing fat off the poor. She disentangled herself from the peons and walked toward him. The padre's eyes sharpened, and he bowed low. She inclined her head. He greeted her with great devotion—her last donation had paid for the new altar—but his breath was much the same as ever. She took a discreet step back. His teeth had rotted into brown stubs riddled with holes. That he had achieved his present girth with a mouth like that was, according to Badinoe, proof of God's miracles. The padre finished praising her and she bestowed the usual compliments, then asked if she could speak with him in private.

He led her into the church. A frantic flapping sounded in

the rafters, and a pigeon swooped down and landed on the altar. With surprising speed the padre ran toward it waving his black-sleeved arms. She stayed back, nudging a cuticle into place. The altar embarrassed her. The church was simple and poor, with bare whitewashed walls and pews that were nothing but rough-hewn slabs of wood. Then there was her altar, the kind of thing that had looked perfect at the hacienda, but here seemed excessive and overbearing. The padre shooed away the pigeon and wiped his sleeve over the spot where the bird had perched. She announced that La Herrida had passed away.

"Ah, La Herrida," he sighed, assuming an expression of sorrowful contemplation. "She was famous for her age. One hundred and twenty, is that possible?"

"I believe so," said Dolores, neglecting to mention that she was also a witch. "Padre, I would like you to do her funeral."

The padre brightened and said that it would be an honor.

"In Pristina," Dolores added.

The padre laughed until he realized she was serious and then he turned pale. "I cannot bury her on unconsecrated soil."

"Well, then. Why couldn't you consecrate it?"

"I? I cannot do such a thing. Even if I were the bishop, I would have no jurisdiction in the United States."

"What are man-made borders to a man of God?"

"Señora. Por favor."

"I have something that should help your teeth." The padre's round shoulders rose to cover his ears. "And that communion wine that you said you needed? I can provide you with plenty."

"Do you really think that something can help my teeth?"

"Hood's tooth powder. The governor's wife swears by it. I can get you an entire case."

The padre smiled. "How wonderful that there is such a thing, but what you ask is too much, señora."

"She served God for one hundred and twenty years and you would deny her a proper burial?"

"Bring her here. Here I have the power. Here the ground is consecrated."

"She did not live here. She must be buried where she lived. She lived one hundred and twenty years on that soil."

"But the patrols, doña." His voice betrayed his fear.

"They won't bother you. I promise. You do not need to go into Pristina proper. The only place you need to go is the cemetery, which is in the caves, where your congregation lives. It is outside of Owen's control."

The priest's mouth twisted and twitched. "I cannot."

Dolores took his hand in both of hers. "I swear to you, Padre. I will take care of the patrols. This is all that I have ever asked you." He studied her for a good long time. "How can you not? She was a good woman. She helped the sick. She needs a proper burial."

He sighed.

She squeezed his hands in hers. "You will do it, won't you? You understand that you must?"

He nodded miserably.

"I'll take care of the patrols."

She emerged from the church, practically skipping. The key was not being afraid. That's what hamstrung everyone, this fear. She understood it; she'd experienced it herself, but no longer. Washington had cured her, or more accurately *leaving* Washington, that endless train ride, face to face with what she was returning to. She had imagined, in that time before the accident, a different ending, a not-returning. She had heard of people who had done such things. James had too. What raving conversations they had had! And then Victoria,

the blood so bright on her dress. As if there really were venge-
ful angels watching every infraction. But why strike Victoria
who had done nothing wrong? The injustice of it! There was
nothing just about God. She fingered her crucifix, wondering
how her mother had believed so calmly and completely.

A cloud hung over Oblaba, pregnant and dark, casting the
huts and shacks in a weird violet light. She hurried down
a nameless street, and people crouched in their small dark
windows watching her go. The church bell rang the hour. She
picked up her pace. She had to be home when Owen dropped
Victoria off, talk to him about the patrols. She'd checked the
town records. She had legality on her side.

Halfway to the crossing, a dog with a wrinkled snout
leapt from behind a mesquite bush. "Down!" she yelled. The
dog nuzzled her thigh and made inarticulate, almost catlike
mews. She pushed him away. He followed, sniffing at her
coattails. He probably smelled Cerb'rus, the black lab Owen
had bought to protect Victoria from any further tongue slash-
ers. So far Cerb'rus had learned to slobber over visitors' faces
and sprawl belly-up, whimpering to be scratched. It would
have been smarter to teach Victoria how to shoot. But only
the patrols were allowed guns, and Victoria was too small
for one of those clunky hunting rifles. The dog leapt upon
her again, his breath worse than the padre's. She pushed him
down then, in spite of her hurry, stopped to knead the loose
ring of skin around his neck. "Poor dog."

The sky grew dimmer by the instant. The dog started to
mew again and butted against her knee. She gave him a last
pat, wiped the greasy feel of his fur off her hand, then picked
along the roots and pebbles. The dog followed her. They came
to the river, its waters almost blond in the weird storm light.
She walked down to the bank, a steep slope studded with

wind-bent reeds. The boat, a creaky old thing that looked like it would sink any moment, lapped against the shore on the opposite side. She put down her bag, stuck two fingers in her mouth, and whistled. Across the river, a man in a red neckerchief poked his head from a stand of bamboo.

"Hola!" she yelled through cupped hands. "Ayudame! Estoy atrasada!"

He shouted something that she couldn't hear, then disappeared. She squatted on her bag. She would be late. She would miss Owen, her chance to talk to him, and Victoria would be angry that she wouldn't be waiting on the front porch, greeting her the instant she got back. The dog arranged himself next to her, proprietarily. She scratched the hollow behind his ear, getting her fingers greasy again.

The man finally ducked into the boat, unhitched, pushed off. His oars dipped in and out of the water, steady, confident, unheedful of the ominous sky. The river looked slow and lazy, but it wasn't. An undercurrent grabbed things that broke below the surface, steered them off course, drowned them. They'd had to rig the boat to an underwater cable so that it wouldn't be swept away. Now she could hear the squeak of the oars in their locks. Was he in Mexico now? Or the United States? You never knew where the border was; it shifted with the river, which shifted itself, running a few feet north, a few feet south, recharting its course every few years.

Dolores tickled the dog's ear with a piece of grass and told him he was a Mexican dog, from the Mexican side, and that she would be leaving him for an American dog from the American side. She laughed out loud, picturing them meeting, the wrinkle-snouted stranger and enthusiastic black Cerb'rus, sniffing asses, American and Mexican flags poking out from their holes. The wind came back, colder than it had been earlier, carrying pellets of icy rain. She pulled the shawl over her head and adjusted the lapels of her greatcoat. The dog gave her a doleful look, as if against his will she had dragged him out to this exposed spot. "Well, go then," she said. He switched his weight from one paw to another, but didn't get any farther than that.

The boatman reached the shore, and the dog trotted over, looking as if he planned to jump in. The man swung an oar at him, and helped Dolores into the boat. She fastened her eyes on the boatman, so as to avoid the dog's gaze, but she did not like the way that the man looked at her either, so she turned her attention to the water. The surface was now choppy, cut into by raindrops and the knife-blade oars. Owen called this stretch of river the "treasonous bend" and refused to come down here. He must have, though, early on, recruiting peons for his mines. She'd heard about that, him on his horse, galloping from hovel to scattershot village, opening his mouth, promising them jobs, some guy behind him, Van Sickle probably, collecting X's on the dotted line. And when he decided to comb Mexico for a wife, he must have crossed here too. But he certainly hadn't since; anyone who came this way he accused of being a Papist or a smuggler. It was her territory.

The boat sighed onto the shore as the sky started to sleet. Dolores paid the boatman, both of them moan-laughing, teeth chattering. She ran down the narrow path, sleet skittering off the bamboo stalks and stinging her face. In the clearing her horse pawed at the freezing mud.

It was dark by the time she got to Casa Grande. The windows glowed and the horse, coat flecked with ice, stumbled up the road. She yelled her arrival, but her voice was lost to the storm. She tossed the reigns to the stable boy, grabbed her bag from the pannier, and ran toward the main house. In the middle of the yard she stopped and shuddered. The weathervane, a heavy oversized fish, was spinning so furiously it seemed as if it would rip itself from the roof. She had to talk to Otto about taking it down, or at least checking to make sure it was fastened tightly.

Cerb'rus bounded over from his position by the fire. "Miss me, Cerb'rus? Or just jealous of the Mexican mutt?" She buried her fingers in the warmth of his fur.

"His name is not Cerb'rus." Victoria called from the top of the stairs.

"I'm sorry I'm late. Meant to get here earlier, but this weather—"

"His name is Snake Dog."

"Snake Dog?"

In a softer voice Victoria called out to the dog: "You like Snake Dog better, don't you?" She patted her knees, urging him to come to her. Dolores scratched the crinkle behind the dog's ear. "Come on, Snake Dog!" Victoria shouted. Cerb'rus didn't move.

Dolores stopped scratching him, but he still didn't leave. "We're having my aunt's chicken soup for dinner," she said. "It's a good night for soup. Sopa del circo. I think you'll like it." Victoria pouted at the dog, her eyes big and shiny. "For God's sake, Victoria. If you want to pet him, come down here and do it. You can't expect everyone to come running to you."

Victoria muttered something.

"What?"

"You said *for God's sake*," Victoria whined, "but God's a misunderstanding. A misunderstanding can't have a sake."

"I don't see why not."

Victoria's tongue darted out. Dolores averted her eyes before she could see the full disaster. The always overly long tongue was now forked like a snake's, and Victoria was the prouder for it.

* * *

She lay in the tub trying to warm her bones with water and her spirits with mescal. Only one shot of mescal; she couldn't become a sot or she'd play right into Owen's hands. Her knees triangled up, pale, bony, caps dry: they didn't seem to belong to her, dislocated by about an inch from the rest of her body. Realness lay in the magnified mass under the water. At the base of her thighs the hairs wavered, like the stringy kind of algae that grows on rocks in streams and pools in the mountains. She snorted at the image, too idyllic. More like cactus—thorny, thirsty, scratching those who came near it. Strawberry cactus or devil's head or jumping cholla. She pictured Victoria's head tearing through the spines, not the baby's head but the seven-year-old's, black braids, accusing eyes, slit tongue. She frowned at her drink and dumped it into the bathtub. "Idiot," she muttered to herself and grabbed the soap. She scoured standing up and rinsed with fresh water from the basin.

Alma only knew how to read in English so Dolores had to translate the recipe. When she finished, she stayed on, mincing garlic and listening to the rain. Alma hovered over the soup pot, skeptical in the beginning but softening up as the aroma came together. "See?" Dolores said, pouring herself a nip of sherry. She offered Alma a glass. The woman refused, but if she were angry or insulted, she didn't let on. Dolores fingered the crucifix that hung around her neck. Alma saw and turned away. She was, in spite of her allegiance to Owen, religious. Dolores knew because she'd caught her crossing herself years ago. She fished a clove out of the soup and sucked on it thoughtfully, careful not to break it.

"What do you think of the padre?"

Alma looked at her blankly.

"You must have gone to Oblaba—before Mr. Scraperton came."

Alma tossed another clove into the pot. "That was a long time ago, Mrs. Scraperton."

"I've asked the padre to speak at La Herrida's funeral."

Alma stirred the soup in silence. "Do you think it needs salt?" she asked finally.

Dolores poured a nip more sherry and took it into the parlor. She looked into the fire and sipped. She had mad ambitions for the funeral. She wanted professional mourners yanking their hair, a band playing a grand, swelling dirge, thick clouds of incense obscuring people's vision, getting into their throats, making them cough. Of course she could not pull off such a thing. But a priest, a priest would do. A priest stood for all that. Please don't let him back out. She offered up a prayer, tensing her toes, her eyelids, her fingers. Along with the priest, she needed people, not loads, just a priest and a handful of Pristinians who were willing to honor the old woman—that would be enough, more than enough, to make Owen furious.

And it was altogether possible. Pristina wasn't the homogenous bloc that she'd imagined. Owen's moving out of Casa Grande had made this clear. After he left, the town had separated into three parties. The first, the majority, in line with Owen, acted as if nothing had happened. She was Mrs. Scraperton in good standing, and they treated her with the same reserve and studied blankness that they always had. The second, the vanguard, made up primarily of committee ladies, any one of whom would happily shove her current husband down a shaft in order to be the next Mrs. Scraperton, staked out her offenses, catalogued and stockpiled them. They had fervor but they were cowards also; none of them would make a move until Owen cast the first stone, and he hadn't even picked up a pebble. The third and smallest party was the encouraging one, the people who might prefer a Zizima to a Pristina, as Badinoe put it, referring to the old pagan goddess of the mines. Potential Zizimans—people who still had some respect for what they didn't know. The engineer's wife who'd grown up in London and talked to Dolores as if she'd been there too. The skinny Swiss bookkeeper at Offitz & Carruthers who bowed low whenever she came into the room, and said *An honor, señora*, in his terrible Spanish accent. The baker's assistant. Millie Bradshaw. Rosa Izquierda. With each person it manifested itself differently, an ironic twist to a phrase, a glance, a half-hidden smile. It was all very vague; they were hardly the partners in crime that she and Badinoe were, and perhaps they were fooling themselves, but she didn't think so.

Yet even if there were Zizimans, they lived in Pristina. They wouldn't openly cross Owen and go to a Catholic funeral. That was asking too much. She stood by the fire, pondering her predicament, certain that there was a way, some way, to win, until Alma brought the soup out in a silver tureen. The steam, fragrant and heady, brought back Marina's low-ceilinged hall, the cousins snickering and kicking each other under the long dining table.

"Dinner, Victoria!" Dolores yelled up the stairs. She called a second time, then climbed to the second floor and knocked on her door. "Vic," she whispered.

"I don't want your soup."

Dolores pinched her lips, a trick she'd developed; it stopped her from snapping and calmed her at the same time. She pinched her lips for ten seconds and then entered. Victoria, hunched over her desk, didn't turn around. She was writing something, her pen scraping loudly against the paper. Dolores sat on the bed.

"It's got almonds and chicken and saffron. It was my father's favorite soup."

Victoria jabbed her pen in the inkpot.

"What are you doing?"

"I'm labeling my snakeskins."

This time, the lip-pinching trick didn't work. Dolores grabbed the pen. They struggled, ink spilling on their fingers, the desk, the fossils. No words, just grunts. Finally Dolores got Victoria's wrist in one hand and pried at the fingers with the other. The pen came out. Victoria, panting, opened the drawer and took out another.

Dolores retreated to the window. Rain spattered against the pane. The drops were hidden by the darkness until they hit the glass; even then you couldn't see their centers, only their white-rimmed borders. "I'm not stopping your father," she said. "He can come back whenever he wants."

Victoria made a sound of disgust.

"It's true," Dolores said, watching a drop expand as another fell into it.

"Then why did you go to Oblaba?" Victoria asked.

"Why?"

"You did, didn't you?"

"Yes." Dolores turned away from the window and faced her daughter. "I went to get the priest for La Herrida's funeral."

Victoria stared at her. "Why?"

"Because La Herrida was not a believer in the Principles, as you well know. She deserves a funeral more in keeping with her life. Just taste the soup. If you don't like it, you can have something else."

"No."

Dolores took a step toward her. Victoria made a fist around the base of the pen. Dolores kissed the top of her head. Her daughter's scalp was as hard and unyielding as if she had pressed her lips straight against her skull.

The next morning, gullies from the storm crisscrossed the yard and a lechuguilla plant leaned over sideways. Victoria ran around the property, gleefully inspecting the damage. "Look, Mom!" she called, as Dolores stepped onto the porch. She ran toward her, cupping a succulent flower in her hands, a splashy red blossom that must have blown in from a distance.

"How lovely," said Dolores, leaning down for a closer view, grazing her daughter's forehead with her own. "I wonder where it came from? We don't have any of those on our property."

"Maybe miles away," Victoria whispered, gently touching the petals.

"Shall we take it inside?" Dolores asked. "Put it on the breakfast table? We can float it in that little glass bowl we never know what to do with."

She followed Victoria into the house, grateful for Mondays, which were always better than Sundays. Victoria jabbered throughout breakfast, excited by the storm's destruction, and appeared genuinely interested when Dolores told her that when she was a girl, her father named her the official storm inspector of the hacienda. She had had a book in which she recorded the depth and width of the arroyo and the state of the fences and roads. How proud she'd been, reporting her findings to her father, feeling almost as powerful as the storm itself.

After Victoria went to school, Dolores had the boy saddle Nickel and rode to town to talk to Owen. She'd been busy combing through his library and found a bunch of useful quotations on religion, including one by the great John Brown himself. How satisfying, how Naturally Satisfying, to throw Owen's logic back at him!

The storm had hit town harder than Casa Grande, rutting the streets and throwing the shutters off balance. People cleaned up industriously enough, but there was an underlying shoddiness that they wouldn't be able to scrub away. Last year's financial panic had shot down mercury prices, making Owen stingier than ever—no new paint jobs, windowpanes, indoor plumbing. Casa Grande, on the other hand, looked great. Dolores had inherited a neat little sum from Tía Ana Carolina, a clucking old hen who had cut her off after the Australian ranch hand incident, but who, on her eighty-fifth birthday, shocked the family by buying a bicycle and redoing her will, naming Dolores her sole inheritor.

At Pristina HQ, a boy in overalls cleaned the mud from the windows, and bald-headed Grierson sat at his typewriter, fingers flying over the keys, creating an impressive clatter that ceased the moment she walked in.

"Good morning, Mrs. Scraperton."

"Good morning to you too. May I see Owen, please?"

Grierson shook his head. Owen and the engineer had left early that morning to look over a distant working, and they weren't expected back until evening. Dolores pinched her lips.

"Perhaps I can help you?" Grierson said.

She asked him for pen and paper, then stared at the paper, deflated. She had wanted to see Owen's face when she flaunted her freedom-of-religion quotations. She tapped the pen against her palm, thinking about leaving, but she had to do something for the padre. She began to write. There were loads of legal, diplomatic, and moral reasons why the priest could not be hampered, but putting them down on paper was hard. Why did arguments fall so flat the minute they

touched the page? People came into the office, talking in normal voices which dropped to whispers when they saw her.
Many turned around and exited, as if being in the same room
with her brought them bad luck. She finally finished a draft,
then drafted a second in much better time. She reviewed the
language. It was fine. Dry, but fine. Except that she didn't
know how to sign it. At last, she wrote, *Your Wife, Dolores.*

"I'll leave this on Owen's desk," she said, folding the letter and putting it in an envelope. She expected Grierson to
stop her—Owen allowed no one in his office unless he was
there—but the man merely nodded. People didn't know how
to treat her. She walked to the door of Owen's office and
twisted the knob. Grierson continued to type, his rhythm
slow and measured.

Dolores had been in this office plenty of times, but always with Owen, the two of them in the midst of some tense,
clipped interview while a line of managers and sneaks shuffled outside. Now she wandered around, assessing the room
as if she had never been there before. His Beacon Hill rug,
soiled with miners' footprints, his mineral case, his china basin with the blue windmill painted at the bottom, his sofa,
also from Beacon Hill, that served these days as his bed.
She pressed her palm against the cushion. Stiff and lumpy
and stubborn as Owen. She looked around for sheets. None
were missing from home, so he must have bought fresh ones.
She wanted to know if he'd chosen plain or colored, but she
couldn't find them anywhere. Maybe he didn't use sheets.
Maybe he thought that they were frivolous. She deposited his
note on the scale that stood on his desk. He ought to notice
it there, a creamy envelope on a mottled brass tray, weighing,
she checked, an ounce and a tenth. On the other side of the
desk, his chair, a green leather armchair that needed to be
reupholstered, had been pushed back as if he'd left in a hurry.

She drew her finger along a crack in the leather. A wrinkle. His throne was aging. She decided to sit in it. At first she sat on the edge, then sank back; it was comfortable in spite of its condition. She fondled the spiraled wooden handrests, wondering what he would think if he walked in to find her, wishing that he would.

Back in the main office, the sun shone through the newly washed windows and onto Grierson's bald head. He was still typing. She cleared her throat. He glanced at her without breaking his rhythm. She asked for another piece of paper. She'd decided that the best way to get a decent crowd for La Herrida would be to have two events: a procession and a funeral. The procession would be priestless. Sympathizers from town could join in and fall out of line before they reached the cemetery; that way, they could pay their respects to La Herrida without imperiling their standing. Grierson typed one-handed as he opened a drawer, fished out a sheet, and gave it to her with a flourish. In large, bold letters, she wrote, *La Herrida: 1788–1908*. The dates might have been false but they might have been true. La Herrida had had something about her that removed her from what usually made sense.

Grierson, watching her, stopped typing. She underlined La Herrida's name two times, feeling his eyes on her pen. Under the double line, she put the time of the funeral and the time and route of the funeral procession. *A secular procession*, she wrote, *open to all. Please come honor our oldest citizen's memory.* She glanced back at Grierson. For all she knew, he could have been a raging Owenite or as wry and duplicitous as Badinoe. That's how most people were, neither possible Zizimans nor committee women, but blank walls you could fill up with whatever fancy you wanted. For no reason other than the flamboyant way he had handed her the second sheet of paper, she decided that he supported her.

"Goodbye, Mr. Grierson," she said, giving him a knowing smile.

He blushed and bobbed his head up and down. "Have a fine day, Mrs. Scraperton," he called as she swung out the screen door. There. Perhaps the way to get people behind you was simply to assume their loyalty and act upon it. To make such a show out of believing in them that they would feel badly not returning the favor. Could this be Owen's trick? Pristina was but a pack of mad, polite followers loathe to hurt his feelings.

At Clarity she stopped, her path obstructed by a stalled mule train. The driver whipped and cursed as a dozen knotty, knobby, sterile mules ignored him. Dolores walked around to the front of the train and almost bumped into Birdie Wilson. The woman jumped back stiffly. Dolores fanned herself with the funeral notice. Birdie straightened her pile of papers; Dolores cocked her head to read the print. They were announcements for the Annual Beautification Committee bake sale.

"Ah, the bake sale," she said. "How yummy."

"Yes," Birdie sniffed. "You know, you ought to drop by and get your daughter something sweet. She's looking awfully skinny."

"She's growing, that's all."

"I do hope so," said Birdie, clucking.

Dolores crossed the street angrily. Victoria ate like a horse. Except for last night, refusing dinner. Why had she made soup? Victoria had had soup forced upon her the entire time she wore the tongue splint. How idiotic. Six straight months of liquids. Dolores smoothed her forehead with her index finger, hoping that Birdie hadn't found out about the soup, and if she had, that she wouldn't tell Owen. If she was smart, she wouldn't. Owen might like to interfere, but he didn't appreciate being interfered with. But those committee ladies didn't possess a drop of intuition between the lot of them. If Owen had half a brain, he'd banish them. They were hardly a good advertisement for Scientific Naturalism. But he wouldn't. Too many old Owenites had headed west, sick of mercury, virtue, chits-not-cash. The population was thinning.

A trio of miners doffed crumpled hats as Dolores stepped onto the porch of the O&C. Every inch of the community board was taken up with charts, invitations, pleas, queries. In the center was Birdie's bake sale announcement. Dolores tacked the schedule for La Herrida's funeral procession on top of it, leaving only the *a-l-e* sticking out. Inside, the Swiss bookkeeper was not in the back room, only a cat with one blue eye and one gray preening itself in the drawer of a broken cash register. She bought a spool of black thread and picked up the mail. When she came out, the miners on the porch had disappeared, and the people on the street stopped what they were doing to look at her. Word about the procession for La Herrida had already spread.

Dolores walked down the street, the center of a noiseless bubble. She turned into the park and headed toward the fountain. The fountain was not efficient or didactic or scientific—it was beautiful. Owen had some sort of excuse that beauty acted as the engine of evolution and therefore ought to be studied and generated in order to spur the race along. But forget about that. It was lovely in itself, the way the mercury flowed over the rim, its mobile, mirror effect. She reached into her purse for a penny. It landed heads up, a smudged copper profile of the Indian princess. She caught it as it slipped over the side. It was dumb to pin her hopes on a penny, especially one that couldn't sink to the bottom. The wishes she'd made here had taunted her, almost coming true, then stopping short. Fifty feet of railroad. James. Yet she could not stop making them.

* * *

Later that evening, Badinoe sat on the porch of Casa Grande, ankles crossed over the railing, while she fixed the drinks. Thanks to Ana Carolina falling off her bicycle, she had a beautiful set of etched glass tumblers and a Moroccan tray on which to carry them. She rubbed a smudge off a glass, found some napkins in a drawer, and poured almonds hot from the oven into a silver dish left over from one of Owen's despised Virginia forebears. Badinoe shouted something. She licked the salt from her fingers.

"What?" she called.

He didn't answer. She brought the tray out to the porch. The air was thin and blue and cool, the shadows already long. Badinoe handed her an envelope.

"What's this?"

"A boy came with it," he said. It was from Owen.

She pressed the envelope between her fingers then slipped it under the Moroccan tray. "Drink?" she said brightly.

Badinoe took his glass and turned it, apparently absorbed by the light shining through the amber. She settled on her rocking chair and tightened her shawl. They drank in silence. A corner of the envelope peeked out from under the tray. She tucked it all the way under.

"Almond?" she said, offering Badinoe the bowl.

"Thanks." He popped a couple into his mouth, then sank back in his chair.

"You thinking about your book?" she asked. He had been working on a natural history of mercury for months now, and often came over so immersed in his facts and paragraphs that it took a good half an hour before he could utter a sociable sentence.

He smiled. "Nope. You've managed to distract me from it. I'm thinking about your funeral."

"Mine?"

"Yours."

"Why are you against this funeral?"

"I never said I'm against it."

"You are. You think that I'm making a mockery of La Herrida's death and putting Cleofas in a terrible position."

Badinoe chuckled. "So why do you ask?"

"Because you're wrong."

"And what do you hope to achieve?"

"What kind of talk is that? You sound like Owen. All his goals and achievements."

Alma stuck her head out the front door and asked if Badinoe was staying for supper. He shook his head and drew a cigar from his pocket.

"You sure?"

"Sure, I'm sure. I've got to prepare myself," said Badinoe.

"What do you mean?"

"I thought I'd check over my will, see who gets my three-burner Perfection."

"You don't have to go if you don't want to."

"Don't worry, Dodo. I'm coming." He snipped off the end of his cigar and blew a smoke ring.

James had smoked cigars, and cigarettes too. He always had something in his mouth—if not a stick of tobacco then a pencil, a twig, something. They were props, ploys for playing with time or with her or with himself. She understood this perfectly; what she couldn't understand was a man like Owen getting by without any props whatsoever. Last time she saw him, his mouth hadn't moved once. No twitches, no lip tightening, no words. She had bumped into him on her way back from the harness store. He had nodded at her, his gaze direct and infuriatingly calm. They just stood there, looking at each other. Then he tipped his hat and walked on.

She had wanted to be the one who left first, but she hadn't been able to.

Badinoe reached for the almonds and dislodged the tray. The corner of the envelope came back into view.

"You don't mind if I open it?" she asked. "It'll be about the priest."

"Of course not." She stood up and walked toward the front door. "Where are you going?"

"Getting the letter opener," she called back. Stupid, yes, but the first note Owen sent gave her a paper cut that bled for a week. She went through the drawers in the foyer and found it, a miniature sword with a bronze hilt and a sharp steel blade. She returned to the porch wielding it like a swashbuckler. Badinoe gave her a skeptical look; he saw right through her. She sliced across the top of the envelope. The letter was hardly a letter, merely a couple sentences, typewritten.

Dear Mrs. Scraperton:

I have reviewed your message dated this morning, January 11, 1908. Although I will do my best to ensure peace, I cannot guarantee the padre's safety. As you know, the men's passions run high. In the event of disturbance, please see to it that Victoria does not attend the funeral.

Faithfully yours,
Owen

Faithfully yours? It was a formality, conventional and meaningless, but it stung.

"Well?" Badinoe asked.

"Well, nada." She crumpled the letter. "He says nothing, only that Victoria can't come. As if I could drag Victoria there in the first place. She thinks I'm the great desecrator."

"I don't know if she'd go even if Owen were doing the honors," said Badinoe.

"Of course she would."

"I don't know. She was scared of La Herrida."

"Victoria? Scared?"

"She thought that she botched her surgery, don't you remember?"

"I don't know what you're talking about."

"She thought that she put a curse on her."

"A curse?"

"La Herrida got after her one day, shaking her stick and muttering in that way of hers. Victoria took it for a string of incantations. She thinks that's why her tongue is still split—"

"Split? It's a tiny slit, less than half an inch, I wouldn't call it split."

"Fine," said Badinoe. "But she thinks it's because of La Herrida. That was almost the first thing she said after the cast came off."

Dolores was silent for several minutes. "I had no idea."

"You were there. Don't you remember? When I took off the cast?"

Dolores shook her head. What she remembered was glaring at Owen, and him glaring at her. She gulped down the last of her drink and went inside for more. When she came out, Badinoe was gazing at a deep pink sunset. She sat down beside him and took a puff off his cigar. He patted her hand and smiled.

"You know what they call you up in the caves?"

"What?"

"Santa Dolores."

She laughed, too harshly, more of a bark.

The morning of La Herrida's funeral, Dolores appeared at

breakfast in a high-necked black dress that crackled with starch. She told Victoria not to go to school or otherwise leave the property. Victoria asked why. Dolores said that there might be trouble. Victoria buttered her toast, taking care to get all the corners. When she had completed the job, she looked up, her expression puzzled. "Trouble?"

"Having to do with the burial of La Herrida."

"Ah, yes." Victoria had gotten better at acting, but it was still pretty easy to spot. When she acted, she understated things, whereas her genuine self plunged into hyperbole. "But I have a test," she said.

"Your father and I both want you to stay home. For all I know, school's closed anyway."

Victoria chewed. "Very well, I hope you have a good time."

"It's doubtful, sweetheart. Funerals are not generally fun," Dolores said, pulling on her gloves.

Halfway down the hill, she looked back. Victoria had climbed to the roof and was leaning over the balustrade. Dolores waved. Victoria waved back, then turned, so gracefully it looked as if she were dancing. With a pang, Dolores recalled an afternoon years ago, before Washington, she and Victoria spinning and bowing, earnestly counting *one-two-three-four*, trying to choreograph their own dance.

She walked to Pristina under a cold white sky. There was no sun, but an all-pervading glare that cast barely perceptible shadows. When she neared town, three figures blocked the road, hands on holsters. She knew who they were long before their faces came into view; Poc had crutches, de Las Casas had an empty sleeve pinned to his shoulder, and Vicente, the man who towered between them, was identifiable by his size and his signature top hat. No one knew why he was a patrol; the reason given, that he was too large to fit in the tunnels, was a lie. They could have assigned him to a surface mine or the reduction works. Owen probably just wanted someone on his force who could outrun and outwrestle anybody he came up against.

"Good morning," she said. Vicente stared at her with grave brown eyes and didn't say a thing. "And Las Casas," she continued, "good morning to you."

Las Casas squinted at the spot where the road disappeared into the horizon. It became clear that they would neither speak to her nor move out of her way. She walked over to Poc, the oldest, and greeted him by name. His beard blew in the breeze. She stepped around him, expecting a hand to grab her elbow, but none did. She kept walking, her footsteps loud and ungainly, her breath uneven. The town looked abandoned, the shutters drawn and the doors closed, the thin trails of chimney smoke the only sign of people within. She shivered and rubbed her arms. The only thing that broke up the desolation were the patrols. At the end of every street she made out their forms, always in groups of three, standing still.

She knocked on Cleofas's door. A man peeked out—not Cleofas, someone Dolores had never seen before. She introduced herself. The man conferred with someone inside, then opened the door with a bow. Dolores was surprised to find a dozen or so people, laughing and nudging each other and helping themselves from plates piled high with nougat and honey squares. She did not recognize any of them. They were not locals. From the way they stared at her and peeked out of the window, she suspected that most of them had come more out of curiosity than grief. Still, she was pleased at the heft they'd add to the procession.

In the center of the room, the coffin lay on four chairs, a plain, unvarnished box with round indentations of hammer blows circling round each nail. Inside, on a red velvet pillow that Dolores had donated, lay La Herrida. They had put her in a white dress with embroidered flowers and vines around the collar. Her head poked out of it, brown and withered as a dried apple. Dolores was about to kneel and kiss the forehead, when she saw the lone figure sitting quietly behind the coffin. "Hello, Cleofas."

He stood to greet her, but would not meet her eyes. "Good day, Mrs. Scraperton."

"No need to get up. What a gathering you've got here."

"Family," he said simply. He returned to his chair and resumed his vigil. Dolores sat down beside him, and together they looked upon La Herrida until Dolores heard footsteps on the street. She wandered over to the door, admiring Cleofas's ability to sit with such divine stillness. There was no one outside; the street was empty. She closed the door, embarrassed, then checked her watch. It was almost ten o'clock, the time she'd given for the procession to start. She paced by the door. Someone else had to come. Where was Badinoe? The ten o'clock whistle blew. She took another look at her watch. They could not be late. The padre would leave on the slightest excuse. She sighed and nodded to the relatives. They pushed back their chairs and brushed the crumbs off their clothes. Only then did she hear footsteps that weren't her imagination. Badinoe, in a crisp black suit with his whiskers trimmed, stood on the stoop. He looked older than usual. She realized he was leaning on a cane.

"Not to worry," he said, seeing her expression, "only the knee, a little off again."

She hugged him, feeling awful for having doubted him, and ushered him inside, offering coffee and the last honey square. He shook his head and said they better get going. The relatives counted to three and hoisted the coffin on their shoulders. Badinoe hobbled over to Cleofas and murmured his condolences, then followed the relatives out the door. Cleofas remained on his chair, looking at the space where the coffin had been.

"Cleofas, my friend, it's your grandmother's funeral. You have to come."

Cleofas stood up without looking at her. He adjusted one of the tin-framed documents that hung above the mantle. It was the deed on the house, his X and Owen's signature side by side on identical dotted lines. Dolores declined to tell him how worthless it was—Cleofas only owned the mud bricks that made up the house, not the land it was built upon.

"If Mr. Scraperton were to ever try anything," she said, "you have my word, I'll take care of you."

"Because of Mr. Scraperton, my son can read. He has sent me letters in his own hand."

"I'll take full responsibility," said Dolores, but she could see from his eyes that her words were useless.

Outside, the men hitched the coffin to the wagon, squabbling over the knots. The livery had rented them their worst cart, the bed warped and streaked with different colors of paint, the wheels wobbling, on the verge of rolling off. They creaked down Thrift then Clarity and past Central Park. No one came out to watch. No one even opened a window. At Pristina HQ, she heard the clacking of Grierson's typewriter behind a closed venetian blind.

Then, straight in the middle of the road ahead of them, someone appeared. Not Owen, but a young man with a bounce in his step. He wore a bright white shirt and held to his chest a bouquet of red roses. He came closer and closer and didn't evaporate. Shining eyes and a triangular, finely wrought face. The relatives started to shout and wave. The man broke into a smile. Badinoe whistled.

"Ysidro," he said, grinning.

Ysidro? He'd left Pristina years ago, a gangly, dreamy kid who had delivered fish to their house, hardly this visitor—but for the roses. She could imagine Ysidro with roses. He'd had a fanciful streak. He used to bring Victoria buckets of river clay, free of charge. They'd squat out in the back together, making funny little statuettes that they'd set to dry in the sun.

Reaching them he bowed low, sweeping his arm like a true caballero. The roses were made out of fabric, but he really was Ysidro. He had a mole on his earlobe that she didn't know she'd noticed before but when she saw it, she recognized it as his. She told him how glad it made her, him being there. He responded in a rich, unapologetic Spanish, his voice rolling deep and true through the shuttered street. An accolade to her. She had done right by his abuela and he thanked her from the bottom of his heart.

He marched next to the coffin and their procession gained from it. How could you ignore the whiteness of his shirt and the redness of his roses? The relatives squared their shoulders, the horses walked straighter, the cart stopped squeaking so loudly. At the reduction works, they finally saw people. Most of the workers toed the line and ignored them, but some youths by the ore carts peeked from under dusty hat brims, and a thick-shouldered canister roller stopped to sneer. As they reached the end of the yard, a man in blue flannel waved—a discreet wave, like he was catching a fly, but a wave nonetheless. Dolores grinned triumphantly, a feeling that stayed with her past the reduction works, the tailings, the warehouses and wastelots, until they reached the base of Cemetery Hill, where the emptiness of the switchbacks up ahead made her queasy.

They trudged upward. She could see miles and miles of desert. All was desolation, no horse, no mule train, nothing except Badinoe panting louder as the grade grew steeper. The wind got stronger, howling and snapping at their clothes. They gained another switchback, and a handful of dogs appeared. "Looks like the dogs are the only ones that aren't afraid of Owen," Badinoe said. But at the top, people were gathered by the cemetery fence, holding their hats so they wouldn't blow off. Lots of people, their skirts and jackets flapping, and their cheers rising over the wind. *Doña Dolores! Doña Dolores!* Cave people, every single one of them it looked like. Dolores had no idea how many there were. She held out her arms to grandfathers, infants, muckers off shifts. La Herrida's relatives marched through the cemetery gate, the coffin now light on their shoulders. The cave people fell in behind them. They stopped at a mound of dug-up earth. At its head stood the padre, clutching his Bible.

He directed the relatives on how to lower the coffin into the ground, anxiously watching as the ropes squeaked and the box lurched down. The moment it hit the bottom, he began to speak. His voice, always thin, now trembled, and the people leaned forward, straining to hear. Dolores made out a few Latin phrases, but for the most part it was wind that she heard, howling and murmuring and shrieking. The peons shivered in their thin clothes, and Dolores noticed the dirty cracked toes of the man beside her. Repulsive toes. She didn't understand how a moment ago she had felt so triumphant. She was not a scientifico or rabble-rouser or missionary; she did not want to move out into the hills and wash their feet.

A crow landed next to the grave. It strutted back and forth, eyes flashing, and addressed the crowd in raw, harsh caws. The padre crumbled a clump of soil over the coffin, his relief palpable. The sermon was over. No patrols, no battle, no nothing. Dolores leaned against Badinoe, wishing that he'd put his arm around her, but his attention was focused on

Ysidro, handsome Ysidro, who rolled a cigarette, then kissed it before tossing it inside the grave.

"You know, his mother was the first one buried here," Badinoe said.

"Ysidro's mother?"

"Yes. She died in childbirth a couple days after she and Cleofas got to Pristina . . ." His voice trailed off. "Look!" he whispered, chuckling. Someone else had been watching Ysidro, a girl whose braids whipped around the instant she was detected, who slipped into the crowd then out the other side, and ran down the hill with a graceful, galloping gait, her dress, a blue dress that Dolores had stitched herself, giving her away.

Dolores watched from the top of the hill, her heart pounding with joy. "How did she get here? Alma was under strict orders to keep her at home."

"You can hardly blame Alma. The girl's got a mind of her own."

Dolores shook her head, trying to tamp down her elation. There was no reason for celebration. This was not a change of allegiance. Victoria had not marched in the procession, after all. She had probably come to the funeral just to spy. But not for Owen! Owen had forbidden her. She had come for herself, an independent, galloping girl, a blue speck fleeing down the white road, causing the joy to spring right back in Dolores's heart.

1911

Pristina, Texas
October 22, 1911

Dear Father,

I write to you from the town of Pristina, located ten miles from the Rio Grande in Southwestern Texas. There are some four hundred refugees from the Mexican War camped in the hills nearby, and we expect their numbers to grow as Madero's insurrectionists are proving themselves fierce and tireless, spurred on by understandable Wrath.

You would be interested by this town, how I wish you could come by and visit! At its center stands a mercury fountain. I have enclosed a picture postcard of it, but you cannot experience its strange and beguiling power unless you stand right in front of it, watching it move. As I understand it, the founder of the town, Mr. Scraperton, believes that mercury has mystical properties and that the mining of it is good for the Soul. He is a compelling man more driven than any I have known. He welcomed us to the town personally and gave us a tour of the Mercury Workings, then his wife joined us and showed us the kitchen she had set up for the refugees, a right impressive couple, she Mexican and he from Massachusetts. They are proponents of Racial Harmony and Unity and showed us a street where a Negro family and Whites and Mexicans all live side by side in neat little houses, with water troughs out front and shutters painted red and yellow. You can imagine the stony faces of the boys in my troop, all from Arkansas and none with a father like you! But they behaved themselves, nary a grumble about Carpet Baggers and nigger lovers until we got back to our encampment. I remained quiet, remembering your counsel, and not wanting to create an unnecessary rift, especially *so soon upon my arrival. After supper the captain lectured us, saying that we are not defending the town, but the Nation, the Border, that these things must be held sacred, no matter the ideas of some of our citizens. The boys nodded along, as did I. I trust that they will fight manfully when the occasion arises, for they are at bottom good boys, at least that is how they seem to me.*

Affectionately Yours,
Will

Pristina, Texas
July 3, 1912

Dear Father,

Our new captain is of a sour disposition, and I find myself looking back fondly on the cheer of Captain Wiltshire, though perhaps even Capn Wiltshire would have been wilted (!) by this heat, over 110 today, in the shade. Still, the climate has been good for my lungs. For the first time in years, I sleep deeply through the night and no longer wake up gasping.

We spend a lot of time cleaning our rifles and wondering when we will be relocated. There is a rumor, very popular among my fellow soldiers, that we may be sent back to Alpine—they were stationed there before, and much prefer it. I have not been there, but they tell me that it is a larger, more temperate town, with a population mainly White and of a normal character, as opposed to the Whites of Pristina, with their Experiments and Aims—though the longer I stay, the less extraordinary the towns-folk seem. Indeed their enthusiasm and conviction remind me of a certain set of Methodists I trust you remember! It is as you always said: men are men, no matter the color of their opinions and plumage.

You inquired about my fellow soldiers. They are a motley lot, the most remarkable of them being Daniels, who towers over the rest of us, a slack-jawed giant for the most part sweet, but prone to outrageous furies. I suspect he may be addled in the mind, for his furies are of an irrational sort. The buzzing of a fly, for instance, can set him howling and jumping and swinging his fists, daring any of us to take him on. The captain refuses to discipline him, and simply watches, laughing along with the rest of the boys. At times like these I remember you saying that enlisting was a folly. Yet had I stayed home, I would have not been able to appreciate its familiar and dear comfort, but would have daily accused myself of Cowardice. You yourself did not stay home, Father.

Though I have not yet had a chance to prove myself in battle, I am confident that I will soon. Last week, Jarrow and I climbed to the top of the Chisos Mountain and watched the smoke rise from a burning village. It was less than fifty miles away!

Love from your son,
Will

Pristina, Texas
October 10, 1914

Dear Father,

    Today I received notice that my petition has been dismissed. I suppose if they allowed me to leave, they'd have to do the same for every one in the troop, for though our reasons are different, no one wants to be here. There nothing for us to do. The war is elsewhere. Here is only listlessness and bickering. The boys pass around flasks at midday, and half of them no longer shave their faces. Every now and then one of them is roused to create a drama just to pass the time. Last week, Daniels and his followers conducted rifle practice on a herd of goats. The animals were in a canyon and the rock walls echoed with the sound of bullets. Those of us not there imagined a true battle had commenced—how we scrambled over each other trying to get there first, only to find three soldiers shouting at a bunch of dead animals, and the goatherd hiding behind a rock. Just a child, maybe ten years old, with his hat all shot up. The Good Lord must have been with him, though, for he wasn't hurt, not even grazed. The next day, the father came, asked for money for his goats and a new hat for his son. The captain laughed him out. And so it goes.

    My consolation is the landscape. I take long hikes through the mountains and investigate the desert, more prickly with life than I had imagined. I enclose sketches of the Montezuma Quail, who I have had the fortune to find nesting! I would greatly appreciate your sending me Green's Guide to Ornithology & Oology and also Becket's Geology, both of which you will find in the trunk under my bed. How is cousin Anne? Give her my best, and tell her that coyotes really do laugh.

Until Christmas,
Will

1914

♣

Badinoe approached the pagoda, curious. He'd seen its roof, the bright red of it poking up from the beige hill, and he had experienced the effects of its bulb, refracting slivers of light that could blind you if you happened to ride by when the sun hit just so. But he had never seen it up close before. Now he fingered the rail, uninvited, hesitant. He climbed the steps, three steps, painted with Oriental flowers, the brushstrokes so delicate and gauzy they looked like ghosts. The steps, the grillwork, the bulb, the tiles, the sliding doors, each piece had been wrapped in muslin and shipped from China, along with an imperial carpenter to oversee its construction. It had been a gift from the emperor to a Californian who owned what used to be the largest mercury mine in America. Owen got it, along with tons of cut-rate equipment, when the California mine went bust. Badinoe walked around its perimeter, floorboards faintly groaning, taking in the cobwebs in the rafters and an abandoned bird's nest. Apparently the Scrapertons didn't use it much. They should have put it down in the park where the kids could play on it.

He hadn't been at Casa Grande for several years.

He remembered perfectly the last time he came. He had reached for the knocker, expecting Dolores, her easy invitation to take a seat on the veranda, the old tarnished tray of mescal, the two of them sitting side by side, watching Victoria run around the front yard, entertaining them with proudly recited facts, cartwheels, snippets of dance, before wandering off, completely forgetting them, investigating some intrigue of her own. He had reached for the knocker, but before he could even touch it, the door had opened. Instead of Dolores, Owen had stood there, scratching the dog on the cuff. The impact hadn't been only from Owen at Casa Grande, although to see him there would have been enough, but also the easy way he stood, the clothes he wore, not the suit, but a checked shirt haphazardly tucked in, a fold draped over a cracked leather belt. "Hello," he'd said casually, but with an undercurrent of force, as if he had every right to his casualness, as if he had been living happily and uneventfully in Casa Grande all along and anyone who thought he had been sleeping on the lumpy sofa in his office was deluded.

It had taken all of Badinoe's courage to say, or rather croak, "Owen, what a surprise." Owen studied him for a while. Then he smiled, as if to acknowledge that this was indeed an event. Badinoe had taken it for a minor victory.

Then she appeared. In the moment before she noticed Badinoe, he saw in her eyes what he had never seen there before, a light that equaled Owen's in its happiness. "Oh," she put her hand to her mouth. "Gene, Hello. I didn't know that you were here." The effect was of a gracious apology, as if she had inadvertently stepped on his foot, and was so sorry, but it was done and over, couldn't be helped. "Can I get you a drink?" What she had said every night, but now with Owen right there, lounging against the porch rail. Oh! The supreme embarrassment of that moment. Badinoe had emptied his glass out in a second, afraid to look at her, looking instead at the etchings on the Moroccan tray. Only afterward did he realize that she had meant to propose a toast, for she was still holding her cup. "To you, my friend," she'd said, taking a sip. Owen gazed at her and past her, serene and thoughtful, probably composing his New Direction speech at that very moment. Maddening how it still tugged at Badinoe. He'd had no claim on Dolores. They had not been lovers. Merely drinking companions, conversationalists.

He trotted down the pagoda steps and banged the knocker against the front door. Footsteps sounded, clacking and erratic, and the door opened: not Dolores, but the governess, a blocky Australian with frizzy hair and a huge gap between her teeth. He couldn't remember her name—Hedda? Higga? Or perhaps not the governess? She smelled of garlic and spices. They were sisters, the cook and the governess, one Hedda/Higga, one Frida/Fredda. He didn't deal with them; they were healthy as could be, sashaying through town, gloating at the miners.

"Hello, Doctor. Victoria will be happy to see you."

"Yes, Dolores asked me to come. Is she here?"

"Mrs. Scraperton? She's driving. I don't know when she'll be back. Victoria's in her room. Shall I take you there?"

"No, thank you, I know the way."

He trudged up the stairs. What did he expect? Dolores had been under the impression that the girl was faking. There was no reason for Dolores to hover over her, or him, if she thought all was well. Victoria hid under a white sheet, a groaning lump on a rumpled bed. He poked her. She giggled. She was fourteen years old, but her laugh was as infective and pure as that of a little girl. He smiled in spite of himself and peeled the sheet off, revealing her fresh skin, her sparkling eyes.

"You're not the least bit sick, are you? You're not even faking."

"Hi, Dr. Badinoe!"

"Hello."

"Actually, I'm dreadful," Victoria said, squirming up

higher onto the pillow. "Look." She raised her upper body a few inches off the mattress, threw her neck back like Marat stabbed in the bathtub, and produced a vigorous death rattle. He settled himself on the chair beside her bed and felt her pulse. She had Owen's coloring, including the thick swath of eyebrow that went straight across the nose, but she had Dolores's spark. There was no reason to worry about suitors; if she didn't turn out beautiful, she could charm people into believing the contrary. "Do you want me to stick out my tongue?" she asked and, before he could answer, extended it fully. She pointed to the tips. One prong wiggled while the other stayed still.

"Did you practice that?"

She nodded. "It's worn me out. That's why I'm so sick."

"Is it that you don't want to go to school?"

"No, it's that I thought it would be nice if you came over."

He looked at her skeptically.

"I miss you."

"Ah, dear girl. Why don't you come visit me at the office? I'd love to have you. I have all kinds of wonderful new books to show you."

"Anything about Lambulus?"

"Lambulus?"

"The Roman explorer! You were the one who told me about him. Remember? He got kidnapped by Ethiopians and was held captive for years, then he finally stole a boat and escaped."

"No recollection."

She looked appalled. "His years in prison destroyed his sense of direction? Instead of sailing to Rome, he ended up on a far southern island? A fate that might have driven others to despair—yet an explorer never despairs, as long as he is free! He explored everywhere, taking notes and writing it all down for posterity. The most curious discovery he made was a village where everyone had forked tongues. They could hold two conversations at once! But what I don't understand is how. Did they say one thing frontward and another thing backward? Did they speak in code?"

"Good question. I don't know. We'll have to write a letter to a Lambulus scholar, see what they have to say."

"Do you think I could have a conversation with both a snake and a person?"

"With you, anything is possible."

"What are you going to tell Mother?"

"You promise you'll go to school tomorrow?"

"Yes."

"I'll tell her you had a case of temporary convulsions, but now you are fine."

She nodded seriously. "Good." She gestured for him to come closer, then rolled down her sheets and blankets. At the foot of her bed, a milk snake, red, white, and black, lay coiled up and sleeping. "I found him last night," she said. "Isn't he pretty?"

He whistled inward. "I'll say."

"How could I leave him all alone?" She covered the snake gently with the blankets. "It's a secret."

He drove the buckboard into town, amused, wondering if he should tell Dolores that Victoria was hiding a snake in her bed. But why? Milk snakes weren't dangerous, and if Dolores wanted to know, she should have been there.

Town was a mess, a swarm of angry drivers and tangled harnesses and black automobile smoke. Pristina got bigger by the minute. The Rivera Chimney, an immense lode that Jorge Rivera had discovered the Christmas of 1911, combined with

Owen's grudging acceptance of alcohol, had drawn recruits from all over the country. Owen crowed and crowed. "Nature smiled upon them!" "The New Direction is the right direction!" Dolores, his Dolores who had led him from his ornery ways, was "Nature's Oracle." It was almost the only time he talked about Nature anymore. He'd gotten so swept up in the business of running a major enterprise that he'd relegated the addresses on Scientific Naturalism to the ladies from the Edification Committee. His speeches now consisted of slogans and raised fists. Pristina was big, big, and getting bigger! They would be the biggest mine in the world! They would overtake Almaden! Badinoe snorted. Pristina might have beaten a California upstart, but it would never come close to Almaden. The Romans, the Moors, the Fuggers and Rothchilds had all dipped into Almaden and barely left a mark. Next to that, Pristina was a flea on the tail of an elephant.

He turned down the side street that led to the steam room. A few buildings down, Daniels, the giant of Troop A, blocked the street. His uniform was wrinkled. His jaw flexed and unflexed in a dangerous manner. He leaned over Rosa Izquierda, who faced him bravely, or foolishly, her arms crossed over her chest, her color high.

"Hey, Rosa, need a lift?" Badinoe shouted.

"Thanks, Doc," she said, her lace-up boots stepping backward, her eyes still burning bright and angry. Daniels grabbed her arm. "Hey! Get off of me!" The soldier lifted her a couple inches from the ground, laughing at how light she was.

"Daniels!" shouted Badinoe crossly.

The soldier looked at him blankly. "Yeah?"

"I'm going to tell your captain about this."

"Ow!" Rosa yelled, trying to twist out of his grip.

"What's wrong, chiquita? Qué pasay?"

"Daniels?" a quiet Southern drawl. "Hey. The captain's looking for you." Another soldier, a skinny freckled boy named Anderson, walked toward them. "Come with me, Ale House. She's okay. You can let her go." He spoke softly, soothingly. "Here, want a licorice? They're the kind you like. My dad sent me them."

Daniels put Rosa down, eager for the licorice. The girl hurried over to Badinoe who helped her into his buckboard. Her body shook with rage. They watched Anderson lead Daniels away, both of them sucking on licorice, their bullet belts shining in the late-afternoon light.

"I hate them," she whispered, tears streaming down her face.

"Did he hurt you?"

"Not too bad, a bruise or two."

"Do you want me to examine you?"

Rosa slipped out of the buckboard. "Not now, I'm late. I'll be fine. Thank you, though!" She hurried away, her blue dress soon disappearing into the bustle of the avenue.

Badinoe had never thought the day would arrive when he would extol the virtues of the patrols, but at least they were consistent. If you followed the rules, they wouldn't bother with you. The soldiers, on the other hand, had nothing to do but bother you. They were bored stiff, pining for the European War, valor, glory, fair-skinned girls, or even Mexico, still in turmoil and flames. Instead they'd been stationed in a town where no one wanted them, guarding against a nonexistent threat.

In the steam room he found poor Paulo Martinez, bloody gums and silvery sweat running down his chest. What affected Badinoe most were his downcast eyes. "You won't tell anyone, Doc?" His fingers wavering, pleading. In spite of all of Badinoe's efforts, mercury poisoning still shamed the men horribly. He prescribed goat's milk to Paulo, and wrote him a note to give to his shift manager, insisting that he be reassigned to a surface working.

It was dark by the time he came out. He headed over to HQ to file the report but stopped when he saw Grierson waving and jumping.

"Doc! You've got to get over to the carpenter's! The German one, Otto! He's hung himself!" Grierson's eyes shone with excitement. "He got a letter from the Kaiser's army—turns out he was a sergeant. Millie didn't even know! They wanted him back. They must be desperate, damn kikes."

Badinoe entered a buzz of neighbors and sharp electric light. Millie fluttered about, pink-faced, prettier than usual, more amazed, for now, at her husband's unexpected past than the fact that he had killed himself. His corpse lay upon a too-short table, his knees knobbing over the edge. No shoes. He had taken them off, perhaps so as not to soil the chair where the envelope still lay, embossed with the Kaiser's seal. His socks were grayish and frayed, the left toe-seam laddered with lime-green thread. They'd left the noose around his neck, but loosened it, so that he looked like an office clerk who, returning from work, had slipped his tie into a more comfortable position.

Badinoe touched the knot of the noose, tenderly. Charles had also used this method. He hadn't seen his corpse, only imagined it. Charles's landlady had discovered him; she was a prim lady who had sniffed ostentatiously when Badinoe came visiting, but who in the end had had the generosity to let him know what happened.

Badinoe drew up another chair and took a seat, balancing his case upon his knees to use as a writing surface. The form stared him in the face, comforting in its businesslike sensibility. Straight solid lines asking only to be filled in. He uncapped his pen. Name. He conferred with Millie. *Otto Kasler Oberschall.* Date. *November 14, 1914.* Cause. He paused. *Blockage of the windpipe.* Neighbors ebbed and flowed, the women clutching different-colored jars of preserves, the men holding their hats. They patted each other, they murmured and puzzled, their expressions stunned and intrigued.

Millie now held the summons from the Kaiser in both hands and was moving around the room showing it off. "A sergeant in the army, can you believe it?" They were taking the summons for the reason, as if the Kaiser's agents would travel across ocean and continent for the sake of one errant soldier. Perhaps it had been fear. If the Kaiser could find him here, who else could? Who knew, quién sabe?

Outside, late arrivals filled the darkening street. Dogs came too, wagging their tails and sniffing, and Owen, driving up in the Stanley Steamer. He drove almost as much as Dolores, but he hadn't mastered her smoothness. The car jerked to a halt, and a crowd immediately surrounded it. Owen brushed the people away and entered the house, eyes ablaze. This was Pristina's first suicide. Badinoe wondered how he would approach it at the funeral.

He found himself blushing, remembering the funeral for La Herrida. He had been hobbling along, self-righteously thinking that he was the only one honoring the old woman in the midst of the whole Catholic-political circus—that is, until Ysidro appeared, his white shirt unbuttoned at the top, his clavicle golden. All pious thoughts had dissolved.

Charles's clavicle had been beautiful also.

Badinoe stayed up, working on his book. No point even trying to sleep, the image of the noose too fresh in his head. How he missed Dolores. His other friends were not so good for talking. With them he felt as if he were mainly talking to himself, but she had a way of understanding what was beneath the words. Though what good could even she have done on a night like this? He remained at his desk until the five o'clock whistle blew. Then, greatly in need of circulation, he poured some old coffee in a canteen and left his house. Outside, the miners walked to work, their lanterns bobbing in one hand, their lunch pails swinging in the other. Badinoe nodded hello and was soon caught up in a web of greetings and gruff morning jokes. He'd miss these men, the dauntless, thoughtless bravery of them, if ever he finished his book and actually left.

Out at Future Boulevard the new houses squatted in their neat little lines. He wasn't as comfortable with the folks out here, sometimes felt himself getting as miffed as a committee lady by the things they would say. Past Future Boulevard, the desert took over. He entered into it gladly, the stiffness gone from his legs, his footsteps sounding firm, detached, wise, as if they belonged to somebody else. He came to a thicket of chaparral where he had once found La Herrida gathering leaves in a big burlap bag. She never had given him one bit of information on what she did with all those roots and barks and leaves. All those years of courting her, and everything that he'd learned from her, he'd learned from spying, snooping, sniffing.

She had only said one thing directly to him. He had been standing next to her, offering her a plug of tobacco, when the schoolteacher walked by, bobbing up and down under his black umbrella. Not an odd sight, MacIntosh never went anywhere without it, allergic to the sun, he said. But La Herrida had raised her eyebrows as if she'd never seen such a thing. She elbowed Badinoe and said in well-pronounced English, "Like a crane with an umbrella." The phrase was so unexpected that Badinoe thought he had misheard until he considered MacIntosh: those skinny long legs with his knees bent forward as if leading the way. He really did look like a crane. How could this woman, who had probably never spoken English in her life, come up with that? And how had she known what a crane looked like? Cranes were marsh birds, waders, and she had lived her entire life, as far as he knew, in the desert. He had looked at her in astonishment. She had cackled amicably then returned to silence.

He walked eastward on a narrow path as the sky took on a rosy hue. The sun would appear in a moment. He stopped by a century plant and stood there, shivering slightly. He had become attached to the desert at dawn, the fierce sweet smell of it, the insects and honey-scented thistles and scamperings of unknown things. The first rays of light lit the flatlands, and the breath got caught in Badinoe's chest, so beautiful it was, a consoling beauty that made him close his eyes and wrap his arms around himself.

He opened his eyes, sensing that he was not alone. A man in a uniform approached, waving in greeting. It was Anderson, the soft-spoken young soldier with the licorice, a pair of binoculars swinging from his neck.

"Good morning, Doctor."

"Morning," Badinoe said tersely.

"Taking a stroll?"

"Yep."

Anderson looked at him directly. "You don't like us much, do you?" The question was not belligerent. His eyes were light blue, candid. Poor kid. What was he doing here? "How is Rosa?" the boy asked.

"She'll be all right."

Anderson nodded. "That's good. Daniels can be . . . tough." He adjusted himself so that he was now side by side with Badinoe, both of them facing the mountains. "Pretty, isn't it?" said Anderson.

Together they attended to the sunrise, silently watching as the mountains turned from gray to purple. Badinoe gestured toward the boy's binoculars. "You on patrol? On the lookout for insurrectionists?"

"Sure. Or a Montezuma quail, that would be nice."

Badinoe cracked a smile. "You're a birdwatcher?"

Anderson clasped his hands behind his back. "I dabble in it. My field is oology, the study of bird eggs, but the birds do not lay until spring." His field? The kid couldn't be older than twenty. "I just completed my first monograph."

"Congratulations," said Badinoe. He couldn't help but mention his own project.

"A natural history of mercury? That sounds brilliant. I'd love to look it."

A more intense pink gathered behind the peaks, and then the sun finally made its appearance. The light hit the boy's face, showing off freckles and the tough sheen of his skin. Badinoe asked him if he'd ever heard of a crane in the desert. Anderson said yes, he had. Last Christmas, down by the Rio Grande, there had been some sandhill cranes, stopped there on their way south.

"You interested in cranes?" Anderson asked.

"In a roundabout way," Badinoe said.

Anderson hesitated, then offered, when he got leave in a few weeks, to take Badinoe down to the river and see if they could spot one together.

"A sandhill crane?" Badinoe said.

"A sandhill crane," confirmed Anderson, reaching for his tobacco pouch.

But why not? Perhaps he'd find a feather, bring it back, poke it into the dirt above La Herrida's grave. And there he was, abundantly glad. Anderson, smiling young Anderson, offered him a cigarette, which he accepted, and the two of them smoked as the sky grew wider and higher with light.

1916

♠

Behind the Marfa depot lay the world's most short and useless railroad, a fifty-foot track that led from one prickly pear to another. Victoria balanced upon it, transforming it into a gymnastic beam upon which she executed a perfect cartwheel.

"Victoria! We're not at home!" Owen cried as her traveling dress fell over her head. A pair of legs shot up, strong and long and alarmingly pretty.

"Oh, come on, Father. There's no one around."

She readjusted her skirts, all the while maintaining her balance. He sighed, not at her, at the track. He had left it there as a warning, a reminder of the danger that railroads could bring, but how could anyone have received this message? All anyone would notice were wasted resources left to crack in the sun.

"What do you think, Vic?" Owen called from the shade of the Marfa depot's ramada. "Should we resuscitate that old monster?"

"The train?"

Owen nodded. Most of what he'd feared the train would bring had come anyway, and to no great calamity. Besides, he no longer cringed at the idea of being directly connected to the big cities. On his last trip to Washington, he had positively enjoyed himself, and this even though the Secretary of War never did grant him that interview. He'd visited the Smithsonian and sniffed at the cherry blossoms and helped Clara around the house. It had been impossible for him to summon his earlier rage. If Victoria's injury had been more severe, then perhaps forgiveness would have come less easily, but she had recovered magnificently. Anyhow, he'd been wrong to blame the Bradley boys' perversions on Washington's air; their own clear Chihuahuan air had produced bandits capable of far worse.

Victoria left the track and returned to him, her tongue poking thoughtfully at the inside of her cheek. "Pristina doesn't need a train," she said at length. "Too much hoo-ha. Auto trucks are the way to go. They're cheaper and they go anywhere you want. Did you see that picture of Pershing's truck train?"

Pershing and his truck train had gone into Mexico, looking to even the score after Pancho Villa had done what they'd always said he would: burned an American town to the ground, shot down its citizens and the soldiers guarding them. There were *Get Villa!* posters plastered all over the train station.

The train chugged westward toward the state border. They had a nice compartment to themselves, green upholstery and newly cleaned windows. Owen studied Victoria's profile as she watched the landscape, the dark, thick hairs of her eyebrow, her pert nose curving downward, her slightly pursed lips. She looked uncharacteristically delicate, like a cameo brought to life. It was strange, how faces could change, momentarily transforming into something quite unknown. When he had lived at the office, his image of Dolores's face had gotten mixed up with the face of his father—that is, the face of his father that he'd thought he remembered from the portrait that hung in Clara and Benjamin's front hallway. He'd convinced himself that the red in his father's sideburns was the same shade as Dolores's hair, that the lines of their noses followed the same course, that they shared the same indentation around the temple, that these physiognomic traits were signs of deceit and pride, signs that he should have been able to read, but had been blind to. When he returned to Washington, that recent springtime trip, and again glimpsed the portrait, he saw that he had been wrong. His father looked laughably ordinary, a middle-aged man sitting on a green armchair, trying to keep his eyes open. Younger than Owen. Not the least like Dolores.

He'd asked Clara if he could have the painting, surprising even himself in his desire to take hold of it. A little bit of him. A rapprochement. He would have asked Benjamin directly if he'd known where his father had gone, but Benjamin had died, and Clara, if she ever knew, knew no longer. Her mind drifted about the house, forming arbitrary sentences about windowsills and mousetraps. But she'd clung to the portrait. *No! No! You cannot have it!* Shaking her head fiercely, the remnants of her chins flapping. No matter. He'd get it. He'd take it after her funeral.

Victoria, still looking out the window, at the endless expanses of gamma grass, sighed.

"A penny for your thoughts," Owen said.

"Nothing. It's just an uncomfortable seat." She wiggled around, wrinkling her nose. "Don't you agree?"

Maybe she was thinking about Ysidro. Dolores had been right. The way she looked at him, the way her voice changed when she spoke of him. When Owen first recognized this, he'd considered canceling Ysidro's commission. But the boy hadn't done anything wrong. Indeed, he'd done everything right. He was shining proof that the Principles worked: a boy with nothing but the blood of peons running through his veins, and what did they produce but a brilliant carpenter and burgeoning architect, well spoken, confident, skillful, industrious, not a lazy bone in that body. She was right to admire him.

"Are you sad to be away?"

"No." She pressed her forehead to the window pane. "It's just an uncomfortable seat. I'm just looking out the window. There's so much grass. Isn't there anything other than grass?"

She seemed on the verge of tears. He pressed himself back into his seat, laced his fingers together, and waited for some clue as to how to proceed. She remained focused on the window, her profile to him, not the profile that he had been admiring earlier, but one that was tense and closed, the lips pressed too tightly together. She was seldom like this with him, but he'd seen similar behavior right before she and Dolores started to fight. He leaned forward again, unable to help himself, put his hand on her knee.

"Are you all right, honey?"

Without looking at him, she nodded. He pressed down on her knee. She laid her hand over his for a moment. He sat back in his seat, feeling better.

She knew about the soldiers. She was the only one in Pristina, not even Dolores knew. She'd been organizing the file cabinets in his den and found a draft of a petition he thought he'd destroyed, a secret attempt to get the governor to supplement Troop A with state militia. She had arrived at his office out of breath, waving the paper.

At first he hadn't see it. He'd seen her eyebrows, plucked for the very first time: two artificial arcs, the tender skin between pink and upraised. It felt as if she'd yanked the hairs out of his own head. He assumed she'd come down to flaunt her new look, and he was trying to think of something to say that wouldn't sound like a cry of agony when she held the petition straight up to his face. The shock of it still made him shudder. From the wording, any intelligent reader could tell that Troop A had been his idea, that attributing it to the governor had been a ploy. He had sat her down. He had put his hands on her quaking shoulders. "Honey," he'd said. "What was I to do? The safety of Pristina must be held above all else."

He hated obfuscation, damned it in others, recognized his own hypocrisy, but didn't see what other course he had. They needed protection. No one would agree to it. The original Pristinians wanted nothing to do with the government and the Mexicans distrusted any defense, imagining it led to support for the federales. With her quaking before him, he had launched into a disquisition on the lesser of two evils, warming up as he went. It had felt good to finally unburden himself. But she had stopped him midstream.

"I understand."

"You don't," he had said. "You can't." How could she, at that age? The soldiers had killed Rivera. They had spat upon children for no reason other than nationality. He would not have forgiven it. He would have flown into a fury. He would have seen it as apostasy.

"I do," she'd said calmly, looking him in the eye. She'd torn up the petition and let the pieces fall to the floor. "It's ugly, but necessary. That's what you're saying."

"Are you thinking of Rivera?" he asked after fifteen minutes had passed. She turned to him, more patiently, more kindly than she had before.

"I would say that you are the one thinking about Rivera."

Owen smiled. "He was a good man."

"The soldiers didn't think so."

"I don't think that they thought about it one way or another. They had been drinking. He had been drinking."

"You should have never allowed alcohol."

"Alcohol is a balm for some, not an obscurant. Or perhaps it is an obscurant for all, but some people need that obscurant. Perhaps the sharpness of pure light pains them. I don't know. Ask your mother." He smiled. Victoria didn't.

"You could reinstate the ban. She doesn't need to drink."

"All the new men drink."

"So? Let them go. They don't care about the Principles."

"We need them, Victoria, as you well know. Even with them the miners are overworked, the shifts longer than we intended."

"Then cut down on operations. The mercury will still be there. It doesn't matter how fast you take it out."

"And what of our obligations?" He had spoken too sharply. She pulled away. "Honey, you don't seem to understand. America is at war. We are at war. The army needs our mercury. The Red Cross needs our mercury. They look to us."

She stared out the window, clearly disgusted.

She was right about Pristina's size. If they weren't so desperate for men, they would have been able to maintain a finer population. They could have even formed their own militia. The soldiers would not have come. Rivera would still be alive. Victoria would still be Owen's greatest admirer.

The next day was better.

Victoria sat across from him, lecturing him on the whys and wherefores of the snake dance, the Hopis' first mesa, the importance of Indian art in general and how it ought to be incorporated into a True American Art. He did not understand her passion. What did any of this have to do with mercury?

"Well now, honey, if you like the Indian art so much, why didn't you decorate the façade of the new HQ with a kachina?

Isn't that Mercury you ordered exactly what you are arguing against? What's inherently American about a classical Roman figurine?"

Her eyebrows dipped into a disconcerted V. He chuckled, pleased to have tripped her up for once.

"Well," she said after several moments, "that's an idea. The problem is that I don't think the Hopis have a god for mercury. Only corn and rain, that sort of thing. The Romans are the only ones I know who have a god specifically aligned with mercury. But you would like the Hopi gods, Father."

"Right-o."

"I'm serious. The Hopi gods live underground. That's why they use snakes to talk to them. The snakes are the conduits. They burrow down to the gods' realm."

"Well, if you have to have gods, I suppose underground is a good enough place to keep them."

"Oh, come on, don't you prefer it to the sky? I would think that you would."

Her eyes were shining prettily. "Sure," he said, happy to make her happy.

At Gallup, they hired a motorcar and set off on the two-day trip across the Sonoran Desert. The sky was blue and the earth red, much redder than the Chihuahuan earth, making the greens of the sagebrush and cacti all the more vibrant. They stopped the car for lunch and the scent of the sagebrush was so strong, so lovely, that Owen forgot himself and capered around like a kid.

"It's good to get away," he said as they got back into the car. "This has been said about vacations, hasn't it? An antidote for brain fatigue. Happy birthday, dear." This was her birthday present, delayed. He had been in Washington the day that she turned sixteen.

That night, they set up a tent a few miles past Ganado, and ate a cold meal of chorizo and buttered bread. The coyotes sang and the stars came out. Owen and Victoria lay on the ground, looking up at the sparkling sky. He couldn't sleep, so overcome by the beauty of the night. This was what he had hoped that his men could experience, this energy that the beauty gave rise to, that he could feel roiling in his chest. That's what he had wanted. That's what was to have been the engine of Pristina. Not commerce. Not this . . . this hunger he could feel Victoria accusing him of. She snored softly beside him. He kissed her cheek. He did not feel that he had completely failed. She did not stir. He watched the stars and listened to her breathe until stillness slowly crept over him.

On the day of the dance, they arrived at the foot of the Hopis' First Mesa. They parked the car and climbed up a steep, precipitous trail, stepping gingerly and admiring the gorgeous vistas. Six hundred feet below, the red earth spread out beneath them, dotted with juniper. Above, the sky arched a perfect blue.

"Those Hopis are going to have to dance hard," Owen said, catching his breath. "There's not a cloud in sight."

"They've thought of that," said Victoria. "They've got four days to make it rain."

"Ah, and in monsoon season. They're not stupid."

"Not at all."

They reached the mesa top and arrived at Walpi, a vertical jumble of crumbling red adobes. "The oldest living settlement in the United States," Victoria announced—how she loved to teach him! The plaza teemed with people. Hopis with their bangs and creased faces and colorful shawls. Taller, blue-jeaned Navajos. White ranchers and their wives. Teenage campers in matching hats and neckerchiefs. A well-known

philanthropist from New York City. Owen hadn't realized
how crowded it would be.

"I'm going to get something to eat," Victoria said, stepping away from him. "Do you want something?"

"No, thanks."

"I'll be back."

A photographer in a striped suit spread the legs of his
tripod, ducked under the black cloth, and aimed at a bunch
of Hopi kids who hung off the pueblo's ever-present ladders.
They noticed the photographer, leapt off their perches, and
scrambled over the rooftops laughing and shrieking. An
older Hopi man walked over, shaking his head. No pictures
allowed.

"You can take a picture for me," said Owen, approaching the photographer. He wanted something to commemorate
his and Victoria's trip. The photographer agreed and Owen
stepped up on a ladder to look for her. She was easy to spot.
She had the effect of diminishing the people around her, dim-
ming them somehow. She was hatless, her hair as dark as an
Indian's, glossy in the sun, her face, in this light, golden. She
waved. He gestured for her to come over.

"I've got some fry bread," Victoria said when she got
closer, brandishing a wad of oil-stained newspaper. She
opened the package, letting loose a heavy steam of honey and
grease. "Want some?"

"No, thanks."

She raised a skeptical eyebrow. He frowned at her forehead which on closer inspection was not a golden sheen, but
a swath of oily bumps the fry bread would only worsen.

"It's good," she said, her lips smeared with honey. "Are
you sure you don't want a taste?"

He shook his head. "Too sweet, it rots the teeth."

She laughed and brushed the crumbs off her mouth. "The

teeth get rotted by all sorts of things." She pushed the bread back toward him. She was teasing him, insinuating something that he did not choose to explore, but he liked the way her eyes sparkled.

"Shall we have a photograph taken?"

"Sure."

He stood proudly by her side as the photographer turned his knobs and disappeared under his blanket. At this point Owen felt almost at ease with photography, so much practice he'd had. A few years ago a reporter for *Western Magazine* discovered Pristina. The man had started his career covering the Colorado mining wars and Steunenberg's assassination, and he couldn't believe a mining town like theirs existed: no detectives, no dynamiters, no trace of the WMF? His articles had overflowed with praise, bringing forth other reporters, other photographers, a cavalcade of fast-talking men with skinny ties and short-brimmed hats. Owen squeezed Victoria's shoulders, reliving their enthusiasm. Photographs! Handshakes! Copies of the Principles! Whoever said that he had given up couldn't see what was right in front of them. The Principles were being distributed, and not by Pristina, by outsiders, by impressed outsiders.

Victoria tugged at his sleeve. "Father! You have to look at this pottery! This is what I've been telling you about." She led him to a heap of ceramic objects presided over by an Indian woman in a threadbare shawl. Her old wrinkled face took him in with a wary nod.

"Good afternoon," he said, picking up a bowl that had been dyed black and white, a mazelike design running along the sides. He made a show out of examining it, tracing his fingers along a line and nodding judiciously.

The old woman made an obscure clucking sound. He

wondered if she had any views on the seeds of American art. She squinted first at the pot, then at Owen, and held up seven fingers.

"Looks like a fine specimen, eh, Victoria? Shall we get this for your mother?"

Victoria burst out laughing. "For Mother?" she almost shrieked. "Oh yes, please! Let's!"

"That's no way to talk about your mother."

"What? What did I say?"

"Your tone, young lady. Don't pretend that you don't know what I'm talking about. Next vacation we'll have to go somewhere that she would like too."

"What about Buenos Aires?"

"What about Boston?" he said. "I got an invitation to speak at an education conference. We could all go out, take a look at Radcliffe while we're at it."

He wanted to show her the street where he'd lived, see if the elm still stood at the corner.

She watched the old Hopi woman palm the dust off the pot. "Mother might like it if she'd only look," she said quietly.

"Would you like to give it to her?"

Victoria studied the pot for a moment, then looked at him thoughtfully. "Yes."

"Well then, we'll take it." His words were superfluous. The Indian woman had already understood and was again brandishing seven of her gnarled fingers. "Yes, yes, I know." He ran his thumb down the slit of his wallet and fingered each bill. He enjoyed paying in cash; in Pristina he never got a chance to—personal expenses were pencil marks in a slew of ledgers, and company expenses were done by check. An entirely different experience, this simplicity of bills that anybody might take, or anybody might give; it dropped you into a whirl of freedom, a world of anonymity. The old woman recounted the money then wrapped the pot in newspaper. He watched the headlines fold over, turn into abstract letters, then fractions of letters, losing their gist, becoming something new.

The dance for which they had made this trip, the infamous Hopi Snake Dance, occurred in the sweltering heat of the late afternoon. Owen and Victoria joined the crowd gathered on the rooftops of the pueblo, the better to see the plaza which spread out beneath them, empty but for the snake hut. A drum started. You could not see the drummer, just feel the slow and heavy poundings, the rhythm of which bothered Owen. He turned to ask Victoria if the drum bothered her too, but then more drums and rattles came, piling on top of each other in a chaotic mess, and the men appeared. Owen had read about the ritual. He knew what to expect: the men dusted with the colors of their clans, the bone rattles tied to the ends of their skirts. Yet the sight of them, their bodies already shimmering in the heat, their almost complete lack of clothing, made him want to clap his hands over Victoria's eyes. They reminded him—especially the clansmen powdered with red—of his miners. Women weren't allowed down in the mines. The men swore it was bad luck, but the real reason was modesty. They did not want to be seen in their loincloths.

She stood beside him, calm and dignified, a cocked eyebrow the only sign of discomfort. Perhaps her sangfroid was an attempt to show him that she would be fine in the mines. She was always clambering about it. How could he expect her to take over? How could she direct a mining operation if she were not allowed on the site where most of the work took place? He saw her point. Maybe when she was older it would not be such a problem, when she was of an age where she could be a mother to most of the men. But he could not let her down now. He'd have an insurrection on his hands.

The drumming continued to disturb him, something about the rhythm. Maybe it clashed with the tempo of his own heartbeat. He took a sip of water, then offered her the canteen. She accepted it without taking her eyes off the men. They did not look exactly like his miners. They had black-and-white stripes on their faces, they were wearing skirts. They wound their way over to the snake hut. According to Teddy Roosevelt, who had written an interesting article about it, the Hopis did not remove the venom from the snakes. They took a foul-smelling antivenom before and after the ceremony, in case they did get bitten, but this was rather like an insurance policy. They believed that they would be protected by their courage and purity, that the snakes would only attack them if they sensed fear. A heavyset man with a large red belly kneeled to the ground in front of the hut, then rose with a snake dangling from his mouth. The snake was almost as long as the man, and yellow. It undulated, slippery and fluid compared to the solid bulk of the man. And so it went, each man kneeling down, then standing up with a snake dangling like an obscene tongue. The men and their snakes formed a circle in the middle of the plaza. They shuffled round and round and dangled round and round in the heat-stroked blaze of the evening.

Owen focused on the snakes, the better to block out the drumming. He understood Victoria's fascination. For him, it had been insects. When he was a kid, he'd loved lightning bugs, butterflies, cicadas. Especially cicadas. He had been amazed by their life cycle, the seventeen years sucking at tree roots, the end of life burrowing up, the throbbing racket after so much silence. The cicadas had surfaced that summer he spent in Washington. He had collected their shells, crisp, brown, and empty, clinging to twigs and bushes and so thickly scattered over the sidewalk you could barely make out the red bricks below. He'd started to unhook one from a twig when he realized that a nymph was still inside, slowly squeezing out, wet and pale. He captured it and brought it back to his room, then sat and watched for what must have been hours. The nymph's skin dried and its wings hardened. When finally it could fly, he pried open a window warped by the summer heat, and released it into the muggy haze. It had been the summer after his father left; he had a boyish hope that the bug could somehow find his father, serve as an emissary.

This was all the Hopis were doing now, he thought, feeling cheerful all of a sudden. They were sending snakes to serve as emissaries. Maybe religion was just that, the imaginary world of childhood adopted by adults. He nudged Victoria, wanting to share his idea, and saw to his dismay that she had forgotten all about him, so caught up was she, so rigidly entranced, by the dance.

◆

The summer had been worse than usual, the mercury rising to the 120-degree mark the past fourteen days straight. Dolores's horse walked like a careful drunk, heat-stunned, incapable of doing anything quickly, though it seemed to her that he perked up when they reached Independence Avenue. Weather be damned, the bustle continued, the people crossing and recrossing the streets, shouting to each other: *Three hundred! Three hundred? Three hundred!* It was last week's news but they couldn't stop talking about it. Three hundred dollars for a flask of mercury. Women in twos paused by storefront windows, their fingers moving fancifully, sketching out plans for future pianos, ceiling fans, ice boxes. Dolores stepped into the bank preparing to wire a larger-than-usual sum to her parents, when a strong set of fingers gripped her elbow.

"You are in it! You are in it!" said Mr. Bartlett, his eyes red with rage.

"Mr. Bartlett! Please!"

His fingers bore into her. A burly clerk hurried over and after some struggle detached him. Dolores watched the clerk lead him away, a bruise forming on her elbow. Impossible that this was the accountant who had sat next to Grierson for years, unremarkable as a smooth stone. They said that he'd gone mad with grief, a cousin having died in a battle in Northern France. But others had lost too. Not all became unhinged. What was it that unhinged some and not others? Her mind leapt to James, in Northern France himself. He had left reportage on automobiles to cover the war and was now the *Times'* main correspondent in France.

"Are you all right, Mrs. Scraperton?" The bank manager hovered in front of her.

"Yes, I am." She realized that she was shaking. "But not Bartlett. What are we going to do with that poor man?" The manager took her to the back office where she was fussed over by two clerks and signed the transfer papers in a deep armchair while drinking iced tea. She left the bank feeling strangely powerful.

"Doña Dolores!" Ysidro waved from high up on the scaffolding of the new office building. She waved back, a little curtly. "Do you have a minute?" he shouted. "I'd like to ask you a question." He scrambled down the scaffolding. He looked like those men you saw in the papers, matinee idols with painted lips and slender chests and greased-back hair. He jumped the last few feet to the ground, then paused to tip his hat at Carlotta Reyes, who was passing by in a yellow dress. She turned on her toes and returned his gesture with a mock curtsy.

Dolores barely contained a groan. She used to enjoy reading Ysidro's file, the mountains of innuendo and possibility, although never an outright scandal. But then Owen assigned Victoria to help oversee the building project and the very thought of the file made her stomach flip. Owen insisted that there was no need to worry, but she remembered being sixteen, those afternoons with Kern Hook and his tarnished spur, that curiosity that melted all barriers of shame. Ysidro walked over to her, respectfully, all business.

"The mercury frieze has arrived," he said.

"So?"

"I was hoping that you could inspect it and make sure it's

all right before I put it up. It would be nice to have it installed before Mr. Scraperton returns."

She assented, curious to see the building. There had been grumbling in the beginning, the Anglo builders claiming that Ysidro did not deserve the commission, that he was too young and inexperienced, that Owen only gave it him to mollify the Mexicans. It had been right after the soldiers killed Rivera. But the structure looked good, the bricks elegantly mortared, the cornices handsome, everything tasteful and well done. The inside was cooler than the street and filled with the pleasant odor of fresh paint. Ysidro led her through the high-ceilinged lobby into a side room where the frieze lay on a paint-splattered sheet. It had arrived in one piece and seemed to be fine: a cement tablet embossed with the bronze form of naked youth, his sex decently covered by his money purse.

"It'll look pretty with the sun shining on it," Ysidro said.

Dolores grunted, noting a snake winding round a wand that the youth held in his hand. "Could you get rid of that snake?"

"The caduceus?" Ysidro raised an amused eyebrow. "I think that Miss Victoria would be a little upset."

"Where did she find this?"

"She found the picture in a book of Dr. Badinoe's and ordered it made. It's a replica of an ancient Roman figurine. I think that they used to put these on their roads. She said that Mercury was their god of roads or transportation or something along those lines."

"I don't think that I'm the right person to inspect this. Why don't you ask Badinoe—he's our resident classicist."

Ysidro squatted down to brush a fleck of dried paint off the snake's neck.

Dolores left, filled with gloom and defeat. Victoria spoke

more with Ysidro and Badinoe than she did with her own
mother. She had tried to make peace with her. She had even
helped feed the snakes in the pagoda, holding the sack of kangaroo rats that Victoria had pulled from her traps, the creatures still alive, bulging and breathing and squeaking inside
the burlap. She could sense the softness of their bodies, their
tiny bones. Victoria had tossed them off nonchalantly. Dolores watched the snakes strike, the wideness of their mouths,
the pinprick of their fangs. Victoria had seen her shudder.

"What horrifies you so? It's my tongue, isn't it?"

"Of course not."

"Then why do you want me to do a second operation?"

It had simply been a thought, a passing suggestion she'd
made almost a year before. Perhaps another doctor, a slightly
different procedure, and they could fix what was broken?

"I don't care about that."

"You do."

"You don't know everything that you think you do."

Victoria's tongue zipped out, prongs pointing meanly.
She'd looked like a carnival geek. Why did her daughter hate
her so? Maybe she was overreacting. At times Dolores thought
of asking Badinoe for help. He and Victoria were thick as
thieves. But she could not figure out how to broach the subject, or any subject, really, other than pleasantries. Years had
passed, and he still made her feel as if she were a traitor. After
seeing him, she'd find herself composing eloquent speeches
and enacting heartwarming scenes in her head, justifications
for her reunion with Owen. Not that there was anything to
justify. She was his wife. It was her duty. But she wouldn't
have minded explaining things more fully. Of all people, Badinoe would have been able to appreciate the miracle of she
and Owen wanting the same thing at the same time. She had
wanted to tell him how planless it had been, how he had clat-

tered up the steps and somehow the sound of his boots on the wood had made her understand that things were different. She had peeked through the lace curtain, confused, nervous as a Coahuila virgin. He had stopped in front of the door, hesitant, looking like he might turn back. She had opened the door before he could take off. His pleasure, his obvious pleasure at seeing her, was such that she stepped very close to him, her face turned up, knowing somehow, before he had said anything, that he would say the perfect thing. And he did: "Maybe you're right." He uttered the phrase with a glint of pride in his eyes, and a half smile, that trickle of humor, that underground spring that she forgot existed until it popped up unexpectedly.

How good it had been.

But it was impossible to tell any of this to Badinoe. The way he looked at her snuffed out any hope of conversation.

She rode by the park, stopping at the sight of two soldiers whacking someone or something with the butts of their rifles. She hurried over. It wasn't a person. It was a yucca plant.

"What are you doing?" They stared at her mutely. She repeated her question.

"There might be dynamite under there, ma'am," said the one named Floss.

She slid off her horse and kicked up the yucca spears. Floss reddened. The other, Grubb, tried to choke back a giggle. There was nothing below, only earth, stamped brown and silent. "Looks safe to me," she said.

"Guess it's under control," Floss said to Grubb. Grubb followed him out of the park, doubling over in laughter. Dolores watched after them, glad that Victoria hadn't been there—she'd be incensed about it for the next year.

Mrs. Lennox, looking like a misplaced African warrioress with her militant stride and her six-foot trash piercer, hurried over. Together they inspected the yucca plant. The spears were bent and broken in places, but the damage could be overcome. They bunched the spears together and wound them with string. Mrs. Lennox kept shaking her head and muttering, "The growth, the growth, the growth," by which she meant the growth of the town, which, when the committee ladies weren't blaming Dolores, they blamed for all evil. Indeed, Mrs. Lennox got so carried away by the growth that she forgot any displeasure with Dolores, and waylaid her for a half an hour, discussing her corns and her dinner party Sunday before getting back to the shameful state of the park. "Trash everywhere! They even disfigured the fountain."

"The fountain?"

"The insurrectionists wrote on it." Mrs. Lennox sniffed. "Everyone has it out for us, soldiers, insurrectionists, job seekers. Look." She led Dolores over to the fountain and pointed at the base. Someone had scraped quite discreetly, *Viva Zizima!*

"Zizima?" Dolores squinted at the small block letters. It took a moment for her to place the name.

"No, Zapata," said Mrs. Lennox. "Viva Zapata! The anarchist."

Dolores shook her head. It clearly said Zizima, Badinoe's goddess of the mines, but she didn't see the point of educating Mrs. Lennox on this particular matter. She stood up too quickly, disturbed by the message, and almost lost her balance.

Mrs. Lennox steadied her. "Are you all right?"

"Yes, thank you. It's been a trying day, that's all."

At the back of Offitz & Carruthers, Sam Mathews was running the mail desk. Dolores had never fully recognized the pleasure involved in riding over to pick up her mail until the wars broke out. What had once been an errand laced with possibility and elaborate fancies about who might have written and what they might have said had become an errand laced with dread. She hitched her horse and entered the store. Receiving any mail from Mexico felt well nigh miraculous. The letters that had gotten through had principally been from her parents. Astounding letters, far better than the ones that they had written in peace—the flavor of the pineapple they'd eaten, the names of the pigs on Tomaso's farm, the gossip about strange omnibus drivers. As if living out of suitcases with their land gone and their friends killed had perked them up. But the letters came so rarely, and their absence, this daily reminder of their absence ached like a wound.

She pictured the charred field where their hacienda had been. It was a distinct vision, yet inaccurate. According to her father, the north wall still stood. But she pictured a field, completely leveled, rubble still smoldering. If she lingered over the details, the vision became falser yet: blackened hulks of industrial machinery, bleeding rabbits caught on barbed wire, pineapples rotting in the sun, the pope-blessed sword of Don Xavier. The rabbits were due to James, a passage that he'd written about no-man's-land that had become engraved in her mind. *A zone where nothing but thick smoke, at times black, at times white, gives appearance of life . . . a form going over this desert land something after the manner of a rabbit . . . a hero.* His language had acquired a brutality that hadn't been there in Washington. She'd watched it, through sheets of newsprint, grow tougher and tougher the longer he stayed there.

No one else was there to collect mail. Just her. Sam Mathews put down the pomegranate he'd been eating, licked the juice from his fingers, and grinned.

"Happy to see me?"

"Yes, ma'am." He disappeared below the counter, then re-appeared, and handed her a large brown package. "Take this away, it's crowding my space."

"What is it?"

"The trumpet, I think. From Col. McFindley & Co."

She had forgotten. Tiny Henderson had earned a trumpet for winning the spelling bee, and she'd promised to deliver it in person. "Anything else?" she asked. Sam ambled over to the mail slots. Really ambled. Or if there was a word that meant moving in a slower and more purposeless way than ambling, then that was it. "Well?"

"Plenty of papers," he said. He leafed through the *Times*, the local broadsheets and stock reports. "Nothing from Mex-ico. Didn't your mother send you something last week?" She nodded. "I haven't heard of any serious fighting since."

"I know. Thank goodness," she said.

"You want some pomegranate?"

She smiled. No. She put the papers in her satchel and picked up the package from Col. McFindley & Co. "I guess I'll take this over to the Hendersons'."

"Wait," Sam said, putting his finger up to his nose. "You did get something else, where did I put it?"

"From Mexico?"

"No, no," Sam replied, crouching out of view again. "I had it on the trumpet to show you, didn't want it to get lost in the shuffle." He chuckled. "Here it is." A weathered enve-lope with many stamps. "From France."

"From France?" she repeated stupidly.

"Look," he said, and pointed at a tiny sketch of a car in the bottom corner of the envelope. "Pretty good, isn't it? I liked that."

"I'm sure you did." She took the envelope and stared at it. James had never written to her before. "Well," she said, feeling like she had been standing there too long. She flashed Sam a smile. "Well."

She left without the trumpet, had to go back and get it, then went two blocks past the Henderson house before she realized what she had done. She hitched the horse and stood there for a moment, smoothing her skirt. James had sent Christmas greetings to her and Owen, birthday cards to Victoria, but never, not once in ten years, anything only for her. She didn't know if she wanted him to, couldn't help but feel that a personal correspondence would be disappointing. But of course she was pleased. She took the envelope out of her bag and pored over it. In the center was her name, *Mrs. Dolores X.T. Scraperton*, written in script that looked more cramped than she'd remembered. In the top right corner, a small standard-issue stamp said, *Liberté, Égalité, Fraternité*; next to it, a larger one with a pale brown engraving of a lion statue and a banner that read, *Orphelins de la guerre*. But it couldn't be bad news, not with the sketch of the car.

That Darracq. She thought of it more often than she thought of James. She thought of it whenever she got frustrated with the Stanley Steamer, its immense power, the air in her face, the steering wheel vibrating, the trees a blur. Or stationary, its elegant curves, its creamy, haughty whiteness, the mechanical reality of its insides. That night outside Benjamin and Clara's with the engine gleaming wetly under the misty streetlamps. But that wasn't solely a Darracq recollection—James was there too, handing her tools as she struggled to keep the stole wrapped around her. Chain. Jack. Vulcanizer. The blessed car fading, and James's face coming closer, his eyes bright in the mist. The tools kept coming. They'd paused at each moment of transfer, their flesh pressed to jointly grasped metal. Oil squirt can. Grease gun. A moment of what she imagined seasickness to feel like. A stab of guilt. And pleasure, pleasure, pleasure everywhere.

She grabbed the trumpet and hurried to the Hendersons'. Tiny Henderson was twelve years old and had won the spelling bee with *vertiginous*. She banged through the gate, squeezing the trumpet to her chest. Laundry hung in the front, white and dripping. She wanted to grab a sheet off the line and wrap herself up in it. She stopped and chided herself and reviewed the Hendersons in her mind. Mr. Henderson manned the pumps in Shaft 8. Mrs. Henderson chaired the Pristina Festivities Committee. Their two oldest sons were already working, one in Owen's office, the other, she thought, did something in the new coal mine. They had Tiny—real name, Ted—who knew how to spell, and a baby girl, colicky. As if on cue, from inside the baby bawled. Dolores knocked. Mrs. Henderson, hair in disarray, child in massive, freckled arm, opened the door.

"Mrs. Scraperton!" she said, flustered, dismayed, exceedingly apologetic.

Dolores lifted up the package. "For the spelling champ!" The baby screamed.

"Ted's at baseball practice," Mrs. Henderson yelled over the baby. "He won't be back for an hour."

Dolores cooed at the red wrinkled creature in Mrs. Henderson's arm, not wanting to be alone with the dripping laundry and the letter. Luckily the baby's sobs became more bearable and Dolores was invited indoors. She settled down at the kitchen table and told Mrs. Henderson that the Mercury frieze had arrived and the building looked almost done. Mrs. Henderson listened with some interest. Her committee was in charge of planning the opening festivities for the new HQ. But no one, she complained, had told them when the building would be finished, and how could they be expected to plan when they hadn't been given a definite date? What's more, she said, as she poured the coffee, no one had specified what kind of party—Class A or Class B. If it was Class A, they needed fireworks, and those took forever to order. The whole thing was most disorganized.

Dolores sipped her coffee without tasting it. Her senses were concentrated in her fingertips, and her fingertips were smoothing her bag. She hadn't expected him to write, not even that first year. The day of the boys' attack, he had been the one to save Victoria and drive them to the hospital, but she hadn't been aware of him, only the heaviness of Victoria's head on her lap, the growing red stain on her skirt, the strange silence mixed with gasps. When things came into focus and normal rhythm, she had been in the hospital room, Owen's fingers tight on her shoulder. He had smelled of cigars, which was odd for him, but he had just been in a club. She had burrowed into his suit, trying to lose herself in tobacco and wool. Who knows how long it took before she realized that there was someone else in the room. A dandy in striped trousers. A stranger. James. He had recognized her not recognizing him. Afterward, she had wanted to say something to him, to try to erase that moment. But she hadn't.

Tiny, flushed from practice, stood in front of her, holding out a tooth that hung from a cord around his neck.

"What's that?" Dolores said.

"Panther incisor," he replied, thrusting out his chin. "Curr and I trapped it in the mountains." His mother made a noise in her throat. "Well, Curr did. But I told him where to put the trap."

Dolores presented him with the package. He tore off the brown paper and got to a handsome case lined with red velvet. Mrs. Henderson clapped as he put the trumpet to his lips. He experimented with a couple of notes before plunging into an ear-splitting rendition of "O Pristina!" Dolores tried to look appreciative, but found herself jumping up and leaving in an awkward rush.

She forced her horse to canter. She would have liked him to gallop, but the heat was too much. Still, there was motion, her skirt flapping, air sneaking down her collar. She wondered at herself, this excitement over a man who, after all, she barely knew. Perhaps it was only that. Not knowing. She knew where she was. The sky, huge and hot, the dusty, flat horizon. The taste of the water, the smell of the smoke. The crease in Owen's neck, the slightest bit of extra skin that had gathered round his belly, evidence of a newfound appreciation for cream. She knew it so well. At home, Cerb'rus panted in a hole he'd dug in the middle of the yard. He thumped his tail lazily when he saw her. She knew everything. The dog's breath, the cost of the electric mine trams, the number of girls Ysidro had kissed. She stopped midtrack, freshly incensed at the idea of Victoria working so closely with him. What had Owen been thinking? She told Hedda to make her something heavy and solid for dinner.

"What, ma'am?"

"Something that will put me to sleep."

Hedda, nonplussed, opened the pantry door and stared at the contents. Dolores went to her room, took the envelope from her bag, and lay it on her desk. She didn't open it. She thought about Owen, enthralled by Victoria, watching Indians shuffle on some godforsaken mesa. She organized the piles of bills and notes and catalogs into neat rectangles, readjusted the vase of dried flowers, and came across a cinnabar crystal shoved back in the corner of the desk. A long-ago gift from Owen. She picked up the crystal and held it to the light. The prisms glowed a deep burgundy—glasslike, perfect, smooth. They didn't seem to belong to the rough rock at their base. She thought, not for the first time, that she ought to line the base with felt, so that it wouldn't scratch the surface of her desk. She put it down, gently. He had given it to her during their courtship. She had left it back in Coahuila, but her mother had sent it when they evacuated. It had come in a package that didn't have a note, just a bunch of nonsense things, a porcelain perfume dispenser with a pink airbag, old bronze keys, an unmatched sock. She wondered if her mother had inadvertently sent her a box intended for the trash, or if had she been too busy, madly packing buttons, ladles, family photographs, to notice what she'd chosen to save, apportion, abandon.

Hedda rang the dinner bell.

"Coming!" Dolores shouted.

She stared back at James's envelope, crumpled it in her fingers, then tossed it in the bin.

"Coming right now!" she cried, her voice strong with resolve.

She made it to the door before she slunk back and fished the envelope out.

Dear Dolores,

Paris isn't how we planned. I am alone with a broken arm (nothing heroic, I tripped when drunk) and learning to write with my left hand. I have never written to anyone with my left hand before, you are the first person, perhaps because I never dared with my right. I have learned how to fly and I want to teach you some day, not a balloon though. They have balloons with machine guns and they are no good at all. An aeroplane, but not a military one, a sweet june bug with canvas wings and a rip-roaring engine.

Always,
James

The handwriting was shaky. She wondered if he'd been drunk when he wrote it as well. She stood there staring at the paragraph, floating in a sea of off-white. Her knees wobbled. She sat on the bed, a great silence all around her. Downstairs Hedda called her for dinner but the sound was so faint it hardly registered.

♣

Badinoe had finally set out to do what he had been meaning to do for ages—that is, organize. His manuscript had deteriorated to the point that it was now numbered paragraphs stuffed into the pages of the books he'd been using for research. The books were everywhere, tottering and taunting in piles on his desk and under his desk, in the larder, by the bed. He grabbed the top volume from the nearest stack, and pulled at the paper sticking out of its pages.

Huancavelica. A mercury mine a mile deep in the Andes, run by the conquistadors in the fifteenth and sixteenth centuries; a great boon for the Spaniards, enabling them to refine New World gold and silver in situ with New World anima mercurii. Not so great for the Incas who knew of the mine as "la mina de los muertos." The conquistadors rounded up the strong-bodied men, sunk them down the shaft, and housed them in a subterranean city deep inside the mountains. Once they got in, they never got out. A life expectancy of about four years.

He had made the mistake of telling MacIntosh about Huancavelica, which meant, at the end of school year, Badinoe lectured the graduating boys on its evils. Not the girls. The girls would never work the mines, and therefore didn't need to be reminded how much worse things could get. He had dreaded the lecture at first, but now he had a good time with it. He tossed out a few lines about Pristina being the best of all possible worlds, but mainly he lingered on the naked, muscular Indian flesh and the whips and the chains and the deep, deep dark, basking in Huancavelica's fantastic brutality, so that by the end of his lecture, the boys' lips were wet and their fingers twitched and they ran outside to pummel and wrestle each other in the baking dust.

In quiet moments, he thought about Huancavelica differently. He was impressed by it. To have built an entire city underground. To have constructed by hand and thigh and mind, by pickax and feeble predynamite explosion, torch-lit boulevards, chapels, cantinas, a central plaza where once a year the Spaniards held a bullfight. He couldn't get rid of the image of the bull stamping the earth a thousand feet below the surface, the Indians gathered round the square, naked with their lanterns and chains. The pikes of the conquistadors' helmets glimmering. The bell tolling in the chapel, echoing off the rock walls and rock ceiling. All this for mercury. To coax it out. And the mercury in turn to coax out the gold and silver. That was crux of it, coaxing things out, coaxing out disease, coaxing out love, coaxing out death. Mercury, *argentum vivium*, the coaxing and coaxed, living silver, fluid, ungraspable, poison and cure, that's why the alchemists treasured it. That's why he had to finish this book.

He put the Huancavelica paragraph in the Mining History pile. The next book, *The Metamorphoses*, housed a sheet of paper with notes not by him, but by Victoria. He smiled at her handwriting. Not too large or too small, slanted only slightly, arrogant, sinuous, confident. He didn't think, even during his most promising years, that he'd ever managed anything like that. Certainly his present handwriting was decrepit. But that wasn't him, that was his profession; doctors knew too much defeat for strong, certain lines.

Victoria preferred the mythic angle. Mercury was the son

of Jove and Maia. He was the trickster, sneaking backward in frontward-moving footsteps, tripping up logical Apollo. He had winged feet, a flute, and a magic wand that had the power to lull men and demigods into dreams or sleep. *A classical form of morphine!* she had written in parentheses. At the bottom of the page, she listed Mercury's domains:

Mercury—Hermes
rules over:
Science
    *Magic
    *Inventions
Commerce & Thievery
Knowledge & Lies
Roads, Travelers & Highwaymen
Eloquence

She had also drawn a picture: a winged-foot Mercury hovering behind a top-hatted man, apparently fondling the man's posterior. Badinoe looked closer. No, he was extracting a wallet. A pickpocket Mercury. Victoria had a soft spot for thievery. A few months ago, she'd tried to slip his copy of *Ars Amatoria* into her satchel. Had he been gallant, he would have let it pass, but it was a valuable edition, and her act had startled him. He had grabbed her wrist. The tips of her ears had turned red, but otherwise she recovered remarkably well, wriggling out of his grasp, loose and laughing.

"I'll bring it back," she'd said. "No dog ears, promise."

It impressed him, that self-mastery. He had been nothing like that at sixteen. Then again, she wasn't normal. She was ridiculously precocious. She dove into her father's business with all the seriousness and intensity of a man twice her age, and yet, she was not Owen II; she was broader. She consumed books. At this point, she'd fingered every volume in Badinoe's general library, inspecting the chapters, smelling the paper, giving the first paragraphs a wary once-over. But if those first paragraphs pleased her, then she'd give herself over, sinking down, right there on the floor. No more scowl, but a soft, half-open mouth, imbibing ideas.

Her favorite author was still her father. Her voice throbbed with passion whenever Badinoe offered the least resistance, though she loved that resistance. Badinoe was sure it was why she came over so often. It kindled her. She would literally shine as rhapsodies about the immense happiness that would one day engulf Pristina poured out of her. Poor Dolores. He picked up Shiverlid's *Unabridged Medical Encyclopedia*. It had no papers slipping out, but a dog-eared page toward the end. Badinoe flipped to it and found a Paracelsus quote he'd been thinking about using for the epigraph:

Poison is in everything and no thing is without poison, the dosage makes it either a poison or a remedy.

He wondered whether innocence was a type of poison.

Something was suddenly happening outside. He rolled up the blind. Two soldiers ran down the street, their movements frantic and jerky as marionettes. Badinoe automatically picked up his medical case and met them on the porch. The soldiers' clothes were bloody and their words incoherent. They gestured for him to follow.

Outside the new HQ, a soldier was sprawled on the ground, belly up, arms akimbo. Badinoe stumbled, confused. He had been expecting a civilian. The soldier twitched. His arm rose from the dirt and his hand moved to something that stuck out of his neck.

"Stop!" Badinoe shouted. Too late. The soldier yanked

out the object, and blood spurted up, a jelly-red fountain. Badinoe rushed forward, grabbed a rag from someone, and tried—unsuccessfully—to stay the rupture.

Badinoe sat back on his heels, the soldier's identity sinking in. It was Anderson, the oologist from Arkansas, the only decent one in the lot. The boy's blood seeped into the sand, staining it an awful hue. The object in his hand was a triangular, sharply notched trowel, the teeth of the notches shiny with blood. Badinoe closed his eyes. In the middle of that bloody face, his lids were pale and clean. Badinoe tried to stand, but faltered. A Mexican who had been leaning against the scaffolding held out his hand.

"Gracias," said Badinoe, pulling himself up. "Qué pasó?"

The Mexican's eyes shone with anger. He shook his head, unable or unwilling to speak.

"Is he dead? Is he dead?" Bailey, perhaps the most dim-witted of the patrols, ran toward them, out of breath and excited. Badinoe nodded. Bailey struggled to catch his breath and fussed around with his clipboard, a contraption that hooked up to his belt so that he could write with one hand. "So," he said, drawing a pencil from his shirt pocket. "The subject is dead?"

Only a few weeks before, Badinoe had escorted Anderson and Rosa Izquierda down to the Rio Grande. They had all waded barefoot in the river, grabbing at the bushes on the side so they wouldn't slip in. Rosa caught a catfish with long whiskers and Anderson ogled it in his shy Southern fashion. They drank some beer. Badinoe had built a fire and grilled the fish, and Anderson taught them the names of the birds that skimmed the surface of the water.

"Doc," Bailey said, "I need to know if the subject is dead for my report."

"I told you."

"You did not say it. You nodded. I need it spoken."

Badinoe rubbed his eyes, wishing that the soldiers had gotten Dr. Gaylord instead of him. But Gaylord was at the mines today.

"Yes. The subject is dead."

Bailey wrote down *dead* with a blunt stub of pencil. He looked back at Badinoe. "Cause of death?"

"Look for yourself."

Bailey shifted his weight uneasily. "Can't you help me out a little? What do I say? Open trauma?"

"You can say he was stabbed by a trowel," Badinoe said. "What else is on that report?" Bailey looked up blankly. "Who killed him?"

"Ysidro Herrida, sir."

"What? You sure?"

"Sure, I'm sure." Bailey stuck his pencil behind his ear, and nodded toward the scaffolding. "They got into a fight, the carpenters and the soldiers. Herrida comes down with his mortar trowel and stabs Anderson in the throat."

The Mexican who had helped Badinoe up spat.

"Es verdad?" Badinoe asked him.

"Querían matarlo," the Mexican muttered.

"He says they were trying to kill him," Badinoe said to Bailey.

Bailey shrugged. "It was a fight."

"He came down?" Badinoe repeated. "From where?"

"From up there," Bailey said, pointing his chin toward the scaffolding. Badinoe looked up. Light pierced his eyes. He stepped back confused. The sun refracted off something at the top of the building. A piece of metal. The Mercury frieze, he finally saw. They had just installed it.

"They were cementing that statue in there," Bailey said, noting the direction of his gaze. "Herrida was scooping ce-

ment with that trowel when the soldiers came down the
street. He got angry and hurled it at them."

"He threw it or he stabbed Anderson with it?"

"Both. He threw it and then he came down and stabbed
Anderson."

Badinoe changed angles so he could see the frieze better.
It glowed in the sun, blank-eyed.

"Where's Ysidro?" Badinoe asked.

Bailey pointed down the street. People were packed from
one side to the other, and more poked their heads out of
second-story windows or stood on the roofs of the stores. A
murmur rose up from them, an insectlike buzz that broke into
distinct voices as Badinoe entered their midst. A skinny boy
with white-blond hair sat on his father's shoulders, craning
forward. "Don't see a thing!" he shouted. "Only soldiers and
a pack of people! Don't see *him*!"

Badinoe used his medicine case to push aside elbows and
hips. A baby bawled. A boot heel crushed his little toe. He
swayed against the shifting weight of the crowd. The baby's
wails rose until a gun exploded. Then silence. From the front,
a clipped voice that sounded like it belonged to the captain
of Troop A commanded the people to disperse. The crowd
didn't obey, but it loosened. Little bits of cool air drifted
through it, and then a thick current, and Badinoe caught this
current and managed to break through.

Up front, the scene was strangely calm: an open stretch
of street in the middle of which Van Sickle and the captain of
Troop A conferred together. A little off to the side, behind the
butcher's water trough, a group of Mexicans stood in a tight
formation. Surrounding them were the boys from Troop A,
pointing guns.

The captain walked over to Badinoe. "How's Anderson?"
he asked.

"He's gone, sir." The captain's jaw tightened. His eyes were pale blue, the whites yellow as if stained with tobacco. "Captain?" said Badinoe.

"Mm?"

"Is Ysidro hurt?"

"Hell if I know." He flicked his hand at the Mexicans behind the butcher's trough. "They won't give him up."

On closer inspection, the people behind the trough weren't all Mexican. There was an old mucker from Vermont, Gwen Hagen, Deborah Plum, but mainly they were young workers from Ysidro's building crew, Sole Jimenez, the secretary of the Demilitarization Committee, and a couple men Badinoe didn't know.

Van Sickle hooked his thumbs through his belt loops and raised his upper lip. "Now hear this," he said to the phalanx. "Herrida will get due process. You've got my word."

Sole Jiminez produced a single, high-pitched "Ha!" that apparently spoke for the group.

"We're going to be here all night," the captain muttered.

The crowd behind them shifted, and out squeezed Rosa Izquierda. She walked across the glass-splintered paving stones, the sun glossy on her hair. The soldiers stared as she linked her arms through Sole's and Hector's. They knew that she and Anderson had gone to the river together.

"Captain," Badinoe said, "I need to examine Ysidro."

The captain laughed. "Sure, Doc. Why don't you just look him over? They's the ones that won't give him up."

A soldier pointed his gun at Rosa. Badinoe left the captain and stood between the gun and the woman.

"You joining us?" Sole asked.

"How's Ysidro?" Badinoe responded. She made an inconclusive sound in her throat. "Is he conscious?"

"Kind of."

"It's no good, him standing out in the sun."

"We're not letting him go, Doc. They'll kill him."

"Can you take him to my office?"

Van Sickle snorted. "If he's going anywhere, he's going to jail."

"I don't know if he's in any condition to move," Badinoe explained. "My office is closer. You can post a patrol outside."

"We're liberal with some offenders," Van Sickle said, "as you well know. But murderers don't get no leniency. He's going to jail."

The crowd behind was silent, straining to hear.

"See, Doc?" Sole said. "They want him alone in that jail. You know what they're going to do then."

Badinoe rubbed his face, wishing that Scraperton were back from vacation. "Let's move him to the jail, Sole. I'll do a medical evaluation. You'll get a copy and Mr. Scraperton will get a copy. No one's going to do anything stupid."

"You don't know what you're talking about, Doc."

Perhaps she was right. But it would be cool and quiet in the jail, and Ysidro could lie down. "You can post one of your people outside," Badinoe suggested. "Nothing will happen with a witness."

"A witness can't see anything, they built the jail that way on purpose."

She was talking about the new jail, a grim brick building out by the warehouses and the tannery. He'd been thinking about the old jail on Thrift Street, an adobe hut that hardly got used anymore.

"The old jail," Badinoe said.

"No," Van Sickle said. "That's for Class-C crimes."

"For God's sake," Badinoe snapped. "Put him there until Scraperton comes back. I'll take responsibility."

The negotiations continued into the ever-expanding after-

noon. Eventually both sides agreed on Badinoe's original proposal. They started to move. Ysidro's phalanx kept formation,
and the soldiers kept pace with their rifles pointed, and the
captain and Van Sickle took up the rear walking like dignitar-
ies at a parade. Behind them came the crowd. They passed
Badinoe's office, and Badinoe remembered Anderson knocking on his door, a fresh copy of *Military Oologist* tucked under
his arm. "Look, Doc!" They'd published his article. "Look,
Doc! *Private Q. William Anderson!*" His name printed, bold black
against the white page. And he, Badinoe, idiotically jealous,
his own manuscript in tatters.

They arrived at the jail, a tiny rectangle of adobe, about
eight-by-eight on the outside. The door was a grid of iron
bars fastened by a heavy padlock. Van Sickle unlocked it and
kicked the door open.

"All right, Herrida. Home sweet home!"

The phalanx stiffened and wouldn't break ranks. "Basta,"
Ysidro said, pushing through his defenders. He stumbled into
the dim room and Badinoe followed. Van Sickle banged the
door shut behind him. The room was empty and smelled of
prior occupants' urine. It had one window, on the west wall,
through which a shaft of dusty light entered. Badinoe asked
Ysidro to step into it.

Ysidro remained in the shadows. "Thirsty," he said.

Badinoe got a canteen from his medical case. Ysidro trembled badly, but got some water down. Returning to the door,
Badinoe asked Sole for a mattress, a lantern, and two buckets
of water. She got the water immediately and sent someone to
find the mattress and lantern. Ysidro managed to make it to
the window. The slant of sunlight poured over him, illumi-
nating the edges of his clothes and the clotted tips of his hair.
His face was cut up and swollen and his earlobe dangled.

"Is he dead?" Ysidro asked.

"Yes."

"Who was it?"

"Anderson."

Ysidro exhaled. Badinoe arranged alcohol, mercuric bichloride, cotton, needles, thread. The door clanged open. A patrol pushed a straw pallet and a lantern inside, then clanged the door shut again.

"I never meant to stay, Doc. I came back for Abuela and Guillermina, but I never meant to stay. I wanted to go to New Orleans."

Badinoe pulled the pallet into the light. It was lumpy but someone had put a fresh sheet on it. He helped Ysidro lie down. The young man clenched his jaw and stared up at the ceiling. He had an ugly gash wound, probably from a spur, broken ribs, internal bleeding. Badinoe gave him a flask of whiskey, then bound and sewed and disinfected. Ysidro drank about half the whiskey, and the rest dribbled down his cheek. It grew dark and Badinoe lit the lantern. The binding around Ysidro's ribs glowed. The rest of him was bruises and swelling and red mercurochrome stains.

"Have you ever been to New Orleans?" Ysidro asked. Badinoe nodded; he'd been there on leave from Cuba. "Tell me about it," Ysidro said.

But he couldn't remember. He remembered instead where he'd never been, his own images of Huancavelica, the central plaza with the candlelit streets and the flame shadows flickering on the gapped stone ceilings.

"I'll tell you about somewhere else," he said. "I'll tell you about a Spanish matador, who got in trouble with the king—"

"A woman, right?"

"Yes, of course. The matador took a fancy to the king's woman—"

"No, he didn't. He didn't have the balls."

"Yes, he did. And the king's woman fancied the matador too. So the king sent the matador to Peru. Everyone knew the real reason, but the official excuse was that the miners in Huancavelica needed to be entertained. The matador and the bull he would fight boarded the same ship and sailed across the Atlantic, through the Tropic of Capricorn, around Cape Horn, into the Pacific. They got to Peru and climbed the Andes. Then they were lowered into the mine, first the bull, then the matador. Down one thousand, two thousand feet until they got to the black heart of the mountain, where they found a boulevard lit by torches with hundreds of Incas lining either side. The Incas were chained, and their chains jangled, but their cheers were powerful and honest. The matador thought they were cheering for him, but they were cheering for the bull. They'd never before seen a Spanish bull, and they took him for a god. When they got to the central plaza, the church bells tolled and the fight started. The matador waved his red cape, and the bull pounded toward him. The reverberation of his hoofs caused a tremor, and the tremor traveled through the mine. In a far-off stope, a hated overseer kept his crew working even during the bullfight. The ceiling crashed down, crushing the overseer, but all of the men survived."

Ysidro seemed to be asleep. Badinoe stood up.

"I've been to a cockfight," Ysidro said, "but never a bull-fight." He looked like he was smiling.

"Can I get you anything else?"

Ysidro shook his head.

Badinoe called for the guard to let him out. By the door, he felt something under his foot. The floor was littered with notes, flowers, and sweets that had been pushed through the bars. He gathered the gifts and took them to Ysidro.

"You have many friends," he said. But now Ysidro slept.

♥

In his wandering years, Ysidro had known a night or two in jail, but he'd always gotten out the next morning, never had walls, the same four, day after day, grind into him. He knew it could be worse. Men got locked in railroad cars, in blackout cells, in barns packed with hundreds of others. Here he had breathing space and light: a window, a door, and a hole, a small, circular hole that might have been drilled for a pipe, but no pipe had been put through it. The hole he liked better than the window, which was barred and looked onto the mud bricks of the municipal warehouse. The hole faced east, and in the mornings, a narrow ray of light came through it. As the day went by, the ray slid across the floor, and he imagined the sun doing the same thing across the sky. The door let in the most light, and its bars were not as ugly as the window's. But it didn't have a curtain, and you wanted a curtain when you relieved yourself. He had shoved the waste pail into the darkest corner, but it was not completely hidden. Every time he managed to squat over it—not an easy thing to do with cracked ribs—there'd be a stirring at the door, and he'd turn to find some woman smiling at him compassionately.

Women and men both came. The women smiled, the men didn't. The men stood outside his door, clenching their hands around the bars so that it looked like they were the ones in jail. Their faces were screwed up, and their voices hoarse with smothered feeling. They brought him rumors and news, most of it having to do with the upcoming trial, his trial. They worried that it would be held in Crow, and they talked against it. He knew their talking wouldn't do any good. Crow was the county seat; it had lawyers, a peak-roofed courthouse, a jail with toilets. Where would they stage it in Pristina—the front porch of Casa Grande? But these men had never left town; anything other than having Mr. Scraperton settle the case they found unnatural and unjust. He didn't know how much better off he'd be in Pristina. He'd made more than one enemy here, but they were right about Crow. Last year they'd strung up a Mexican just for stealing a chicken.

He liked it better when the men and the women didn't come. Then he propped himself next to the door and watched the birds that hopped on his stoop. He had gotten to know the birds, and he had gotten to know Hobart, the only decent guard in the lot. He knew how Hobart's shoulders stretched the fabric of his shirts, and he knew the delicate way he wiped the sweat off the back of his neck. Sometimes Hobart turned around and they talked about things. Hobart was a big man, with hanging cheeks and a hook for a hand. His original had been crushed between two ore carts. It was a real accident, not one of those productions that the auto-crips staged in order to become a patrol.

Now the key rattled in the lock. The door slammed open. Not Hobart, another patrol, an ugly auto-crip named Handsome Stan.

"Cell search!" Handsome Stan announced gleefully. "Hey! Look at me when I talk to you!" He flashed his torch in Ysidro's eyes. Ysidro blinked. "Glad to see me?"

"Sure, Handsome."

The patrol drew himself up. "What did you say?"

"I said good day, Patrol Smith."

"You bet you did. Get up." Handsome Stan kicked at his pallet.

The cell searches had been going on for about a week now. The patrols had dreamed up some nonsense about him working for Pancho Villa, allowing them to kick around his pallet and slash up his food in case old Pancho was trying to smuggle him in a razor blade. Handsome Stan kicked over the slop pail. "Shee-it! Why don't you watch where you put this thing?" Ysidro grabbed the pallet before it could get wet. "Shee-it! My shit smells like primroses compared to this. What have you been eating?"

He knew perfectly well. He was the one who mashed Ysidro's food into a pulp.

"Clean this up. It's disgusting."

"I can't without a rag."

Handsome Stan leaned into him. "What did you say?"

"You have to get me a rag first." He'd been through this the day before. The Pristina charter had a clause about fair treatment of prisoners. You did not have to lick up shit or pick it up with your bare hands.

Handsome Stan stomped off swearing. Another patrol, a limping blonde who Ysidro did not know that well, returned with a rag and a pail of sudsy water. He opened the door a crack and shoved it in.

"Hey, Herrida. Looks like you're going to be shitting with us for a couple more months."

"How's that?"

"Word on the trial came. You're up for Crow on November 7."

By evening, word about Crow had gotten all around town. The men and women who supported Ysidro came out onto the street and shook their fists and yelled. They didn't want Crow. Crow meant an Anglo judge who did not believe in Natural Unity and jurors who would be the same. Ysidro didn't care so much about Crow. What he didn't like was the date. Two more months to wait. Two more months of the men clenching their hands around his bars, and women smiling and pleading with their soft wet eyes. Two more months of going over and over in his head the things that he should have done, that he was capable of doing, but that he hadn't. He wanted it over with now. Throughout the night, Ysidro heard windows breaking and people running, and he gathered from the shouts that the barracks and the houses of the Anglos who were openly friendly to the soldiers were being attacked. He was surprised by the chaos, that it could occur in Pristina, that it could be on account of him. He felt ungrateful for not appreciating it more, but what he really wanted was to go to sleep, to not have to think, and it was too loud for sleep.

The morning after, the feeling in the air was odd and subdued. Outside Ysidro's door, broken glass and overturned trash cans lay in the street. The loudspeakers crackled on. It was Mr. Scraperton. Due to the disturbance, the opening gala for the new HQ had been canceled.

"Shoot," said Hobart. The ladies outdid themselves cooking up food for events like that. "But maybe it's just as well," he sighed. They'd scheduled him to work that night, which meant he would have eaten too much, then fallen asleep on the job. He always fell asleep when he ate too much, and if they caught him asleep, they'd cut half his week's pay.

"They wouldn't have caught you," said Ysidro. "I would have protected you. I would have said you were up all night doing a cell search."

Hobart grunted, pushing himself up. A car had stopped in front of the jail. The doors opened and out came Jeb Smith and some other men. Jeb handed Hobart a piece of paper and said, "We're taking the prisoner." He said this like he didn't know Ysidro's name, even though Ysidro had fixed his roof last summer.

"Huh?" said Hobart.

"Read." Hobart looked at the paper, then polished his hook against his jeans. "You can't read, can you?" Jeb said. "We're transferring the prisoner to Crow. Be safer there."

"I can read," Hobart responded.

"Well, good for you," Jeb said, looking down the street. "Let's hurry it up. We don't want to turn this into a going-away party."

Hobart unlocked the door. The men grabbed Ysidro by the armpits and snapped his wrists into handcuffs. Hobart looked at Ysidro, and Ysidro looked back. There wasn't anything to say. The men dragged Ysidro into the street. He couldn't see, his eyes were so used to the dim of the jail. They pushed him into the back of the car, and the engine started. The car turned down the alley and shakily made its way between the jail and the municipal warehouse. Ysidro's busted bones bumped up and down. He wondered if the car would shake all the way to Crow. The engine hissed like someone trying to clear the phlegm from his throat, then they stopped. The jail was only a few yards behind them.

Jeb Smith cursed slowly and evenly and the other men argued about what was wrong. Ysidro peered out the window. They were next to the empty lot where the marching band practiced. On the other side of the lot was Commerce Street. There, a woman in a gray dress stood on a ladder cutting streamer from a lamppost—they must have been decorations for the canceled HQ gala. The streamers glided down, the red and white of Pristina, snaking and rippling. As they landed they were grabbed by children who danced around ripping them to shreds.

The men got out of the car. One ran off to find Hagen,

and another, the mechanic. Jeb pulled Ysidro out, saying that they were taking him back to the jail. Ysidro inhaled a couple times, trying to memorize the smell of the air. It was gasoline air but it smelled a lot better than the slop-pail air of his cell. He turned to get one last look at the children, and the children saw him. They raced across the lot, waving their streamers and shouting his name. Jeb pushed him faster and got him in jail before the children could catch up, but the children had seen him coming out of the broken-down car.

By that evening, everyone in Pristina knew that they had tried to take him away, and they also knew that Hagen had fixed the car, and that Ysidro would be brought to Crow at dawn the next morning. They lined up to wish him well; it seemed like everyone he had ever known or dealt with was there, everyone except for Guillermina. After a few hours, he couldn't face them anymore and pretended to sleep.

He must have actually fallen asleep because he woke to the glare of an electric torch shining in his eyes. The soldiers had come to wish him goodbye too. The first kicked him in the temple. He heard something break and hoped it wasn't his skull. Then the others started. He tried to defend himself but he was too weak from the first fight. He flopped around struggling to breathe as the boots kept coming. Somewhere in the blur above him, the captain stood still, smoking a cigar.

They beat him up worse than the first time, probably wanted to kill him, but they, or maybe he, made too much noise. Now gray light came through the door and the doctor leaned over him giving him spoonfuls of medicine. Morphine. He'd never had morphine before. It was wonderful. He slipped outside of his body and watched the doctor work, then he wandered out of the jail. No one stopped him. He went down to the creek, to the alamo grove where he used to go fishing. The alamos were still there. The wind blew through the leaves and the leaves whispered to each other. The doctor interrupted them to give him some coffee. Then people yanked Ysidro to his feet. He had to go to Crow. But he couldn't move. He leaned against the doctor. They had him lie down again. It was very confusing.

Hobart told him later that they had planned to take him away because his presence in Pristina "posed a threat to the public safety." But at the last moment, the Crow people called and said that the jail up there was "packed to the gills," and that they wouldn't have room until the beginning of November. So they had to keep him in Pristina, whether they wanted to or not. He no longer cared where he was as long as he had the morphine. Then he could go wherever he desired. He returned to California and El Paso and the endless railroad tracks cutting through the plains. He went places he hadn't been also. He visited New Orleans and wandered through the crowded wharf and heard the blasts of the boat horns. But he didn't always have the morphine. When he didn't, he had his wrecked-up body. The soldiers had left him with interior stings and exterior stings and aches and numbnesses and itchings; there were hurts that throbbed and hurts that were constant and twistings and spasms and heavinesses and swellings. The doctor told him more of his ribs had been broken, and his muscles twisted and his ligaments ripped. At first he tried to tell which pain corresponded to which condition, but this was an impossible task.

The men and women came, but not as often anymore. Once a lawyer visited, someone Mr. Scraperton had hired. He was a stooped, thin-haired Anglo who'd been in Crow for the preliminaries, but hadn't bothered to come down and meet him or see Pristina. He stayed for about an hour. Most of the time he looked through the bars of the door, twisting a toothpick around in his mouth. He said they should go for temporary insanity because clearly it was insane to charge against a soldier in clear daylight with half the town watching.

Another visitor was a skinny lady from the Edification Committee. She dropped off a tablet of paper and some books which Ysidro hadn't asked for and didn't touch. A few days later, she came with new books. The third time, she got the patrol to let her in. "Look what I've brought you," she said. *The Birth of Pristina.* He didn't smile back. He'd read the book in the fifth grade; it was written by Mr. Scraperton and bound by the Appleby Company of Greater Fort Worth. But she hadn't meant to insult him—it was the very book he'd read in the fifth grade. Carefully, so as not to further damage the spine, she opened the back cover. Glued upon it was the list of students who the book had been assigned to. Up at the top, he found his name.

"Look," she said. She thumbed through pages that were soft and gray from years of fingering. The margins were filled with sketches—his sketches, he'd even signed some. He took the book from her. He'd kept to the text, illustrating the earth convulsing, the mercury migrating through cracks and fissures, the steam escaping at the hot springs. The drawings were done in pencil, and they'd smudged some, but they were still distinct. He remembered pushing the lead deep into the page, the shiny bluish tint he got if he put enough pressure on it. The best picture was on the last page of Chapter 3. The page only had one sentence on it, which meant lots of room to work. His original picture was of a volcano with flames and lava shooting out of the top. Above that, clouds of ashes floated in a starry sky, and on top of each cloud, an animal. They were there still: a panther, something that looked like a dragon, a coyote, and an antelope. But the children who had been assigned the book after him had drawn animals standing on the shoulders of the first ones, and more animals on the shoulders of these, so that now it looked like each cloud was driven by a crooked totem pole.

S **'all right,"** Victoria said, stroking Ramses through the burlap. He pushed his body against her hand, somewhat consoled. He didn't like traveling. "'S'all right, 's'all right." Her lisp was more pronounced when she spoke to snakes. She'd loosen the prongs of her tongue, give it latitude; with people, she talked almost perfectly. A few miles from home she stopped. The site was marked by an old adobe wall, a mesquite tree, a patch of sand just right for practicing. She sat on the wall, the bag on her lap. There were mica-flecked rocks where snakes sometimes warmed themselves, but there weren't any there now, which was just as well, as Ramses behaved better when the other snakes weren't watching. He poked his head out of the bag, his scales black and white and tomato-red, glowing in the evening sun. "Okay, boy." He slid down her thigh and rested beside her. She put the flute to her lips.

According to the books, he wasn't affected by the music, but by the vibrations and the hypnotic motion of the flute. Though she wasn't sure about those books. They treated snakes like they were nothing but dumb lines of instinct and muscle, and she and Ramses had more between them than vibrations and promises of kangaroo rats. She could sense his moods, and he sensed hers. When she felt lonely or glum, he wrapped himself around her in the most comforting manner. And he liked her music. More than once he had nosed her the flute, asking her to play. She'd stupidly mentioned this to Ms.

Peabody, her old governess, and as a result was subjected to endless lectures on empirical proof. She knew what empirical proof was, but the thing between her and the snake was important too. Her father would have understood. He always said that too much empiricism skews science.

But she couldn't talk to her father anymore.

And why did she think that he would have understood? Why take anything that he'd ever said to have any meaning? He was a liar. But he hadn't—he couldn't have always been. She remembered helping him move Rudolfa Quiñones into town. It had been ages ago, right after they installed the water system. She remembered his face, beaming, as he showed Rudolfa the glass panes, the wooden floor, the water trough; how he'd scooped water into his hands and drunk it up, demonstrating its purity, and Rudolfa switching between laughter and breathlessness, running after him.

Rudolfa's daughter had been attacked by the soldiers.

He used to say that progress was like following a stringer, one of those threadlike seams that lead to an ore body. A stringer can go for miles through sheets of bedrock, and it doesn't always lead anywhere. But you have follow it. You are patient and you have faith. She'd been like that with the New Direction, even though it was too lax and too influenced by Mother. But the soldiers were different. They were not a new direction. They were a negation. They were treason. They were the worst part of America coming to destroy what he'd created, and all because he wanted to protect his property. Property! And he bragged about being clear-sighted!

The flute keened into a shriek. She had to stop. She had to be calm. She had important work.

He hadn't noticed that she didn't speak to him anymore. Well, she hadn't completely stopped, but she only spoke of facts, meetings, percentages, the cycle of business. Nothing important, nothing like before. But he didn't notice; he beamed his dumb-brilliant smile, thumped her shoulder, called her Vic-a-doo. She rubbed her face into the sand. She wanted to bleed, to scratch off her skin, to scour everything away. She'd never asked for his inheritance, biological or otherwise. She could no longer go to the demilitarization meetings; her shame was too heavy. She stroked Ramses softly. What had she done? Not much. A dumb Mercury statue. She'd meant it as a sign, a warning: the god of thieves and liars presiding over his office building. Instead it had put Ysidro in jail. And now he might be killed. She lifted Ramses and looked in his eyes.

He followed her to the tree and back, first with the flute, then without. Then he made the trip alone. She picked him up and kissed him. Every day he learned more. He curled around her shoulders, and she stroked him. Her arm hurt from digging. Two hours of digging, every day for weeks. But it was good; she was developing new muscles, and the hole was almost finished. She reached for her bag and tied a small package to the end of Ramses's tail. "All right," she said, "try thisss." The snake moved along the rocks, but the package slipped off. She tried another knot. And another.

It was almost dark, and they'd miss her at home, but she'd found a knot that worked, and felt the need to celebrate. She lit a torch and hung it from the tree. Ramses curled on his burlap bag. She walked into the flat patch of sand and closed her eyes. She pictured their scales slipping over their ribs, their smoothness, her own skin and muscles and joints. She rotated her neck, then her spine, then her hips. She moved in slow arcs, testing the limits of bone and tendon. The movement took over, gathering her into its own force and logic, propelling her up, down, out toward the wide-open desert. She felt like Ramses was inside her. All of them were. She talked to them, and they talked to her, but not in words. They were shimmering, spiraling, shedding skin. Then she had no skin. All was heat and beauty.

The dance ended. She shivered in her sweat-soaked shirt—not a wretched shiver, but a triumphant one. She thought of Ysidro. He also had snake in him. She'd watched the way that he'd grabbed the scaffolding and pulled himself up, slipping through the bars like an acrobat. She wanted to dance for him. She wanted him to see her at her most beautiful. She wanted them to dance together. She put Ramses in the bag and buttoned her coat. She had put her hand on Ysidro's shoulder. She had felt the warmth underneath his thin cotton shirt.

♥

The sky was blue and the scaffolding of the new HQ was blond against the red brick. Up on the roof, the workmen hammered and sawed and laughed and boasted. Ysidro climbed toward them. He had a pail in one hand and the mortar trowel in the other. He had to go slowly. The sun glinted off the bronze god, making it hard to see. As soon as he got to the top, he would give the men their lunch break. They would sit on the roof with their feet dangling over the edge, their chorizos and tortillas in their laps, their canteens by their sides. They'd tell stories, and when they were through, they'd look over the roofs that were so much lower than that of the structure they were building, and they'd look past the roofs to the hills and the head frames, and past the hills and the head frames to the mountains. But he couldn't get to the top. He kept climbing. The sawing and hammering went steadily on, getting louder and louder.

He woke. The sound of construction continued—men were building something in the lot behind the jail. He lay back on his pallet and closed his eyes. The mortar trowel had slipped. At this point, he was no longer sure if it had slipped by accident or design. He kept remembering it differently. What was certain was the sun glaring off the statue and the laughter of the soldiers below, loud and coarse, the kind of laughter that went straight to your spine. The soldiers had never been checked, not for Rivera, not for the Quiñones girl, not for the casual kicks and cigarette stealing and thoughtless insults. You were supposed to be above it. They were poor white trash shipped in for an emergency. They were beneath your dignity. That's what the gringos said, but they didn't have to deal with them. Ysidro let the trowel slip. It fell five stories and almost blinded Daniels. The laughter stopped. Daniels howled. Ysidro went down the scaffolding. Why? To retrieve the trowel. Of course, he didn't have to. He could have run up to the roof. But the soldiers would have chased after him, and his crew was up there—he would have gotten them all in trouble. Ah, he didn't regret it. It felt good to have faced them. He only regretted that in the blur that followed, he didn't get Daniels or the captain or Grubb. Anderson wasn't worth killing.

The hammers and saws stopped. He listened to the workmen's conversation and gathered that they were making the Columbus Day floats. At dusk, the men left and it was quiet enough to hear the scurrying of the mice. They had burrowed a hole in the one patch between the floor and the wall where the concrete hadn't spread. Ysidro had named them Lola and Lobo. Lobo had scars on his tail where no hair grew. Lola had a way of looking at him sideways that reminded him of a girl he'd once met at a dance hall. He collected some crumbs from his plate and arranged them in a circle, and watched the mice eat.

The next day, the hammers and saws started up again. The Columbus Day parade always had three floats, one for Industry, one for Science, and one for Nature. A couple years ago, Industry had been an oversized mercury flask with Carlita Reyes coming out of the spout in a silver leotard; that had been the most popular float they ever had, but the ladies from the Edification Committee hadn't liked it. This year, they seemed to be making a ship—Ysidro heard them arguing about how to rig a sail. There was also some confusion

over a snake and a beak. He couldn't make heads or tails out
of that. He asked Hobart if he knew, and the man shrugged.
Hobart thought parades were a bunch of foolishness, but not
what came afterward. He opened his arms, hook and hand
balanced in happy anticipation: "I'll bring you a mountain of
ribs, and one of Hatty's sweet potato pies too."

The men hammered and sawed for over a week, and in
the evenings the band practiced, until finally the great day arrived. The women scuttled back and forth, carrying bunting
and sawhorses and shouting how perfect the morning was.
Their fancy flowered dresses made Dr. Badinoe, in his black,
look faded and dreary. A reporter trailed behind him, but the
doctor didn't pay him any mind. He muttered something to
Handsome Stan who flashed his broken smile and unlocked
the gate.

"Morning," the doctor said, stamping the dust off his
boots. "Time to change your bandages." He frowned as he
unwound. "You haven't been doing your exercises." Ysidro
was supposed to walk around the perimeter of his cell twice
in the morning and twice in the afternoon, and he was supposed to try to squat, and he was supposed to try to touch
the ceiling.

"I'll start. I promise."

The doctor spent too much time fiddling with his case.
"Don't bother," he said quietly. "There's been an epidemic at
Crow. It's cleared out some space in their jail."

"They're sending me up?"

"Tomorrow."

Ysidro stared up at the ceiling, wondering if they'd be using
the car again, and if it would shake. He should have asked the
doctor for morphine. He would. It would be his last request.
They'd have to give it to him. He stretched his arm out and

tapped around for the writing tablet and pen. He lay there biting on the end of the pen and holding the tablet above his face for a long time. He wrote nothing.

A trumpet sputtered out a few notes, then a trombone and a bassoon. People gathered on the street. He heard patrol whistles, a guy hawking grilled corn, mothers calling their children. He'd never known his mother and his father was now gone, and for that he was grateful. The air got thicker with the press of people. He felt more and more of them, pouring out of their houses, crowding on the sidewalks, pressing their ideas and words and eyes into each other. Now the band squeezed through the alley. He felt their footfalls, the brass, the humorless pound of the drums. He winced and hobbled to the door. Better to watch a parade than stare at a blank writing tablet thinking you gave up your life for a girl who knew the right way to balance a bucket of water on her head.

He couldn't see the band. His view was blocked by spectators clutching little Pristina flags with some miniature American ones thrown in there too. But he could make out the floats. The first was the ship he'd heard them making. He recognized it from his school days, the square-rigged masts, the sails decorated with iron crosses: the Santa María. It looked good, the breeze blowing, puffing the sails. He hoped some of his men had worked on it. When it got closer, he saw that it was drawn by Scraperton's car. Victoria sat at the wheel in a tight sequined dress. He stared. It was strange seeing her in a dress like that. She was a mannish girl; you'd see her in riding britches or loose checked dresses with worker's boots. A half a dozen children done up as Indians and conquistadors rode in the backseat, waving and throwing pieces of candy at the spectators.

The next float was a two-story cage with men packed inside—he thought some joker had designed a jail float until he realized it was an enlarged model of a double-decker shaft lift. The last float, the one dedicated to Nature, explained the confusion over the beak and the snake. It was a huge papier-mâché road runner with a swiveling head and a rattlesnake in its mouth. Children rode on the float, pulling strings that moved the head and shook the snake. Some of the women on the sidelines pretended to be scared and screamed, but the children were serious and ignored them.

Then came Miss Mercury done up in a modest dress, then the boy who had won the oration contest, then finally, at the rear, Mr. Scraperton. He rode on a black horse in his black suit with his square shoulders and his square jaw. He looked the same as he always did; he'd looked that way since Ysidro first remembered. The man gazed deep into the crowd, and the people cheered. When he reached the spot in front of the jail, Ysidro felt a quiver in the back of his neck. He passed on, and Ysidro watched him go, the square shoulders and the tail of his big horse swishing.

After Mr. Scraperton, the crowd dispersed leaving the street cluttered with stomped-on confetti and corncobs. It grew dusky. The smell of meat got strong, and Ysidro hoped that Hobart would remember to bring him something. He did. "A picnic," Hobart said with a wink. He opened a basket and took out ribs, potato pies, deviled eggs, saffron cake, candied citron. He arranged them on the threshold of the jail and slid a fully loaded plate under the door. It had been a long time since Ysidro had eaten food that hadn't been slashed and mashed. Hobart tucked a napkin into his shirt and spread another over his lap. They ate slowly, murmuring with appreciation. When they finished, Hobart laid his good hand over his belly and sociably curved his hook around one of the bars. They talked for a while. But Hobart was tired, so tired that in the middle of a sentence he fell asleep.

Ysidro lay on his pallet. The fireworks boomed and shrieked, people gasped and applauded, and Hobart softly snored. Then there was something else, a scuffle in the corner. One of the mice, Lobo or Lola, darted past Ysidro's feet. A snake had come through the mouse hole. A slow and strange-moving snake, dragging something by its tail. Ysidro rubbed his eyes. He hadn't taken any morphine; his aches and pains proved it. The snake got closer and the thing it dragged skittered on the concrete. It was a heavy piece of paper, folded over and over again, and it was attached to the snake by a loop of string. Ysidro slipped the paper out of the loop and something metal clanked to the floor. A key. Hobart kept snoring. Ysidro pocketed the key and squinted at the paper. It was too dark to make out the writing. He edged himself closer to the door and read from the light on the outside wall of the jail.

> *Succor awaits! When the road is clear, whistle like a screech owl. If your whistle is returned, unlock the door. Once you are out, scratch the lock so it looks like it has been picked. If you are caught, swallow the key! I await you in the alley.*

> *A Friend*

Ysidro crumpled the note and stuck it in his pocket. It had to be a joke. He looked for the snake, but it had disappeared. Outside, a couple of men staggered by laughing. Ysidro put his hand in his pocket and felt the key and the note and the spool of thread he'd carried around for ten years. The band started up a reel. He'd always liked the dancing, spinning around with the Japanese lanterns and the girls in their dresses, but the Anglos didn't. They left early, coming down the street in twos and threes. He squeezed the key, and the metal cut into his palm. Someone had gone to a lot of trouble for a joke.

A few songs later, the road emptied. Ysidro gripped the bars and pulled himself up. Still no one. He whistled. Not like a screech owl, like a midnight train coming into a town on the plains, a low, quiet moaning that wouldn't attract attention. A single whistle came back. He slipped his hand through the bars and tried to fit the key in the hole. The angle was difficult, and his shoulder was so stiff he could barely move. Someone laughed and the key jumped out of his fingers. For a moment he saw it golden, shimmering in the light, then, with a dull clink, it landed in the darkness. The laughing got louder. Bartlett wavered up to the jail, reeking of sweat and brandy. He threw himself against the door, rattling the bars and yelling about firing squads and mustard gas.

"Shhh," said Ysidro.

"What's he doing snoring?" Bartlett said, kicking the toe of Hobart's boot. "The world's going to hell and you're all sleeping and dancing."

Ysidro heard the key skitter. Now he saw it, the top curve of it, glimmering, a couple inches from the gate. Hobart stopped midsnore and Bartlett waved his flask at him.

"Let us drink to the cavalry."

"Let us not," Hobart said.

"What are you afraid of?" shouted Bartlett.

"Shhh. Don't make me arrest you."

Bartlett let his arms drop to his side, mumbled something incomprehensible, and stumbled into the dark. Hobart sighed. Ysidro closed his eyes, praying that the man wouldn't see the key. A couple more people walked down the street, then it was empty. Hobart mumbled something, then started breathing deeply again. Ysidro crouched. Breathtaking pain shot through his side. He got the key. The street was still empty. He slipped the key into the lock, and this time he got the angle right. The door swung open, smooth as could be.

He ran to the alley, clutching his side. Something large and dark blocked his way, a pale ghostliness hanging above it. A different kind of fear came over him, until he realized it was the float, the Santa María, with the sails barely visible. Someone below it suddenly grasped his wrist. "You didn't whistle!" It was a girl. His head hit an axle as he was pulled underneath. He moaned.

"Quiet!" she whispered. "Did you scratch the lock?"

"Yes."

"Good," she giggled. "I can't believe we did it. And Ramses? Did you bring him?"

"Victoria?"

"Yes, of course, silly. Did you bring the snake?" It was too dark to see her face, but there was a faint glittering from the sequins on her dress.

"No."

"That's all right," she said. "He knows the way home. His name's Ramses, after the Egyptian king. I've got another one named Tiresias. Do you know who Tiresias is?"

"No."

"I'll tell you later. We've got to get going. I've set you up a lovely hiding place. I hope you like it." She flashed on a light. He saw her face for a moment, then she pointed the beam at a small square hole in the underbelly of the float. "You'll have to get in there," she said. "That's not the hiding place. It's just the mode of transportation. The hiding place is much better."

"Does your father know about this?"

The flashlight wobbled. "No. Of course not."

They heard voices on the street and Victoria pushed him

into the hole. He didn't fit. The planks pressed into his bandages, and his knees bumped into his chin. She pushed harder and harder—it felt like she was rebreaking his bones—until somehow she got the door closed. He could hardly breathe, his ribs were so tightly squashed. But worse than his position, far worse, was the darkness. He shut his eyes against it. Outside, footsteps crunched in the alley. Then an automobile engine turned, the float's. Ysidro lurched forward.

They moved into to the heart of town, where the music was loud and clear. A patrol whistle shrieked, then another. The float turned and the music faded. Another whistle. The float dragged on at the same slow rate. Now the whistles stopped. Everything was quiet except for the rumble of the engine and squeak of the axle. Ysidro's bones bumped and his bandages itched; he concentrated on the bluish light coming through the cracks. They went up a hill, a short one without switchbacks. They stopped. He smelled horse and straw. Victoria and a man moved some stuff around, then she asked the man if he wanted a ride back into town.

"No, thanks," he said. "I'm hog-stuffed, better walk."

But the man didn't leave. A stable hand came in and they talked and talked. Then a new set of footsteps, sharp and adamant. Ysidro knew who they belonged to even before he started talking. He congratulated Victoria on the float.

"Thank you, Father."

"Best one we've had so far," Scraperton said. He slapped the side of the hull, and Ysidro felt the planks vibrating. Finally everyone but the snuffling horses were gone. Ysidro pushed at the plank, but he couldn't get it loose.

By the time Victoria returned, some time later, he was so stiff that he could not move. "Hurry," she whispered, pulling him. They ran crouching along a rocky path then climbed some steps and went through a door. She turned on her flashlight and pulled a couple of boards from the floor to reveal a black rectangular hole beneath. She climbed into it.

"Come on," she said. She stood at the bottom and aimed her flashlight at a series of two-by-fours hacked together to form a ladder. He didn't move. He hadn't gone underground since that time in the mine.

"Come on," she said. "What's wrong with you?"

He gripped the edge and lowered himself in. The hole was about six feet wide and eight feet deep.

"I dug it myself," she explained. "I've been working on it ever since I got back from the snake dance." She had tried to make it more bearable by covering the sides with fabric. A quilt lined the bottom. "Do you like it?"

He said it was nice.

She told him there would be a manhunt, and that he would have to stay here until it died down. He eyed the close walls. "It's the best place," she said. "The patrols won't search Casa Grande, and no one from the house ever comes out here because of the snakes."

"The snakes?"

"Yes," she said. "Tiresias and Ramses. I keep them up in the pagoda."

"Ah."

"Badinoe says you'll be fine in a couple weeks—"

"Dr. Badinoe?" he said. She nodded. "Does he know about this?"

"No," she answered impatiently. "Nobody does. Nobody knows. I slipped sleeping powder into Hobart's coffee, I designed the float, I dug the hole. It's my plan. I only brought Badinoe up because I asked him about your condition. You have to do your exercises, and you'll still be pretty busted up. But if you have to, you'll be able to move in a couple weeks.

By that time the search will have cooled off, and we'll get you down to Mexico."

"Who's the we?"

"I told you," she said. "You and me." Her face was hard and she had a little bit of makeup on.

"Why are you doing this?"

"I got you into this, I'll get you out."

"You didn't get me into this," he said.

"Yes, I did. It was that Mercury frieze. It was my idea."

"What?"

"You dropped the trowel when you were putting in the frieze."

He remembered the sound of their laughter. "They would have found some other reason," he said. "They just wanted to fight."

"You don't understand anything," she said. "But that's all right."

She pulled back the fabric from one of the walls. It was timbered with more two-by-fours; in between them were shelves stacked with water bottles, baskets of food, and provisions. She melted the base of a candle onto a radish-shaped saucer and gave it to him. He watched the flame.

She pulled aside another curtain. "See, I thought of everything." She pointed out a pail, a can of lye, and a shovel. He thanked her. "Do you need anything else?" He asked for a painkiller. "Of course," she said, frowning. "I should have thought of that."

"Don't worry about it."

"I'll get you something as soon as I can." She paused by the ladder and stared into his face. "Well, good night," she said.

After she left he inspected his provisions, finding a rag and water and even a triangular shard of mirror. He gazed at his reflection with a dull curiosity. An ugly purple gash ran across his cheek and the bones stuck out more than he remembered. He had a straggly beard. He found a razor and shaved, then turned the mirror to face the wall. He wanted to lie down, but first he wanted matches. He needed them at hand's reach, in case the candle went out. She had to have stocked matches, but he couldn't find them. His fingers shook as he opened every canister and box. At last he found some in a rusty tomato tin and put a handful into his pocket.

The smell of the earth was everywhere. And the muffled silence. He hadn't been underground since he was a boy. He hadn't been afraid then. The fear came afterward, with the dreams. One in particular that still came back to him: He was trapped at the bottom of a shaft. Up at the top, his abuela looked down, laughing. He tried to quiet her by throwing a rock at her, but she was too far away. The rock hit the wall of the shaft, then crashed down onto the head of a miner, who brayed like a mule and fell to the ground. His abuela kept laughing. He kept throwing rocks. The rocks kept crashing down onto the heads of miners. A big heap of bloody miners piled up. Then the pile came apart and the miners rose. Some of them had faces of mules and some had faces of blue-eyed burros, and some had regular miners' faces smeared over with red muck. But no matter what kind of face, the whites of their eyes were phosphorescent and bulging. Ysidro ran. They chased him down slippery tunnels, their brays echoing in the dark. He got to the precipice where the gallina ladder had been, but it wasn't there. He edged closer. There was no way down, only blackness. The brays got louder and the hoofbeats pounded the tunnel and everything shook.

He hadn't been able to sleep much. The dreams didn't count as sleep; they were something else. His father forced him to take Dr. Badinoe's sleeping pills, but they just made the dreams worse. His pupils grew so large you could hardly see his irises. After a few weeks, his abuela took him outside and held up different things for him to look at. Then she made a special tea. After he drank it, he slept for three days and three nights and had no dreams at all. When he woke, his abuela was sitting in the chair beside his bed. She leaned close to his pillow, her breath sour with tobacco. She made him repeat some words and blow on a candle and promise to never work in Mr. Scraperton's mines. If he ever went back on his promise, she said, the dreams would return, and this time they would be real.

He lit matches one after another. He sniffed at the sulfur and smoke traces and tried to block out the smell of the ground. He didn't understand what the girl Victoria was doing, or what she wanted. He wanted to know what she was doing, but he didn't think he wanted to know what she wanted. He rubbed the spool of thread in his pocket. Sometimes he pretended that he would still give it to Guillermina. He'd gone up there a couple times. She shared a shack with her father and a cripple named Hammock, and made money embroidering napkins for the ladies in town. It was a lopsided shack with burlap sacks nailed to the windows and hogs snorting in the dirt out front. She never came out, but last time he went up there, she pushed aside one of the burlap sacks and looked directly at him. It was not a stare. It was a soft, pouring look that entered right into him and melted his bones. He took out the spool of thread. The discs of wood were black with sweat and grease. The thread, hardly red anymore, was frayed and snapped.

The pain ebbed and flowed. Insects with soft bodies and many legs crawled out from the walls. Days passed, or hours, he didn't know; he lit new candles before the old ones went out and avoided the darkness. Victoria returned at some point. She wore a white cotton nightgown, and the candle-light glowed through it. Ysidro lowered his eyes and studied a bloodstain on his jeans. She knelt beside him. She wore her mother's perfume.

"I should be able to get you something stronger," she said, slightly out of breath. "But for now, take this."

She dug into a satchel and handed him a flask of whiskey. She watched him drink, her mouth moving as if she were do-ing internal calculations.

"That's enough for now." She took the flask before he was finished and stuck it between her legs. "They're going nuts," she said.

"Who?"

"The patrols—they have no idea what happened."

"Good," he said.

She eyed him impatiently; she'd wanted him to say some-thing different. He told her she was clever and she flushed with pleasure.

"They've torn through everyone's house," she laughed. "They've found all kinds of clues. They're trying to pin it on Pancho Villa."

"What if they find out it was you?" he asked.

"They'll never find out." She twisted the flask between her thighs. "Of course," she added softly, "once we're in Mexico, they'll figure it out, but by then it will be too late." Her eyes wandered over to his. There was a question in them that he'd seen in the eyes of women before. He ignored it.

"You have to start exercising," she said abruptly. "You've got to get in decent shape." She pulled two cans of peaches from the shelves and made him stretch out his arms and hold them while she counted. When she got to ten, he lowered his arms and she gave him a sip of whiskey. They kept at this, extending the time he held the peach cans from ten to twenty counts, and in this way, he managed to get through most of the flask. Then he dozed.

When he woke, she lay on her side, facing him. She didn't have any question in her eyes anymore. They were black and wanting and fierce. They looked like Scraperton's.

"What time is it?" he asked. "Shouldn't you get back?"

She rolled over. Her silence was sharp and angry. She stayed on her back for a while, then curled up and drew her finger through the candle flame.

"Father can hold his finger in a flame longer than anyone," she said.

She looked as though she were expecting a reply so he nodded.

"Do you hate him or love him?"

"Who?"

"Father."

"Neither," he said.

She squinted into the candle like it was a faraway sign she was trying to read. "La Herrida hated him. I used to hate her for that, but I don't anymore. Was she really your great-grandmother?"

"More than that," he said. "Great-great-great, but I called her Abuela. That's what she wanted." And she hadn't hated Scraperton. She'd been too tough or too stupid or too smart to hate or to love. She'd had enemies, and these people she fought; and she'd had patients, and these people she yelled at. That's all people were, patients or enemies. She'd been as bossy and certain of her claims as Scraperton.

"I went to La Herrida's funeral," Victoria said. "I wanted to see what a cleric looked like. Did you see me there?"

"No." He'd seen Guillermina though. She had been wearing a black dress with a purple bow around the waist, and her eyelashes had been blacker than the dress, and her breath a thick whisper. Victoria poked him in the chest. "Ow!"

"I was there," she explained. "Cerb'rus started barking and I thought mother would discover me and I'd get in trouble. I hated her then, but I don't now. My father is a liar."

She kept talking. He dozed off again. When he woke, she was now sitting very close to him, and the look had come back in her eyes. He moved an inch or two away. She rolled her tongue all the way out and pointed the prongs at him.

"Are you afraid of it?" she whispered.

"No," he said.

"I didn't think so. It scares some people because it's forked like a snake's. But we're not . . . Do you know why people are afraid of snakes?"

"No."

"It's not because they're poisonous. If that were the case, then they'd only be afraid of rattlers and corals, but they're afraid of every species. I think it's because snakes mean knowledge, and people are afraid of knowledge."

"Your tongue is fine," he said. "It gives you a nice little lisp."

She didn't seem to hear. "I never told you about Tiresias, did I?" The question in her eyes had seeped into her voice. He pretended to fall back asleep. He didn't want any girl at the moment, especially not her. She nudged him. "Listen. Tiresias saw two snakes." She moved closer. "He was walking in a meadow, and he saw two snakes twisting in the grass . . . copulating. He struck them with his staff. At the moment that his staff touched the snakes, Tiresias became a woman. He stayed a woman for seven years, and during that time he felt all that a woman experiences. Then he went back to the meadow and the snakes were copulating again. Again he struck them. This time, he turned back into a man."

She was quiet for a while. He figured she thought that he was sleeping. She leaned her chin on his shoulder. "So," she said, "the snakes gave Tiresias knowledge of both sides." Her hair tickled his cheek. "One night, when Jove and Juno were in bed, they got into a dispute about who enjoyed it more, women or men. Are you awake?"

"Yes," he mumbled.

"Tiresias said that women enjoy themselves more," she said with finality.

He guessed that she wanted him to challenge her, something like that. He could feel the heat rise off her skin. He felt badly; she'd be lucky if she got as much as a kiss before they married her off. It wasn't the tongue, she could fascinate people with that. It was her father. He seemed to hover above her and inside her too. She put her hand on his chest. He shuddered.

"Please, Victoria, that hurts," he said.

"The whiskey didn't help?" she whispered.

"It helped a little, but not enough."

She removed her hand. He closed his eyes.

"Good night," she said, standing up. Her voice was flat and defeated. She inhaled. He realized she was about to blow out his light, and he started. She moved back from the candle, a bit of hope flickering in her eyes.

"Don't blow it out," he said. "I like it lit when I wake up."

She kept gazing at him. He closed his eyes again.

She didn't come back for a long time. He burned through three or four boxes of candles, and got uncomfortably close to the end of his supply. He exercised, and with each successive candle, he forced himself to work harder. He got so he could walk the length of his coffin hole seventy-five times. Or more. Or less. He got snagged with his counting and forgot where he was; it drove him mad, not being able to keep track. He forced himself to calm down. He did the peach can exercise and practiced rising on his tiptoes and balancing there.

He knew the river. He'd worked as a fisherman until the day after his fourteenth birthday when he pocketed Abuela's money, traded some fish for a wagon ride, and set off on his days of exploring. There was a place by the gorge where a granite cliff rose up five hundred feet. It looked like it blocked the way to the water, but on the side of the cliff, behind a thick stand of reeds, was a cave. It led to a passageway so narrow that you had to suck in your stomach, but at the end was a safe place for crossing, with boulders to hide behind. All he needed was a rope to guard against the current, and he could pinch that from the stables. Or from the float—there'd been coils of rope hanging from the masts. But he couldn't make it to the river until he beat back some of the pain. The pain occupied him more than his plans, his regrets, the darkness that waited behind the flicker of the candle. He tried to pace it away and count it away, and sometimes he managed to sleep it away, but it always came back.

Then she came back. He was lying down, delirious in the middle of a fever, and she stood over him wearing riding britches and holding a crop diagonally across her chest.

"Still hurting, Ysidro?" She tapped his foot with her boot. She was out of breath and sweating and had a triumphant look in her eye.

"A little."

"I brought you a present," she said. "But I'm not going to tell you what it is."

She squatted next to him. Through the stench of his fever, he could smell the outdoors on her, the thistles and the

sun and the hot smell of sand. She said that she'd just gone
with her new governess out to the canyons, then taken the
shortcut home, leaving the horse to straggle back along the
old ranch road.

"I'll be free of her for the rest of the afternoon," she
laughed. "She's a stupid old cow, afraid of a bandit behind
every bush. I'm not afraid of bandits." She took a breath, then
she was on top of him, straddling his ribs. He shouted in surprise and pain. She squeezed his ribs with her thighs. "That
hurts, doesn't it?" She grinned. "I've got something for you."
She unbuttoned the top of her riding shirt, revealing a rawhide string. "Guess what it is?" She pulled at the rawhide.
Something weighed it down. As she pulled, the thing rose
between her breasts. He forgot about the thing and stared at
the contours of her breasts. She let the rawhide go and unbuttoned another button. Her skin was smooth and not mannish
at all. He looked away, but she put her hand on his chin and
guided him back. The leather string slid smoothly over her
skin. Another inch of rawhide drew up, now a drawstring
pouch. She loosened the string and pulled out a blue glass
bottle.

"I got you some morphine," she said. "You won't hurt
anymore."

The bottle glowed in the candlelight. He wanted to grab
it out of her hands, but forced himself not to. He had to resist. He'd gotten too attached to the stuff. Her face loomed
over him, the sharp angle of her jaw, her fiercely plucked eyebrows. He pushed her away.

"What's wrong?" she gasped.

"I don't want your medicine."

"Yes, you do!"

"No. I don't."

She moved to get on top of him again. He pushed her,

hard, but she was strong and came back, her hand snaking into his pocket. She pulled out the emergency matches.

"Ha!" she said. "I thought you might have tried something like that." She grabbed the candle.

"No!"

She blew the flame out and everything went black except for the reddish glow where the candle had been. "Shhhh," she said. "You want me to turn on the light?"

"No." The reddish glow faded. All was black. He hugged himself to stop the trembling. "Yes."

He heard the cardboard box slide open, the sulfur scrape against the sandpaper strip. He had never been so grateful for light. It wrapped around the wick, softening from white into yellow and orange.

"You're shaking," she said, touching his forehead. "You're all wet." She smoothed his hair back. Her hands were calm and commanding. She propped his head up on her thigh. "Now why won't you take your medicine?" She poured a spoonful. The liquid rose a hair's breadth over the rim and hovered there, not spilling over. "Open."

Something deep inside him opened, a spring of sparkling, pure water. It lapped at his insides, dissolving the pain. He nestled deeper into her lap. It felt good, the way she stroked his hair. He shouldn't have been so mean; she wasn't like Scraperton. She was like her mother. Benevolent. Helping the people up in the caves. He'd been in love with her mother as a child. Everyone had. He put his hand on her thigh and she hummed a lullaby.

The world became permeable and forgiving. The water that had been lapping inside seemed to be lapping outside too; he was in a bathtub. She was kissing him, unbuttoning him, her breath and fingertips pouring over his throat and limbs. He ran his fingers through her hair; it was wonderfully soft. He held a strand to its full extent, amazed at its length, its glimmering blackness. She pulled down his pants and flicked her forked tongue over the insides of his thighs. His legs were bare and pale and didn't seem to belong to him. He could hardly feel his sex either, but it rose.

She wriggled out of her riding britches and her shirt and her underthings. She took off everything except for the rawhide pouch that held the morphine. When she kneeled before him, he slid his hand between her thighs. It wasn't easy. He wondered vaguely why she pretended to know what she was doing, most girls were just the opposite. But he knew what to do. She softened. He was above her, then she above him, with the medicine pouch swinging pendulumlike over her navel. It seemed to him then that everything that had happened had to have happened, that there was a logic and a beauty to everything. A centipede crawled up his sleeve, and he brushed it off. It landed on the quilt and cocked its head at him. *Sleep*, it whispered. He flicked it into the corner.

Then she had her clothes on. She knelt over him and tugged at her rawhide string, giving him a last glimpse of her medicine pouch.

"I'll be back." She kissed him.

He kissed her too, then the centipede returned.

He awoke clear-headed knowing he had to leave right then— with the morphine working enough to ease the pain, but before he started getting pangs for more. He tied up a bundle of food and water, and hauled himself up the ladder. A nail caught on his jeans, tearing a hole in his pocket. As he yanked himself free, the spool of Red #4 fell and landed on the quilt below. He stared at it for a moment then continued up, pulling himself through the trapdoor, hoping he wouldn't encounter one of Victoria's snakes. The pagoda was black except for the outline of a bluish rectangle marking the door. He felt for the knob and turned. The air, cool and fresh, rushed into him. The stars glittered all around. He saw lights shining in Pristina, but none in Casa Grande. He wanted to laugh. He was no longer afraid of anything or anyone. He wanted to announce it to all of them, but he didn't. He ran across their property, toward the river.

1919

♣

Max Hernandez slumped on the examination table, his belly pale and tender against his leathery arms and neck. He had a bullet wound in his left shoulder. He'd been fighting alongside Manuel Urrandago. Now his eyes were fixed on the front door of Badinoe's office, alert to new danger. In an instant he was racing out of the room. Badinoe turned, the disinfectant still in his hand. He expected a patrol, but instead he got Dolores raging toward him, a wave of black with balled-up fists. At first, he didn't understand. Then he thought that she was mad about him helping Hernandez, who'd gotten shot fighting Scraperton's men. He drew himself up dignified and righteous, inwardly reciting Hippocrates and the Rights of Man. But she didn't give a damn about Hernandez. Her eyes blazed and her mouth curled into furious words. She called him a destroyer, a bitter drunk, a blathering snake. She tore off her hat—the first time he'd seen her remove it since her hair began to gray—and swiped it at his face as if she couldn't stand to touch him directly.

He grabbed the hat. "What is all of this?"

She forgot about not wanting to touch him, and slapped him across the cheek. He cupped his palm over the sting.

"Dodo?" he whispered.

"Don't call me that!" she screamed and punched him in the eye. She had on her engagement ring, a silver band on which was mounted a huge cinnabar crystal, sharp as a diamond. It broke open the skin of his lid. The blood blinded him and he felt her shaking him by the collar. "You drunken imbecile," she moaned.

He detached her fingers from his shirt. "I have done nothing and I am quite sober." He wiped the blood from his eye. She put on her hat. There was soot smeared on her neck and dress. She tied the hat string and marched out the door.

He staggered after her, but lost his balance and had to grab a porch post for support. She was the only person on the street, moving unsteadily with shreds of posters blowing at her ankles and bright broken glass sparkling in the sun.

The air was sour with lingering cordite and buildings still smoldering. Pristina had been at it for two days. The mercury market had bottomed out, along with production in general, the whole overinflated industrial promise popped like a punctured zeppelin. The entire country was at it. High-heeled telephone operators waving placards, Bolsheviks crawling out of basements, lone-wolf lumberjacks organizing. Pristina might have been able to avoid it if Owen could see straight, but he still imagined that the people trusted him, that he could do anything and everything without explaining why. Last week, he decided that they could no longer afford the subsidy on blasting powder, and cut it without telling anyone. When the miners went to Offitz & Carruthers, they discovered it cost twice as much as usual. All they would be eating for the next week was rice. Then he closed Shaft 8.

Still, he could have pulled it off. Still, he had the voice. But when he closed the shaft, he spoke only of the tragedy of boarding it up, the mythic grandeur of it, nothing of the men who'd worked it, some of them for over twenty years. It was perplexing how glaring his mistakes had been. When Manuel Urrandago and his committee marched to Casa Grande and asked what they were supposed to do, thirty men out of work and the rest barely able to buy the material they needed to keep working, all Owen could say was, "Do you think I control the price of mercury? You ought to be grateful!" He said other things too, but the men remembered *You ought to be grateful* and chanted it when they stormed Shaft 8.

Badinoe washed around his eye, the water warm and thick with sediment. The water supply had been poisoned, so now Pristina was back to the system they'd had when he first arrived: the water tanks hauled up from the river, filled with the mud of the Rio Grande. He examined his eye in the mirror. It hid behind a slit, the whole area a swollen mess of purple and red, but he could see out of the other. Blood on the floor, clumps of singed hair, medicine bottles overturned, scissors too hastily sterilized. He poured himself a drink.

A groan rose from the temporary clinic in the house next door. Another. No electricity meant no ice which meant no relief for pain and swellings. And warm whiskey too. But that was all right, he rarely took whiskey on the rocks. He swirled it around with his tongue. His clock chimed, some hour. Time streaked forward and backward, stale and ripe and festering. He hadn't slept in days, but the moment a patient appeared in front of him, his mind straightened, and his fingers stopped trembling, and he knew what to do. Owen didn't understand this. Owen had yelled at him. But he knew what to do. His mind straightened and his fingers stopped trembling. Yet he couldn't do everything. They expected him to do everything. Why did they think he could even do anything? What could you do without medicine? He had none. Someone, the strikers he guessed, had attacked the last shipment. The cart lay twenty miles up the road, overturned, straw and purchase receipts scattered and pinned to cactus thorns.

The groans from the clinic continued, one of them ascending, transforming into a ululating curse. Badinoe would have to use the telephone again. He hated that telephone, shouting at voices far away and indifferent, the static crackling in his ears. He'd used the telephone yesterday, and they'd promised him a new shipment of medicine which still hadn't arrived, and today was their tomorrow. But he had to use it; he couldn't get out of it. He poured himself a half an inch more. It's true—he wouldn't deny it, he never used to touch the stuff before six o'clock in the evening, and now he needed a shot to wake him up and a couple others to get him through the day. He had been forced back into being a war doctor, and he had sworn he'd never do that again. He only had one other doctor to help him, the other two gone, one in the influenza, the other, smart, packed his bags at the beginning of the slump.

Owen should have been grateful that he, Badinoe, remained, but no one in Pristina was grateful, least of all Owen. He had barged in. When was that? Only yesterday? Yes. Yesterday morning. Owen Sunday. Dolores Monday. Both of them barging in and pushing him around. But no, Owen hadn't barged, that was Dolores. With Owen, the door had opened slowly and quietly. He had wavered in the doorway, so pale that Badinoe thought that he had come to him for an appointment. In the street behind him, patrols dragged a woman by her braids, and Badinoe felt for him then, his utopia reduced to a sobbing, hair-pulled Mexican. But that wasn't Owen's way. Owen welcomed the strike. It was a challenge! A vitalizer! A revitalizer! His words pounded out of the loudspeakers, old-fashioned words, such as he hadn't used in years: Paychecks be damned! *We are bridge-builders, connecting Nature to Man, Daylight to Underground, Metal to Flesh, Burro to Boy!* He moved ceaselessly, manning the hoists, hauling ore, filling in gaps from mucker to miner to mule driver, showing off his stamina.

And then he stood in the doorway, blinking and pale.

"Are you all right?" Badinoe asked. Owen licked his lips tentatively. Badinoe felt disoriented; he had never seen the man do anything tentative before. He stepped toward him, worrying that he had gotten shot. Owen lifted his hand, a strange light in his eyes. An appeal. Badinoe paused, wondering how best to help him, and then he hiccupped. It was not a good time to hiccup.

The look went out of Owen's eyes. "You're a weakling, Badinoe. You're a weak, weak man." His nostrils flared. He lunged into the room, found the whiskey bottle, and threw against the wall. "I was a fool to have ever hoped for you."

If Owen wanted him out of Pristina, very well, he'd leave, but for now the groans were too ragged and demanding. He had to get at least one generator working. They needed ice. He changed his shirt and went to the clinic. The nurse made him coffee, and he visited his patients and gave out sugar pills. He needed to find Ralph Burton. Ralph Burton, who could repair almost anything with rubber bands and bent nails, would know how to fix the ice machine. He walked through town, looking for him. Snapped wires dangled from their poles, and trash swirled, and a bird sang. Another bird lay electrocuted by a wire. Badinoe kicked it into the gutter.

Burton's house looked strangely unaffected, even welcoming. The morning glories nodded and the shutters were open, but no one answered when he knocked. He started to leave, then saw Mrs. Burton and her son. They looked as unlikely as their house. The boy wore striped shorts and a matching jacket and held hands with his mother. She had her hair in a pretty bun and carried a tin of Danish butter biscuits. When she saw Badinoe, she waved the tin.

"They're giving them away free!" she called. "Down at O&C! A morale booster!"

Badinoe rubbed his spine. There was a mysterious soreness, not the normal ache—a swollen bump at the small of his back. And now Mrs. Burton gawked at him, reminding him that he also had a swollen eye.

"Who did that to you?" She shook her head in disgust. "Beating up an old man."

"I'm not that old."

"Of course not. Do you want a morale booster?" She brandished her cookie tin and laughed. "But who says our morale needs to be boosted! We don't need a morale booster! Our morale is soaring"—her voice had a hysterical tinge to it— "we've got an Opportunity with a capital O."

"Do you know where your husband is?" Badinoe asked.

"Opportunity with a capital O," she repeated.

She was referring to Owen's latest speech. This one he had delivered in person, on the steps of the athenaeum with the windows broken behind him. The strike was an opportunity. They would root out the rot. They would begin again with hearts and minds tested and tempered by the struggle.

"He never takes responsibility for anything!" Mrs. Burton said fiercely. "Teach the greasers how to read, what do you think they're going to read? He was a fool, we were all fools. He made a hero of that boy Ysidro." She pried open her cookie tin. "Come on," she commanded, "take one."

"Do you know where your husband is?"

She held before him an array of sand-colored cookies partitioned by dainty white ruffles. "The horseshoe ones are the best," she said, "or the jellies. Abraham prefers the jellies, don't you, Abraham?"

But her boy wasn't there. He had wandered down the street and was peering into the shell of a burned-out house. The walls slanted inward and the roof tiles had collapsed. Amidst the rubble were remnants. A bedspring. A ukulele. A wrinkled diaper hanging from a broomstick.

"Abraham!" Mrs. Burton shouted as he squirmed through a crack in the doorway. She shoved the cookie tin at Badinoe's chest and took off after him. Soon she was back, dragging the boy by the ear. He straightened a wire hanger that he had taken from the house and turned it into a skinny cane that he tapped on the ground as if he were blind. Badinoe returned the cookie tin to the woman. "I'm looking for your husband," he told her. "The ice machine's down." The boy stabbed the hanger through the shred of a *Pristina Unite!* poster and held it up proudly.

"Try the reduction works," said Mrs. Burton. "And tell him to come home for supper."

The road to the reduction works was hot and quiet. Badinoe watched his boots move one in front of another, but he did not feel as if he were going anywhere. His back hurt. Why was he saddled with these mysterious injuries? It was the suddenness of the violence throwing things off. Or lack of sleep. He rubbed the swelling, then slapped his thigh. It didn't matter how he'd gotten the bump. Burton. He had to find Burton. That's what was important, fixing the ice machine. But he hesitated once more, feeling as if the clouds in his mind might disband.

"Stop!" A young patrol raced toward him making an X with his skinny arms. There were snipers in the hills. No one was allowed on the road.

Badinoe waved him away.

"But sir," the boy protested, "the road is closed!"

Badinoe walked through the emptiness, whistling a song that the strikers would recognize, a song the cave people loved called "El Sol Mojado." It was about Ysidro. How he could slip in and out, how he had no boundaries. The strike could be traced to Ysidro. Or maybe not. It could be traced to anything: the end of the war, the slump, the veins sapped and spent. But Ysidro figured in there. He had brought people hope after Scraperton lost his appeal. A new flavor of hope that burst from his stories and pamphlets and songs and got into the imaginations of even the obedient ones. If you went to the hills, you could sit for a game of checkers and hear, along with the usual accounts of Mexican bandits, the latest on the general strike in Seattle, or community factories in Russia, or the certified miracles of socialist priests. The postal clerk confiscated what he found, but he couldn't keep up with Ysidro's ruses. He hid letters in seed packets or wadded articles up and used them to cushion glassware and china dolls and other curios that he could now somehow afford. And the mail that was confiscated only caused more rumors and excitement and was perhaps more effective than the material that actually got through.

Badinoe reached the fourteenth verse, an obscure verse that he'd learned in the caves. It told how Ysidro sailed to freedom in the hull of the Santa María. Badinoe had sung it for Victoria, and the color had drained out of her face, confirming his suspicions, suspicions that he'd had ever since Ysidro's jail break, when a bottle of morphine had disappeared from his apothecary right during the time that Victoria had been tending it.

Now Victoria avoided him; he'd only seen her once since the strike began. A crowd had been rushing to put out one of the fires and she'd been walking in the opposite direction, studying her clipboard, so focused on her task that she didn't, or pretended not to, notice the people. They surged forward, but as they were about to crash into her, they hit some invisible wall of will or rank and streamed by on either side. She reappeared at the other end, still studying her clipboard. He shouted to her, but she passed right by.

His eye pulsed. Ice. He had to find Burton. A new wire

fence surrounded the reduction works. At the gate, guards leaned on rifles. "Another fight?" one asked, indicating his eye.

"A stray fist," said Badinoe. "An unintelligible occurrence." He had to find Dolores too. She owed him an explanation.

Inside, Badinoe paused. Whistles sounded, dust rose, men and mules moved from station to station. Except for the soldiers guarding the gate, there was no sign of unrest. He unscrewed his flask. He felt like he was dreaming, or he had been dreaming, and now he'd woken up. This was real, this undaunted industry. He walked by the condensers and the jaw crusher. No Burton, but maybe he didn't need him. Maybe it really had been a dream and the ice machine wasn't broken and there were no men groaning in his clinic. A man with an orange bandanna tied over his nose opened the bottom of the furnace, and heat blasted forth. The man hoed out the burned slag then slammed the door shut. As he finished, another man on the upper walkway opened the loading door and began to shovel in new ore. Badinoe frowned—to protect themselves from the fumes, the furnace men had been ordered to wear coveralls and bandannas, but the man loading ore wore neither. He didn't even have a shirt. He worked like a demon, his muscles flexing in the sun. He hurled the last shovelful into the furnace and pulled the door shut, the screech of the metal painfully loud. Only when he turned and wiped his face did Badinoe recognize him.

He had never seen Scraperton without a shirt before. He'd only seen him in his suit, or in the checked shirt he had on that evening at Casa Grande. Even during the ladder races, when Scraperton competed against loinclothed tanateros in 110-degree shafts, he wore a suit. Now he wore nothing; his chest rose and fell with perfect arrogance and strength and rhythm. Sixty-six years old. Unjust to have a chest like that.

Scraperton saw him, and Badinoe moved back, looking for a shadow, but there were none. He stopped, uncertain why he was trying to hide.

His back hurt and he rubbed the bump. Owen had given him the bump. Yesterday. After Owen had smashed the whiskey bottle, he hadn't left. Badinoe, still moved by that thing he'd seen in Owen's eyes, that appeal, had mastered his hiccups. He didn't see Owen's strength and vitality then, he saw the lines crisscrossing his face, the hair still black but sprouting from his ears instead of his head, skin visible through the course strands. He'd put his hand on Owen's shoulder. He should have learned from Victoria never to put his hand on a Scraperton shoulder. Owen pushed him away, his face closed and blunt, his skin tight with judgment. He pushed him hard, and Badinoe's back cracked against the examination table.

"Gene!" Scraperton called now from the furnace. "I'm glad you're here. I owe you an apology."

The hauling and crushing and sorting and braying stopped. A last load of rocks tumbled down a chute and crashed in a dusty heap. The yard was silent, stunned. Scraperton didn't apologize, at least not to stumble-drunk doctors. Badinoe watched along with everyone else as the man descended the furnace steps and came toward him. His footsteps were precise and unvarying, his boots the same old boots, cracked and red with dust, his pants the trousers of his black suit. His chest, on closer inspection, was matted with white hair and mottled with various spots and splotches, the rib of an ancient mountain. Badinoe forced his eyes up past the corded neck. The face, familiar, flushed and sooty, was fixed on his.

"Gene," Scraperton said and pulled Badinoe toward him. There were no whites in Owen's eyes, only red and black, and his smell was overpowering. "I misjudged you," he whispered, "I misjudged you and I apologize."

Badinoe reeled back, so red were Scraperton's eyes, so foul his breath. Scraperton walked in a wide arc, his arms raised, his ribs showing through his skin, his eyes shining. The men watched, their hands hanging by their sides, their mouths open. Behind them, thick, dark smoke rolled out of the stack.

"I have not known my friends from my enemies," Scraperton said. "I thought I did, but I was deceived. I took the doctor for an enemy but he proved himself a friend."

Badinoe panicked. He had to get out of there. But Scraperton's voice rooted him to the ground. He accused his men of spying on him, of perjury, of blindfolding him with their cowardice. His voice rose, louder than the loudspeakers, louder than the jaw crusher and the dynamite blasts. He lunged toward a frightened worker, licked his lips, and spoke, his voice now low and controlled.

"Or is it I, you think I am a coward?" The worker shook his head. Scraperton laughed and poked him in the chest. "You think I have no backbone?"

"No, sir," the worker said, his face twitching.

Scraperton didn't hear. He glared into the next man's face. "Well?"

"You're no coward, sir," the next man said.

"Then why didn't any of you—not one!—indicate to me that I harbored a traitor under my very own roof?" His words echoed off the steel water tanks. When Badinoe stepped back, Scraperton leapt over and grabbed his arm. "Gene," he whispered. There was a white crust in the corners of his mouth.

"I don't know what you're talking about," Badinoe said, trying shake his grip.

Scraperton squeezed tighter. "Don't you go at it too!"

"I didn't tell you anything. I just wanted to see if you were all right."

Scraperton moved closer. "Don't you understand? It's for the best, a natural corrective. You get too closely involved, forget about the vastness of the scope. The family unit, the family unit becomes bloated, and you see everything in it, when indeed we are threads in a big hemp rope, some are strong and some are snappable. It doesn't matter which thread is where, it is the quantity, the quality. There are all kinds of families, voluntary and involuntary, natural and artificial, airborne and limited to land."

Badinoe backed away. Scraperton smiled. Then he swung around, his arms waving like a conductor. The men sprung back into action, and a load clattered down the chute. Badinoe bolted out the gate. The warehouse roofs glared, and his collar was soaked through with perspiration.

The door creaked as Badinoe let himself into the schoolhouse, looking for some shade and solitude. A spiderweb stretched thick and dusty in the corner. The blackboard was filled with children's drawings of forbidden anatomical parts. He unscrewed his flask and leaned against the windowsill. He had to find to Dolores. He'd sing her "El Sol Mojado," the fourteenth verse. He didn't make it up. The cave people knew— they had written it. Owen must have heard it; Dolores must have heard it too. Yes, she had. Badinoe had already sung it to her. But maybe he hadn't. He couldn't remember. He emptied his flask; it clattered to the floor and spun around twice. He stepped over it to the slit of outdoors, the sky horribly blue. He had to find Dolores. He hadn't said anything that Owen couldn't have figured out. It was all in the song. He could see Owen's expression, pure judgment and disgust. All he'd done was put his hand on his shoulder. Owen had pushed him against the examination table. "A man's duty is to keep a tight ship." *Him*, with the Santa María in his stables. Wouldn't any-

body have said, *And what about yours?* "And what about your
ship, Owen?" But Owen hadn't believed him. He had roared
that he was lying.

Badinoe circumvented the town watching his shadow
shift on the sand. His throat thickened with thirst and his
head spun like the flask spinning on the floor. If only Victoria hadn't stolen the morphine, then the song wouldn't have
meant anything to him either. The assertiveness wouldn't
have entered his voice. If that indeed was what got through
to Owen. Owen shouldn't have pushed him. He only wanted
to help.

He shuddered and stumbled up the driveway. The curtains were drawn. He knocked. He waited. He shouted Dolores's name. A pot-bellied patrol came around the side yard, a
rifle slung over his shoulder.

"No one's home."

"Where's Dolores?"

"Not here."

Badinoe slumped against the door wanting to sneak in
and see if she still kept mescal in the china closet, but the
patrol eyed him suspiciously. In any case he needed to be
sober. He didn't know what he would say, but he had to explain. He stumbled off the porch. In the driveway he found a
ripped sheet of a canvas with a Spanish cross emblazoned on
it. It was from the float. Now he saw the bits of hull and mast
strewn across the yard. The place looked like it had been hit
by a nor'easter.

And there was a pile of ashes where the pagoda had been.

♦

The strike had nothing to do with reason. Hard-working, sensible men marched their families up to the hills to protest Owen closing a shaft that was empty of ore. Malingerers with files an inch thick put in double shifts and bragged about it. Cousins shot each other, women burned effigies, and some prankster rigged a phonograph to Owen's loudspeaker system and played ragtime music as a bunch of failed mystics beat up the postal clerk. As if you could blame the strike on a few fiery letters smuggled to a group of mostly illiterates. Dolores had stopped going to town, too disgusted. She stayed home, alone, the house emphatically empty. She had assigned herself her own mission: to clean Casa Grande. Really clean it. Every wing.

She had recruited Hedda, Graciela, Ana Pilar, and various others. She had set up rows of cots in the ballroom so that the extra help could spend the nights. They emptied out the main house, refinished and polished the furniture. They ripped the brocade from the walls and sanded and plastered and painted. She wanted simplicity. She wanted white. Everything—the molding, the wainscoting, the walls—to be painted white.

She could smell the paint now. She was in the kitchen unpacking the last box—a set of goblets she'd rediscovered, the glass a deep, dark red with a pattern of grapes molded in. She took each one from its nest of straw and put it into the sink. They bobbed in the soapy water, releasing twenty years worth of dust. They had been a wedding gift, she couldn't remember from whom, but she remembered opening the box, and even back then being struck by their beauty. They had never used them; she'd shoved them into the back of the china closet as soon as they got to Casa Grande. Almost vengefully. Not wanting Owen to drink out of them—they were too beautiful and he was too crude. But now they'd use them, when things returned to normal. They could hold water as well as wine.

At some point, Owen and Victoria would have to take a break from their respective missions. This was her plan: They'd come home to a table set with good silverware, red goblets, white linen. They'd eat and talk and somehow things would be all right. A vague plan, true, but at least she had a plan. She blew the dust off the last goblet and sunk it in the dishwater. The house was so quiet she could hear the bubbles pop. An impressive quiet. There hadn't been this kind of quiet when there was still dust in the corners and bric-a-brac in the closets. She had thrown away everything that was broken, useless, ugly. They had gathered it into a huge pile and burned it. It was the second bonfire they'd had. Owen had set the first. The second one she and her help enjoyed properly. They dragged over some chairs and an old divan and watched the flames dance and spit. They stayed up almost the whole night drinking lemonade spiked with tequila and singing. She had rocked on her rocker, remembering the songs from ancient nights with the vaqueros. Somewhere past midnight Ana Pilar and her husband stood on shaky feet and began to dance. Dolores hadn't wanted them to stop. She'd been unaccountably happy.

The first bonfire had been in daylight, yellow flames snapping and twisting against a yellow sky. That was before the housecleaning, soon after the strike began, when Victoria and Owen were still living under the same roof. The morning had been quiet, no gunfire or shouting, and there'd been hope in the air. Owen had cheerfully eaten his cereal, certain that he could get people to see reason. Then he drove off to work. Then he returned. She didn't see him, she saw the car, and seeing it, all hope evaporated. He always parked in the carriage house, but now the car slanted across the driveway, the front wheels edging off the road. The *pop pop* of the guns started up again. She put on her driving gloves—you don't need driving gloves to repark a car, but she wasn't thinking straight. No one was. She turned the ignition and the engine started, solid and reliable, immediately comforting. She didn't want to repark, she wanted to collect Owen and Victoria and a canister of gasoline, get on the road, get out of there. It didn't matter where. Maybe to Refugio's, maybe somewhere else, just drive and keep driving, Pristina behind them, first a speck with a trail of smoke, then nothing.

Owen had then appeared on the steps of the pagoda, a burlap bag in his fist. "Victoria!" he yelled.

No answer. He saw Dolores and shouted her name too, his voice filling up the yard. Something was very wrong. Dolores leapt of the car and hurried toward him. The burlap bag bulged at the bottom. She slowed down and Owen held the bag out to her.

"Take it," he said.

When she stepped back, he dropped the bag on the pathway. "Victoria!" he shouted. The door of Casa Grande opened and Victoria stepped onto the porch.

"What?"

"Bring me a crowbar."

Victoria tucked her hair behind her ear. It was loose and heavy and unbraided. She walked across the yard, affecting an unconcerned gait. Cerb'rus followed. Owen breathed slowly, his eyes alarmingly red. Victoria came out of the tool-

shed and stopped a pace away from him. He reached for the
crowbar, but she didn't let her end go. They stood there,
holding the crowbar, staring at each other. Dolores felt dizzy.
Owen jerked the tool out of Victoria's grasp and marched
into the pagoda. They followed him. He'd stuck a flashlight
in his belt, one of the long metal ones with a textured grip
that doubled as a patrol's baton; it ran up the middle of his
back like a metal spine. Dolores hadn't been in the pagoda for
years. It was musty and dim with a crooked armchair, a crate
of books and yellowed newspapers, dust balls, and hunks of
spat-out rodent fur. Victoria leaned against the wall, her expression composed and strangely elegant. Owen wedged the
crowbar between the floorboards, the wood squeaked and
snapped. That's what Dolores remembered best, the sound
of the wood, for both Owen and Victoria were silent and
their expressions inscrutable. Or perhaps inscrutable was the
wrong word. They both looked determined, as if they knew
exactly what they were doing—Victoria leaning against the
wall, Owen tearing up the floor—as if they were following a
set of rules that they settled on long ago but hadn't informed
her of. The wood cracked and splintered. Underneath was a
deep rectangular pit partly covered with chicken wire. She
knew what it had been used for when she saw it. Badinoe
had insinuated something of the sort, but she hadn't believed it.

Owen climbed down the hole. His torch bobbed around
in the dark. He came back up and stopped a couple inches
away from Victoria. They still didn't speak. They were the
same height and their profiles met symmetrically. They could
have been reversed copies of one another except for sex, and,
to a greater degree, years. At that moment it was not Owen's
age but Victoria's youthfulness, her glowing skin and full
head of hair, that struck Dolores as monstrous. Owen's jaw

twitched as he walked out of the pagoda. A smile played at the corner of Victoria's lips.

Dolores followed Owen. The blue sky hit her like a surprise. He kneeled in front of the burlap bag, his flashlight raised above his head. "No!" Victoria shouted, leaping down the steps. Owen whacked the flashlight onto the bag. Victoria stopped a couple feet away, holding her stomach. Owen kept beating the bag, his swings so powerful you could hear them slice through the air. When it was over, Victoria clutched the bag to her chest. Owen looked at his flashlight, as if inspecting it for damage. His daughter untied the bag and took out the snakes. Milk snakes, two of them, mangled and bloody: she stretched them out on her lap and stroked them. Her tears dripped down her cheeks and chin. Owen spat. Dolores shuddered; for some reason, this spit seemed worse than anything that had come before. Owen didn't spit. It wasn't his way. But there it was, a glob on a dark gray rock, frothy and bright in the sun.

Victoria picked up her snakes and marched down the driveway. Owen wiped his hand over his mouth, like a child trying to erase a bitter aftertaste. Dolores ran after Victoria. Victoria ignored her until she got to where the driveway hit the road, then she turned around, her arms akimbo with a snake dangling from each.

"Don't leave," said Dolores. "It will kill Owen."

Victoria laughed. "He's already dead."

The snakes jiggled in her hand, then they twisted through the air, heading for Dolores. A coldness slapped Dolores's cheek and she screamed.

Back at the house, Owen had taken the float out of the stables and was hacking the hull with an ax. Dolores sat in her room with her eyes closed, listening to the wood crack and splinter. There was silence. Then shouting. She gazed out the window and saw the pagoda in flames. Owen marched between it and the stables, dragging back pieces of the float and throwing them in the fire. The patrols were the ones shouting; they hopped and flapped their hands, uncertain what to do. She hurried outside, just in time to see the roof of the pagoda crash in. Owen watched, his arms crossed over his chest, sweat pouring down his face. She ordered the patrols to get saddle blankets, then helped Hedda and the stable boy attach the hose to the water tank, but when the boy turned it on, only a sad trickle came out. *Like pissing at a volcano*, Dolores's father used to say. The boy covered the hose with his finger, trying to increase the water pressure, but he couldn't get more than a thin arc. Owen smiled and turned away.

"Where are you going?" Dolores yelled as he walked down the driveway. The fire crackled and the wind blew and now the sky was yellow. The patrols returned with the saddle blankets. She took a few then sent the patrols to monitor the other buildings; she and Hedda and Horatio remained by the pagoda, whacking the flames when they tried to spread. Eventually the wind died down. Dolores hugged her blanket to her chest and stared at the timbers inside the flames. Across from her, Hedda and Horatio, shimmering in the heat, seemed to hover above the ground. By nightfall, the flames burned themselves out, leaving a circle of smoldering embers. Horatio finally got to use the hose. The water dripped out, producing loud hisses and great clouds of steam, ghostly white in the darkness.

Dolores didn't sleep at all that night. She sat on the porch as the shutters creaked and the clouds moved in front of the moon. Neither Owen nor Victoria returned. She thought about the snakes, still down at the intersection. She imagined first Owen, then Victoria, stumbling home, coming to the snakes, inevitably turning back. She should have kicked dirt over them.

The next morning, she asked Horatio to find the snakes and bury them. He gave her a little bow and announced that he had already done it. He was about twelve years old and had long eyelashes and a cowlick on the back of his head. There was something in his smile, a pride at having thought to bury the snakes all on his own, that broke down whatever was holding her together. She couldn't speak.

"Gracias," she finally said.

"De nada."

She drove to town looking for either Owen or Victoria. She found neither. She went to Badinoe's thinking that he would know where Victoria had gone, but when she opened the door to his office, he jumped, and his face shifted in a white, guilty panic. She remembered then, him singing that tanatero song, teasing her with the possibility of Ysidro and Victoria. She walked toward him, and he grew paler. He'd been so close to Victoria. He would have loved letting Owen know that he knew.

"You snake. You imbecile."

He sputtered uselessly and she slapped him. The gesture was tiny and dumb. She wanted to burn his house down.

The phone rang. Dolores left the goblets in the sink and peeked out the back door. A ringing phone meant that Owen was on his way; he hadn't completely abandoned Casa Grande. Every couple days, he came back for an hour or two. But it didn't count—he didn't eat, he didn't sleep, he didn't talk. He disappeared into his study, and the telephone rang every five minutes, then he left, and the phone rang a couple more times, forlornly. He had not yet appeared on the road. The only life she saw was a bird marring the fresh paint on the garden fence.

"Tell them he's not here!" she yelled to Hedda. She banged out the back door and shooed away the bird, then frowned at the place where the pagoda had stood. She had raked sand over the charcoal and ashes, but something else had to be done; it looked too barren. She was thinking about a rock garden, a bed of white gravel with small boulders placed at restful intervals, like the photographs of the ones in Kyoto. It would be as Oriental as the pagoda but it couldn't be burned or used to hide anything. Or perhaps they could install another mercury fountain. They had warehouses of mercury they couldn't do anything with.

The price had fallen again. If Owen were reasonable, he'd take heed. But he had not been thinking rationally since Victoria left. He muttered the craziest things. *Antelopes don't strike! Coyotes laugh and lead you to water. There is no strike!* His reason wasn't the only thing slipping; his hair had started to fall out, and his appetite had gone too. When he came home, she brought him trays of food. He sent the plates back to the kitchen empty, but she'd find the food in his trash bin. Last time, she saw something shiny underneath a mess of tomatoes and pork. It was a photograph from Owen and Victoria's trip to the pueblo, still in its frame. Victoria's hair was glossy in the sun, and Owen wore a Stetson; they were grinning and holding a primitive vase between them. The vase had been a gift for her. She remembered Owen presenting it, and herself unwrapping it—and being secretly relieved to find it in pieces. But Owen had looked so disappointed.

Dolores turned from the bald patch of sand. Still no Owen. A smokestack exhaled a wan stream of smoke, and beyond town the hills rose, blunt walls of limestone with dark splotches of trees and scrub and the light zigzag scar of the cave road. Later in the day, the road would be dark with strikers. They were staging a May Day parade, Pristina's first. According to the rumors, Victoria would ride at its head.

Dolores did not want Owen seeing that parade. He knew about it, of course, and he knew that Victoria had helped plan it, but seeing it, the girl, his girl, on her horse at its head . . . He couldn't see that. They had to meet at home, at the dinner table. She returned to the kitchen and dried the goblets, put them on the counter. The phone rang again. That was good; Owen was definitely coming home. When he did, she would keep him here. Somehow. If she couldn't convince him, she could lock him in his study. Something had to be done about the patrols. What if they fired on the parade? They had to be disarmed.

The phone rang. He had to come home, she had to talk to him.

Last time he came, he'd looked so alone that she felt like she was spying on him. "Owen?" she'd called. He didn't hear. "Owen!" She'd gone out to meet him, and he still didn't seem aware of her. She'd patted his horse's mane. Still not acknowledging her, he'd spoken. A family of seven had moved out of their cave to make room for Victoria. They were treating her like a queen. "Let's go see her," she'd said. "Just the two of us. They'll let us in." He'd dismounted and walked into the house.

She looked down the road. Still no sign of him. She'd go to town and get him herself. Nearby, Hedda and Graciela and the others were gathered around something—a goat. They were examining its ear. Graciela ran toward her, her face shiny with excitement. "Doña Dolores!" she cried. "Mira!" The goat had belonged to Samedi Martin, the one whose herd had been mowed down by Troop A. Somehow it had escaped and had been wandering alone these past few years. The mark in its ear was a bullet hole. They looked at her expectantly.

"Veo," she said, and left it at that.

She headed to the car, but didn't have the strength to turn on the ignition. It was pointless. What would she do—tie Owen up and throw him in the backseat? And if there was shooting, perhaps it would be better if Owen were in town, perhaps he would stop it. She slumped against the steering wheel and stared sideways at the house. Her parents were rebuilding theirs. They said they refused to live out of suitcases until their dying day. What if it never ended? they said. What of the Thirty Years' War? The Hundred Years' War? Mexico could outdo them both. The new house wouldn't be the same as the old one. They were building it on smaller scale, they said. A cottage.

They had no idea about the strike, about Victoria, about Ysidro. The worst thing that she, Dolores, had ever done had been to let an Australian ranch hand touch her between the legs, and it had taken years for her mother to recover from that. She smiled against the steering wheel. There was leather wrapped around it, and the pattern imprinted itself onto her cheek. She stopped smiling. Pristina was crumbling and her skin was sagging, and she had twenty years of touching and being touched behind her. Foolish to dwell on it.

She got out of the car. She would make bread. She'd never made it before, but her mother had. She used to ride back home to the smell of it coming out of the oven. She tied on an apron and squinted at the recipe book. It told her to sprinkle yeast into warm water and check that there were no bugs in the flour. She obeyed the instructions. Hedda and Graciela soon burst in giggling; she told them to return the goat to Samedi Martin. They left, looking at her strangely. What was she doing cooking? But who cared what they thought. She sifted. She kneaded. She used to sit in the window seat watching her mother knead. She had muscles like melons, and could make the sturdy old table groan with each thrust. Dolores hadn't seen her in twenty years. Her thin lips, her lobe-stretched ears, her rosary. Dolores turned the dough, pressed and smeared. The air holes blinked. She turned and pressed and smeared again. Her arms felt rubbery; her mother was the stronger. The dough finally seemed to get to the right texture, so she balled it up, rolled it in oil, and placed it in a ceramic bowl with a damp dish towel draped over the top.

She sat at the kitchen table, massaging the ache in her arms. The dough rose. She went outdoors to see if the parade had started up, but the cave road remained an empty zigzag. The road from Casa Grande to town was empty too, except for a solitary bull with twisted horns and a glossy stomach. Something strange was happening with the animals, too many strays lost from their pack. Nothing else. No one else. Silence. A moth fluttering. She thought about making more bread. Another and another batch, putting a loaf in the oven every hour until Owen and Victoria returned. If they never returned, she'd bake forever, the loaves like sandbags stacked around the house.

The dishcloth bulged. She peeled it off and punched the mushroomed dough, which sank with a sigh. She sprinkled flour on the board, divided the batch in two, kneaded. The house sweltered. The fans buzzed. The stain-crimped page of the recipe book wavered up and down. She went ahead and made another batch, and when she finished with that, she made another. She baked the whole morning and then the afternoon. In the periods of waiting, she stood on the back stoop, watching the roads.

No red flags, placards, pickaxes. No Victoria proud on her horse. Only sunlight and green insects humming on the first day of May. When the five o'clock shift whistle blew, Dolores decided that the parade had been a rumor, and she poured herself a glass of sherry to celebrate. By now, she had a bunch of loaves on the counter, some charred and twisted, but some all right. She gazed at them, wondering if she should make more. A floorboard creaked above her. It sounded like it came from Victoria's room so she crept upstairs. Victoria's door was closed. No one answered when she knocked.

"Victoria?" she whispered, turning the knob. She imagined she'd find her nonchalant, arching her eyebrows at her as if nothing had happened.

It wasn't Victoria, it was Owen. He sat on Victoria's bed facing the window, his fingers laced across his stomach. Light poured in, late-afternoon light, but instead of tinting his skin golden, it paled it, turning it an almost pure white.

"Owen?"

He didn't move. Again, no sign that he'd heard her.

"Is everyone all right?" She moved to the foot of the bed, blocking his view of the window. "They didn't have the parade, did they?"

"What?" he said softly.

"Did they have the parade?"

He cocked his head.

"The march," she said. "The May Day march."

"Of course not. Today's the thirtieth."

She sat down on the windowsill. She started to say something but her voice broke.

"What's wrong?" he asked.

"Nothing."

He looked awful. Steely stubble, red bumps from where an insect had bit him, bloodshot eyes. And his hair. It was even scarcer. He felt her gaze and his hand moved over his scalp.

"Owen," she said, "you've got to talk to her."

"Who?" He looked at her blankly.

"Victoria!"

He laughed and threw up his arms. "Victoria!" he cried. "Queen of the Empire!" He pulled his fingers, chuckling madly and shaking his head.

"What's wrong with you?"

"Nothing." He wove out of the room.

"Where are you going?"

"I'm going to shave."

"I made you bread." He disappeared into the bathroom. "You have to eat."

The water kept running. She paced the landing, feeling like he would escape if she left the door unguarded. He took an awfully long time. When the door finally opened, her mouth dropped. He was bald—he had shaved off his hair. He looked her square in the face, as if to say that he was fully aware of what he had done and there was no need for further comment. But she couldn't stop staring at his eyes and his eyebrows, for he had kept those, still black and thick and tangled, running straight across the bridge of his nose, more prominent than ever, surrounded by all that white skin. She smiled; he didn't look bad bald. He looked better than he had on the bed, stronger, younger, more spirited.

"You've got to have something to eat," she said.

"I just brushed my teeth."

She made him go down to the kitchen. He walked down the stairs first. With no hair, you could see that the back of his head did not curve around perfectly; right in the center, there was a barely noticeable depression, like a ball just beginning to lose air. She had never known this before, nor had she suspected it as many times as she had cupped the back of his head in her hands. She grasped his shoulders and pressed her face to the indent. "Please stay," she said. He shook himself loose.

The last loaf she'd taken from the oven was still warm.

She got a knife, but Owen said not to cut it, he'd take the whole thing and share it with his men.

"How many men?" she asked, wrapping it in a clean dish towel. "I've got plenty more."

"Only a couple," he said, and tucked the bread under his arm. He walked out the back door and cut across to the driveway, his suit flapping loosely. Halfway down the hill he stumbled. She ran after him, grabbed him by the elbow, and ordered him to eat the bread right then and there. He unwrapped it and tore off a hunk, then studied it as if he didn't know what it was.

"Eat," she said.

He put it into his mouth, looked over her shoulder, chewed slowly. After a while he swallowed.

"Happy?" he said.

"What are you doing about the parade tomorrow?"

"Depends," he answered and looked over her shoulder again. "Thanks for the bread." He retucked it under his arm and started toward town. He was small and solitary, the sky gigantic above him.

"Owen!" she called. The wind swept up, pelting her cheek with sand.

The panes rattled. The dust they'd gotten rid of blew in through the cracks, reclaiming the house. She poured a second glass of sherry. Cerb'rus thumped his tail under the dining room table.

"Come on, Cerb'rus," she said. She packed the remaining loaves in a basket, then took it and Cerb'rus out to the car. She circled around Pristina, the basket sliding on the seat beside her. A boy approached at one point, a barefoot boy guiding a burro. He looked like Miguelito, one of the firewood boys who played checkers at the athenaeum, but he was skinnier, with meaner eyes. Perhaps his brother.

"Dónde esta Miguelito?" she asked.

"Soy Miguel," he said flatly. She bit her lip. Miguelito with something torn out of him and a protuberant rib cage. She handed him the loaf of bread. He looked as if she were offering him poison.

"Qué pasa?" she asked. He stared at her, hungry and stubborn. No one wanted her bread. She drove on. She reached the turn off to the cemetery and started up, then remembered that the last storm had washed away the switchbacks, so she pulled over to the side. "Come on," she said to the dog. Cerb'rus placed his front paws on the ground and painfully got out of the car. She got her basket and they headed up. By now, the sky was a light purple, and the lizards were black shadows. The trail got steeper and both she and the dog panted. At the cemetery, the gravestones were silhouetted against the darkening sky, crosses for the Catholics and circles for the Owenites.

She stopped to catch her breath. The lights at the reduction works blinked on, then the streetlamps. Beyond the town, Casa Grande loomed on its hill. It used to remind her of a shipwreck, but no longer. "Come," she said to Cerb'rus. The path to the caves twisted and turned, and the light got dimmer, but she knew the way and walked confidently until she got to the barricade. The bottom was neat and solid, the top a precarious heap of rocks and corrugated tin. Cerb'rus sniffed around the base, his tail wagging. She shouted her arrival and a woman in a red bandanna poked her head up over the mound, then disappeared.

"Doña Dolores!" someone yelled. Someone else laughed. Dolores hugged her arms around her chest. It was getting chilly. The woman in the bandanna reappeared.

"No necessitan naranjas!" she shrieked.

"Quiero hablar con mi hija."

The woman disappeared again. A couple children peeked through the rocks, one blond, one brown, Owen's vaunted unity. Dolores buried her fingers in the dog's warm fur.

"Mrs. Scraperton?"

She looked up. José María, who had worked Shaft 8 from the very beginning, from before she had even come to Pristina, leaned over the top of the barricade, holding a lantern. The light spread over the wall, and Dolores saw that the bottom wasn't mortared; if you took a stone away the whole thing might topple.

"Buenas noches," Dolores said. "Dónde esta Victoria?"

José María shrugged. "She won't come."

"I need to speak to her."

José María gazed at the darkness beyond her.

"How do I get in?"

He shook his head.

"Do you want me to tear apart the wall?"

"Please, Mrs. Scraperton. Go home."

"I brought bread," she said.

"We don't need it."

"Take it." Dolores reached down for the basket but it was gone. Cerb'rus had disappeared also. "Where's the dog?"

"You have always been good to us," José María said. "Please go home."

"I'm cold," Dolores responded, "and I have no light to get home by."

José María looked at her a long while. His face was as careworn as her father's during a drought. He disappeared; a minute later, his lantern appeared further down the barricade. He let her in through a crevice so narrow that she had to slip in sideways.

"Warm yourself," he said, indicating a dying fire. "I'll get you a shawl and a lantern."

When he had gone, Dolores hurried toward the basin, the dirt plaza where she would most likely find Victoria. The jacals were lit with lanterns, and soft, quiet voices floated from doorways. Last time she had been here had been during the manhunt for Ysidro. She'd come hoping that her presence would rein in the soldiers, and perhaps it had, but still there had been furniture flying from huts, hogs stampeding, women shrieking. The present calm was due to more than the absence of soldiers. The land had been rearranged. The tangled lines of laundry and drying chilis that had mapped out each family's plot had been rerigged; the trash heaps moved elsewhere; the lanes straightened so that you could see the black openings of the caves.

The basin had changed too. Instead of a dirt plaza, there were tables set with oil cloths and communal cooking fires. The women looked up from their stirring and the men looked up from their guitars. Most stared in silence. A bunch of children hiding under a table giggled. Dolores saw the two who had been spying on her earlier; one wore the bread basket like a wicker helmet. She asked them if they had seen Victoria. They looked at her blankly. "Or Cerb'rus?" she asked. "El perro?" They blinked and smiled. A group of young men and woman brushed past her and she called after them, but they ignored her. When she climbed on top of the table, the men stopped playing their guitars.

"The last time I came here," she said, "the soldiers were tearing up your houses, and I told them to stop. Now my house is being torn up."

The children crawled out from under the table.

"We made a maypole," said a girl in an unraveling sweater. "Do you want to see it?"

A woman came over and clucked at the children and they ran off. The woman asked Dolores to get down from

the table and have some soup, but she refused. She whistled
for Cerb'rus and he didn't come, so she remained standing
on the table with her arms folded. People holding torches
stopped their errands. They had dark eyes and they looked at
her, their expressions no longer blank, but quiet. They surrounded her. They multiplied. Their silence turned into a low
growl then a rumble. They were a mass of dark faces and
burning torches, and then, rising up out of them was Victoria.
She had her hair in many braids and wore a bright red dress,
and she seemed to float above the ground, until Dolores realized that she also stood on a table. Cerb'rus, who had found
Victoria, whimpered on the ground, too old to jump up and
join her.

Victoria faced Dolores, but her words were intended for
the crowd. "My father always told me that I was born to up-
hold Pristina, and so I shall. So shall we all. He would have
wanted it this way."

"What are you talking about?"

"He is dead, Mother. Is he not?" She turned toward the
crowd. "Does anybody consider that man who sold out Pristina to be my father? That man feasting off the spoils of the
war? That man who invited soldiers to trample us, to scoff at
our Principles, to mutilate and kill our citizens? You tell me
that that is Mr. Scraperton?"

"No!" the crowd shouted back.

"That man who gave up the promise of Scientific Naturalism for that old whore of a greenback? Who has fired the very
men who made him rich? That is my father? That is Owen
Scraperton?"

"NO!" roared the crowd. Victoria's cadences reverberated
against the rock walls of the caves, and the people swayed to
its rhythm.

"And he has the cojones to invoke Natural Law and Internal Knowledge?" she shouted. The people shook their heads and muttered darkly. "This man follows no law and knows no knowledge!"

Victoria lifted her arms and sang the first line of "O Pristina!" The guitars started up, and the people joined her song. The music beat against Dolores and she turned away from Victoria to see Guillermina, pregnant, proudly holding her belly. Guillermina made her way over the uneven ground, aware of peoples' eyes on her, calm under their scrutiny. Behind her a group of men struggled to carry a maypole wound with red ribbons. Dolores wondered where they'd gotten such a fine piece of wood, probably stole it from the mines. With a shiver she remembered La Herrida hobbling after an oxcart that carried freshly hewn alamo trunks to the mines. After all these years, Dolores could still remember the driver's expression. La Herrida's curses were not taken lightly. *The man who buries the alamo will be buried himself.* She'd said it in Spanish to make sure the man understood.

"O Pristina!" drew to a close, but Victoria wasn't ready to get down from her table. Her body and voice brimmed with a confidence no one her age had a right to. Troop A. The patrols. The murder of somebody named Nueve Dedos. Cerb'rus, forgotten, panted under her table.

Dolores kept thinking about La Herrida, her black eyes filled with will and weird Indian power. A cool emptiness opened up inside of her. Fear. Owen was in trouble. The moment she allowed herself to think it, she was almost certain that it was true. She scrambled from the table and dove into the crowd, pressing against the hot breath and packed bodies, the coldness spreading through her.

♠

O wen, in the dark, in a cage, with his hands around the bars, imagined John Brown, saw him as in the famous painting, his hands sinewy, strong, and undefeated, squeezing the bars of his cell, not grasping them or clutching them, but squeezing them manfully, as if he were the representative of flesh shaking hands with the representative of iron. The cage jerked. Owen lost his balance and cracked his forehead against the bar. The pain cleared his head: he was not in a cage. He was in an elevator, his elevator. It only seemed like a cage because no one else rode it. He unscrewed his canteen, swished the tinny water around in his mouth, swallowed. Shaft 8's elevator. He wetted his handkerchief and patted it against his forehead: only a trace of blood, nothing grave. Officially he was here to do the last rounds, but really to check out Forrester's stope. No one else knew, only Forrester and himself, a stringer that looked like it would lead to a rich new vein. They'd found the ore chimney that way, closing a crosscut they thought was spent. He jammed his handkerchief in his pocket, impatient to get down there, although he wouldn't be able to do anything until the price of mercury rose. They were throwing pennies at it. Pennies. But it would reach its rightful place, and when it did, they'd blast open the stringer, hire new crews . . . He could feel the mercury calling him. The strikers and his own daughter wouldn't be able to hear it. They couldn't. They idolized money. But money was only the means, the mercury was why you did it.

The elevator swung toward the shaft wall. His headlight illuminated the rock, a jagged field of gray with a splotch of red paint. Graffiti! The strikers had been down here. He shouted for the hoist man, and the car jerked to a halt.

"Mac!" he yelled. "Mac!"

No one answered. The cable groaned and the car creaked toward the other wall. Still no answer. He dabbed his forehead with his handkerchief, then a voice finally came through the dark—"Yes, Mr. Scraperton?"—a hollow, tricky voice, not Mac's.

"Where's Mac?" he shouted.

"I am Mac."

Owen's voice and the stranger's echoed through the shaft.

"If you are Mac, then when did you start working this shaft?"

Silence. A whistle. "Wa-al, right after Gwinnie was born, that makes it 1912."

It was Mac.

"What the hell's wrong with this lift?"

"Wa-al, a hitch, sir, we're working on it."

"We? Who's we?"

The floor dropped as the car jolted a foot or two down.

"You all right, sir?"

"In one piece."

"Smooth sailing from here on out."

The ride resumed. "Wait!" Owen shouted. The cables screeched. "The desecration!"

"Sir?"

"There are slogans on the walls."

"Yes, sir, wa-al, sir, we were going to clean it off, but since we're closing the shaft—"

"Get rid of it."

"Yes, sir."

The markers passed by. One hundred, two hundred, three hundred, four hundred, five hundred, six hundred. Owen sucked the sweat gathering on his lip, rolled up his sleeves, and inhaled. Must, sweat, and metal—a good, honest smell, the smell of elemental merging. It got into your bones, gave you strength and joy.

The cage landed. The men down here, they knew what he was talking about. Their muscles shifted in the lantern light and they worked with pride and steady purpose. He wandered through the piles of goods. Metal hooks and stakes. Canisters of kerosene. A manager came up—his belly large enough to quell any suspicion that he didn't get enough to eat—and asked what he should do about a broken ladder.

You couldn't throw away something that still had a use. Owen's mother had taught him that. You couldn't untie a string from a package without her winding it into a ball. She had kept the balls in the bottom drawer in the hallway. Once, Father came back, quite drunk, singing a drinking song, and found the balls and unwound them, looping the string around table legs, doorknobs, cornices, and curtain rods. *A spiderweb*, he said, *a sticky spiderweb to trap you*.

A man approached with a length of heavy rusted chain. "What do you think of this, sir?"

The man's voice didn't sound right. It seemed familiar, but it didn't seem like it came from the man's mouth. It was the same hollow voice that Owen had heard on the lift. The chain slithered through the man's hands. Stubby hands. Thick oily coils. Owen backed away. People tried to stop him. People brandishing metal and wood, howling questions, whining supplications. He ran down a tunnel. Footsteps pounded behind him, but he wouldn't let them get him. He ran faster and faster. His spotlight bobbed before him, shining on crescents of tram tracks, forks off the path, rats darting out of his way. He soon lost his pursuers. Things kept changing on him, but if he held his mind together, he could escape anything. He slipped into a little-used passage. He knew this mine, its shortcuts, dead ends, intersections, dips and curves, places where you had to crawl or slither sideways. Every year the geography changed, new tunnels, dead tunnels, wider stopes, filled-in stopes, inclines leveled, level spaces blasted through. It was alive, forever transforming itself. You could sense it in the hot, fertile blackness that lapped at the periphery of his spotlight.

Owen stopped and clutched at the rock wall. He was dizzy and trembling. Mercury attacked the weak, the slack, the pallid, those who didn't take care of themselves, those who gave themselves over to drink and excess, those who lost their nerve, their will, their respect for themselves and the ore. He clenched his teeth. Two had fallen out.

He only needed rest—Dolores had been nagging him about it all week. He took off his headlamp and his hat and lay down in the tunnel until the dizziness abated. He adjusted the curvature of his skull into the crevices of the rock floor. The stone pressed into him, insistent and rough. His hair would have made a cushion before he shaved it off, but so much of it had been falling out, thick clumps whenever he ran his fingers through it.

He closed his eyes and dots swam on his eyelids, orange, yellow, green. They formed a picture. Of himself. He stood in the muck on the shore of a swamp, hair growing from every pore in his body. His mouth had expanded into double rows of teeth. A giant lizard came out of the swamp, a hadrosaur with more teeth than he. It lunged toward him, two thousand teeth snapping and flashing under an ancient sun. Owen threw rocks and the hadrosaur caught them in his mouth, crushed them and spat them back, spraying them like machine-gun bullets. Owen slipped in the mud and the hadrosaur came forward. Owen struggled to get up but he couldn't move. It had started to rain.

He opened his eyes. Something dripped into the center of his forehead. He couldn't see where it came from—where had the lights gone? The strikers must have stolen them—no, that was wrong, the lights were being saved, the men had carted them to the hoist. His mother would be pleased, economy, though he wouldn't tell her about Dolores, she wouldn't approve. Dolores sent baskets of oranges to the loafers in the caves. He felt for his headlamp, turned it on. The dripping came from a stalactite on the ceiling above him, a knobby soft protrusion, like a nipple. The mine was giving him milk. He squirmed underneath and opened his mouth.

Not milk. Water that burned his tongue, trying to kill him. He spat it out and jerked up. But it wouldn't kill him. He belonged to this mine and it belonged to him. This was the work of the strikers, they were poisoners, scheming to take away his perception. He had to find Forrester's stope. He needed to press his hand against the stringer, close his eyes, let the mercury talk.

The tunnel twisted, the walls cracked and scarred. Forrester's stope was further than he'd remembered. He scaled a ladder, crouched under a low overhang, arrived at a fork he'd forgotten about. He turned right, and the tunnel widened. He turned left and entered a room he hadn't been in for years. This was gutted earth, the blood leeched out of the walls, the air stale and still. His beam hit a cavity in the wall, a niche with a peaked roof and a wide, flat bottom. Water seemed to be running off this bottom, a small cascade, flowing over the edge and down the wall, but it made no sound. He inched forward, holding out a tentative hand. It was wax, candle wax. He groped further into the niche. More wax and dusty wicks, then something solid. He took it out—a Virgin, crudely wrought, with paint chipping from her cape. He hadn't found a Virgin in ages; the peons had given up on them after the Mariposa collapse.

He entered the next room. No altar, beams buckling on the ceiling, a broken pickax on the floor. Where was he? He couldn't be in the Mariposa, it was miles from Forrester's stope. He entered the next room—only half a room, the rest rubble, from ceiling to floor, rocks and broken beams, a squashed lunch pail. But he wasn't deep enough for the Mariposa, he'd descended six hundred feet at most, two ladders, some downward grades. The Mariposa was at nine fifty, the deepest they'd gone, parts of it sunk down to a thousand.

His boots echoed, making reckless vibrations. He didn't know where he was, so he went back to the room with the altar. His mother kneeled before it. His mother, in a white bonnet with her spectacles on. She lit a candle.

"Mother!"

She stared at the match in her hand, as if she disapproved of it. The flame flickered and she blew it out. He ran toward her. Her eyes were fixed on the altar. It couldn't be her. She prayed in a white church with clear windows and penitentiary pews. Or at home, hands in white crocheted gloves, face scowling into nothingness.

"Mother!"

She ignored him. It was her. She never paid him any attention when she prayed. She had ignored Father too. Ignored them both to pray in crocheted gloves. It had driven his father out of the house.

"Stop!" he shouted. His hand sliced through the air. "There is no hell or heaven, there is sand and rock and sky!" But not here, no sky, earth. He clenched his fist. Where had she gone? She had disappeared into the blackness.

She was dead. She fell down the staircase, her eyes looking up at him, saying nothing. She was buried in Boston.
There was still snow on the ground, old snow mixed in with
frozen mud. The sailor who had given him the ship's cup had
gone to the funeral. He had been fat; he hadn't been fat when
Owen was a boy, but now he was fat and you couldn't see his
whale tattoo and he smelled of stale tobacco. People stood a
few paces away from him. Clara and Benjamin had been there
too, proper in black silk, and James, still a child, squirming
between them in a green muffler. And the others from the
abolition committee. And the colored people she had spon-
sored, shivering and polite. And her wretched priest. And
the naked gray branches of the trees behind them, and the
thin streams of their breath, frozen white, rising from their
mouths and noses.

He walked around in circles. The dizziness had weakened
his insides, his brain. It wouldn't have done any good to tell
Badinoe about it. Badinoe would have laughed, would have
laughed and guzzled his whiskey, liquor dribbling down his
chin. Even if he hadn't laughed, what could he have done
except send him to the sweathouse? Owen could build his
own sweathouse. He could do it right here, light a fire in the
Mariposa where no one ever came. Why hadn't he thought of
this before? He returned to the room with the rubble. Cottonwood beams were jammed between the rocks. He would pry
them out. He had matches in his pocket.

Voices came from far off, men, spies, looking for him. He
paced around the room, spitting the saliva that pooled in his
mouth. The voices came closer. He pressed himself against
the wall and listened. Footsteps, urgent and chaotic, beat
through the crossdrifts. He crouched, burying his head in his
arms. The spies came closer. They were only fifty yards away.
Owen held his breath. The spies yelled amongst themselves.

Owen had to spit. His pursuers agreed to split up, take different routes, then their footsteps grew faint. Now Owen couldn't hear their voices, only the inscrutable breath of the mine.

He lit a match and a flame rose with a hiss. He would sweat it out. He didn't need to tell Badinoe—no one would ever know. Only the mercury, and the mercury already knew. It knew everything. He must have done something wrong. Maybe the chits. He shouldn't have introduced cash. The money had screwed everything up. But the mercury would understand, mercury had weakness too. He grabbed a beam from the pile of debris but it wouldn't budge. He loosened a rock and tried the beam again then removed another rock. They were large rocks; they would have been heavy even when he was younger.

Pain shot through his back and his breath came out uneven. Another rock. A space opened. He yanked at the beam once more and the wood groaned. It moved! He dragged it to his fireplace. He had matches—he would sweat the mercury out. He would find the lake, cleansed. He had to sweat it out before they started to dredge. An entire lake of mercury. They existed, he'd read about them, and now he had one of his own. It was close: he could feel it, shimmering, deep, waiting for him. Something else groaned and he stopped. The walls shuddered. A piece of the ceiling broke off and he watched the dust rise. But he was so close to the lake. The mine roared. He couldn't breathe for the thick frenzy of particles in the air. A furious noise ripped through the pores of his skin.

Silence.

He coughed and lay on his back. Black everywhere, his lamp had gone out.

He could move one hand, one arm. He freed his left shoulder. He squeezed a fist-sized rock and pressed it into his forehead, reawakening the bruise from the bars of the elevator. Someone chuckled, soft, masculine, not unfriendly.

"Drop the rock," the someone said in a deep Virginia drawl.

Owen dropped the rock. His forehead felt clear and light and free. His father, holding a lantern, squatted down beside him. He smelled of hard cider. He was young, younger than Owen, with just a little gray in his hair and red in his cheeks. He took out a deck of cards and fanned it loosely, his eyes twinkling.

"Where is she?" his father asked.

"I'm coming!" his mother called.

His father chuckled again. "Always late," he said, dealing the cards.

They were soft and old, with a red-and-white diamond pattern on the front and the edges worn to a comfortable yellow. Owen picked up his hand and tried to arrange it, a difficult task, considering the way he was pinned. He moved his head into a more comfortable position and studied what he had been dealt. In his father's face, he read nothing but a mild amusement.

"There she is," Father said. Mother came toward them, still wearing the white dress she'd been praying in. But now she was younger, no longer in spectacles. Owen gazed at her. He had forgotten that she had been pretty. He jerked, remembering the cards in his hand. There were crevices in the rocks where he could stash them, but he couldn't reach. His mother laughed.

"Calm down," she said. She placed herself primly on a ceiling beam, picked up a hand of cards for herself, and frowned at them. "What are we playing for?" she asked.

Father shrugged. "Nothing. Just playing for the hell of it."

"We have to play for something," she said.

They decided to play for matches. She led. They played in silence, a companionable not-quite silence, a quietness filled with tongue clucking and fabric shifting and cards sliding. Owen had questions to ask, but he could do that later; he wanted to concentrate on the game. It had been years since he played, almost a lifetime. His father won the first two rounds, his mother the third. On the fourth he slapped down his hand, finally beating them both. Three aces.

"You won Pristina on three aces," his father said.

He was right. Hardly a game. Three aces and an opponent, Nick Wentwright, who was so transparent he could read two pair in the pucker of his brow. But a good loser. He'd sent him the claim a week later, with a bottle of brandy. Owen wanted to ask how his father knew, but his voice didn't work.

"Blood," his mother murmured, smoothing the rough edge of the deck.

Somebody called his name, somebody else, not his parents. The spies, they were coming back. Their voices were harsh, urgent. His mother said something and his father laughed. They were talking about something Owen didn't understand. The spies' voices got louder, their footsteps rang through the rocks. Then his father's light went out, and his parents returned to the blackness. He couldn't hear them anymore. He could only hear the spies, their voices growing distinct. They were not spies. They were his men, and among them not a man, but Dolores.

"Owen?" Her voice filled up the cavern. "Can you hear me?" Her voice was beautiful. It streamed into the rocks and the cottonwood beam.

"Yes," he said.

But she couldn't hear him. "Owen!" Her voice rose, ragged and fearsome; it was still beautiful, but it was no longer a stream, it was a flash flood ripping through the desert. He saw the frothy black waters and the crashing boulders and the bull with its milky eyes, its horns entangled in the roots of a tree from the mountains. "Owen!" she yelled.

"Yes!" His voice cut through his chest bones. Something broke inside.

Outside of the cavern, the voices clamored. They had heard him. He tried to move toward them, but the boulder on his chest weighed him down.

"Where is Victoria?" he shouted. Inside, the thing kept breaking. Each word felt like a blow from a blunt-edged ax.

"She's on her way." Dolores's voice was near, and soft again, lapping from the rock behind his head.

"This is hers," he said.

"Don't talk like that Owen. We're getting you out of there."

"I belong here. Don't let them move me."

"Nonsense! We'll be there in a moment."

The men chipped at the stone and grunted and swore. Now the water was gone and it was rock, all rock. The sound of the axes got further away, and the black grew blacker. And then there was silence.

"Dolores," he called one last time.

"I'm here," her voice came, a faint trickle. He pushed his forehead to the rock, and felt it smooth and young, and galloping toward him, tender.

Epilogue

The year is 1923. Badinoe soaks in a tin tub in his kitchen. His white belly is surrounded by gray water, which is surrounded by pots, pans, flies buzzing around the chorizo, which is surrounded by a continent, and beyond the continent, more water. Then land again. Europe. Spain. Almaden. Almaden that pumped out mercury way back when Pliny soaked in his tub, that survived Moors, monks, Fuggers, Rothschilds, deranged kings, enlightened despots, republicans, that continues to this day. Almaden belongs to Europe. It can slog through anything and everything; it has patience. But Pristina is through. Ephemeral America. Yet its demise can't be blamed on the impatience of Americans. Dolores has tried to keep up operations; the deposits won't let her. It is as if the earth, when it piped the mercury into its creases and folds, didn't want to commit itself to anything too vast, but wanted instead to experiment with elements, colors, shapes, create a kaleidoscope of short-lived possibility. Badinoe has been thinking of kaleidoscopes. He received one in the mail this morning. A gift from Victoria.

They had had no idea where Victoria went. She disappeared when the cave-in killed Owen, didn't even stay for the memorial. Poor Dolores stumbled around in shock for a year. Then a photograph arrived, a wedding picture. The husband with a square face and thick strong features looking as if he's challenging you to step over an imaginary line. He is Victoria's manager. She has become a snake dancer. She stands beside him, slim and graceful, not the least bit cowed, in a daring dress modeled on a Greek toga. Last year, they drove down in a yellow car. Badinoe has a vivid memory of the husband, reclining in the driver's seat, his body relaxed, but his eyes dark and shrewd, taking everything in, making them uncomfortably aware of the adobe walls returning to dust, the boarded-up houses.

Pristina may be a ghost town but the peons remain, tending their squash patches and skinny goats. They require his services and he is happy to oblige. Why return to Massachusetts, to live on the charity of his niece, when he can deliver quinine, pull teeth, stitch skin? If anyone should leave, it should be Dolores, who, if not young, is not yet old. He has suggested this to her, quite nobly, as they have resumed their evening cocktails. If she does go, he doesn't know if he can bear her absence. But she has just bought another horse and is thinking of acquiring cattle. *Where would I go?* she laughed. *Who will sweep Owen's grave? And what if Victoria should decide to come home?* It is the land, Badinoe suspects, the beauty of which once seduced Owen, asserting its pull on her.

Dripping from the tub, he takes the kaleidoscope from its wrapping. Victoria has sent it as a present for his seventy-fifth birthday. He aims it at the light from the window and watches the blue slide into amber, and the amber slide into red. The colors group and regroup, symmetrical and mysterious. It is a handsome kaleidoscope with a leather-bound cylinder and a golden eyepiece, not too heavy, just right for the hand of an old man.

Victoria didn't visit him when she came back, still mad about the song. She went to Casa Grande and ate dinner with Dolores, and the next morning she went to Shaft 8, Owen's burial site. Dolores had had the opening covered with concrete and his name embedded in gold letters. Victoria brought a pillow and sat cross-legged on the concrete for hours. Her husband stood with her a while, then wandered around the silent reduction works, nosing around the shells of the machinery. Then they drove away. But now she has sent Badinoe a present and a note signed: *Love, Victoria*.

He hears the rumble of an engine, adjusts his bathrobe, and, as promised, steps outside. Dolores's aeroplane appears above Casa Grande. She swoops low over the deserted houses, trailing a white banner that twists and snaps. She steadies the plane and the banner becomes readable. *Bon Anniversaire, Doctor!* Now she veers upward and Badinoe's stomach lurches. He went with her once. Never again. He'd felt as if he were being ripped away from all that was precious. She could not understand, she loved zooming through the clouds, her land tiny below. He watches her now, gaining altitude and speed, diving into the huge expanse of blue. The sun shines on her wings. Now she practice the tricks her pilot taught her, loop-the-loops and figure eights, a joyful speck in the sky, showing off for the cacti and swallows, for the moment free.